THE
WHITE
ROSE
NETWORK

BOOKS BY ELLIE MIDWOOD

The Violinist of Auschwitz
The Girl Who Escaped from Auschwitz
The Girl in the Striped Dress
The Girl Who Survived
The Girl on the Platform

ELLIE MIDWOOD

THE
WHITE
ROSE
NETWORK

Bookouture

Published by Bookouture in 2022

An imprint of Storyfire Ltd.
Carmelite House
50 Victoria Embankment
London EC4Y oDZ

www.bookouture.com

ISBN: 978-1-80314-089-6
eBook ISBN: 978-1-80314-088-9

If you have ever spoken against oppression, xenophobia, racism, and hatred directed at minorities, no matter who they are—this book is for you.

PROLOGUE

MUNICH. FEBRUARY 18, 1943

When the call came, Kriminalkommissar Robert Mohr had just sat down to eat his lunch. He had long ago made it his habit to eat alone, at his desk stacked with binders, instead of sharing a collegiate meal with his fellow Gestapo officials in the Wittelsbach Castle's canteen. It was much too cold there, particularly in winter, when the icy chill of the marble floors penetrated through the thick soles of his winter half-boots and the steaming goulash went cold in a matter of minutes. Ersatz coffee—muddy, chicory-flavored water that, in Mohr's opinion, insulted real coffee's name—was a lost cause entirely. By the time Mohr sipped it, it was just as chill-inducing as the stone bowels of Munich's Gestapo headquarters.

Whatever was he doing here? Mohr wondered with a resigned sigh, pulling his winter overcoat on as his eyes scanned the littered desk for his hat. He didn't belong with this new breed, no matter what his former colleague from the Bavarian police had claimed when he implored Mohr to join the Munich division of the Gestapo.

Yes, to be sure, the pay was much better, and the new apartment had two extra rooms and his wife could now afford to hire a maid, who always misplaced his favorite ashtray from the armrest of his chair to the middle of the coffee table.

"Daft woman," he grumbled under his breath, lifting fresh reports written by busybodies who had nothing better to do than denounce their neighbors for not greeting them with a Hitler salute, and wasting his precious time. "How many times have I told her..."

Mohr's back was not what it'd been in his twenties, when he could sleep in a dugout under French artillery fire and feel just grand the next day. He was in his forties now and felt his age in his aching bones whenever it rained outside; the last thing he needed was extra exercise with the ashtray after a fourteen-hour shift at work. All he wanted was to come home, have his glass of cognac and enjoy his evening newspaper without having to get up every two minutes to reach for the blasted ashtray. *Was it too much to ask?* he mused irritably.

Mohr's adjutant Weltman's polite "hurrumph" brought Robert back to the reality of his smoke-filled office. With the impenetrable, dignified expression of an English butler, the young man held Mohr's fedora in his hands. Fresh out of Berlin's Leibstandarte barracks, he'd been serving Mohr for over four months now: silent, sharp as a whip, and with a memory that seemingly held the minutest of details of every case from Mohr's multiple secret police binders.

"Thank you, thank you," Mohr murmured, putting the hat atop his balding head. "The car—"

"Is waiting downstairs." Weltman inclined his chin as he held the door open for his superior.

"Your efficiency is sometimes downright terrifying."

The slightest indication of a smile passed over Weltman's clean-shaven face. "I have instructed Inge to save your lunch and serve it warmed up when we return," he reported with a nod in the secretary's direction, as though in ironic confirmation of Mohr's last comment.

"Who was it that called again?" Mohr patted himself absently, the faint feeling of having forgotten something at the office nagging him as he followed his adjutant down the long corridor carpeted with red runners. Through the lining of his overcoat, his fingers closed around his cigarette case, his Gestapo police badge... Still, the feeling persisted.

"Rector Wüst himself called, Herr Kriminalkommissar," Weltman said, holding out the written report to his superior as they descended the stairs. "He claims that the university building custodian, Jakob Schmid, saw two students throw a bunch of pacifist leaflets from the top floor."

Mohr grunted his acknowledgment as he scanned the paper, squinting at it with his long-sighted eyes. He missed the old days when he had hunted the real criminals—thieves, murderers, rapists —instead of spending his days sorting through stacks and stacks of reports written on scraps of paper, often without the slightest respect for grammar, denouncing family members and former lovers with remarkable regularity. First, there were anti-Nazi leaflets, which had left Mohr's superior, Oberregierungsrat Schäfer, pale with horror and indignation; then, *Down with Hitler* graffiti blatantly painted right on the university's façade, and now this pacifist business...

Producing an off-white handkerchief, Mohr dabbed his forehead with it. Just two years ago, he would have been winded after ascending the damned grand staircase. Now, he had to catch his breath after the short walk down. Perhaps he should have listened to his physician and eased off his favorite brandy...

Easier said than done when something forty-proof is the only thing that keeps one sane in the midst of current affairs, Mohr thought grimly.

Weltman's searching eyes on him made Mohr realize that his adjutant must have said something important that he had missed. Always attuned to his master like a loyal dog, Weltman repeated his words as they exited the building.

"Rector Wüst thinks the students he placed under civil arrest belong to the White Rose."

Mohr stopped in his tracks. Somewhere in the back of his mind, he was aware of the driver waiting by the car, of the fire brigade rushing to the south of the city still smoldering from last night's bombing, of the growling of his own empty stomach... and of the fact that he could be the man who would put an end to the resistance movement that was slowly engulfing the country.

Mohr didn't know what he had expected to see, but it was certainly not this. Seated in the rector's office—beautifully paneled in oak, Hitler's portrait above the mahogany desk, all business, as it should be—a young man in a medic's Wehrmacht uniform was studying Mohr with a look of calm curiosity. Next to him, a dark-haired girl was sitting, flanked by two men, one of them digging in his ear as he stared at the officers in stunned wonder.

From the first look, there was nothing extraordinary about her: a straight nose, a stubborn slash of a mouth, chestnut hair pinned to one side—not as a fashion statement, as it occurred to Mohr, but just to prevent it from getting into her eyes. It was the eyes that gave him momentary pause. Under the knitted dark brows, they studied Mohr with such fierce intelligence that he suddenly felt exposed and oddly vulnerable, as though the roles of interrogator and suspect had unknowingly reversed between the two. Just like her fellow student, the girl appeared to be perfectly unruffled by the presence of the Gestapo in the room.

"Hans and Sophia Scholl," the man to the girl's right declared with a somewhat theatrical triumph about him, his accusing finger pointing at the perpetrators.

Rector Wüst, Mohr assumed. Wüst was short in stature but dressed in a tailored suit of the highest quality. In his lapel, he wore a Nazi Party pin with apparent pride.

"I have all the evidence here," he proceeded, gathering a thick stack of leaflets from his desk and holding them out to Mohr. "We have collected every single—"

"Well," the second fellow, who had finally come out of his stunned state, interrupted in a thick accent betraying his working-class background, "not every single one. Some of the youngsters had already made away with them by the time we..." He quickly receded after noticing a withering glare from the rector.

"And you must be Herr Schmid." Mohr turned to the man he had presumed to be the custodian.

"*Jawohl*, Herr..." Schmid was desperately groping for the correct term of address.

"Herr Kriminalkommissar," Weltman supplied in an undertone.

"Herr Kriminalkommissar." Schmid looked at Mohr's adjutant gratefully before shifting his eyes back to Mohr. "I have witnessed the crime and am ready to testify in court—"

Mohr waved his hand in front of his face, indulging the eager custodian with a smile. "My good man, I haven't interrogated these two yet and you're already calling for a firing squad."

The color mounted in Schmid's face. "But it was them; these two youngsters threw those leaflets down, Herr Kriminalkommissar! They have an empty suitcase with them too, in which they must have smuggled all this propaganda in." Offended, he pointed at the small suitcase that indeed stood by Sophia Scholl's chair.

"Is it yours?" Mohr addressed the young woman directly for the first time.

Rather to his surprise, she nodded without the slightest hesitation. "Ours."

"We're brother and sister," the medical student explained in response to Mohr's quizzical look.

"*Ach*. That's right. Herr Rector did say, Hans and Sophia Scholl." Mohr was silent, studying the siblings closely. Calm and collected, they presented a stark contrast to Wüst, all but fuming in indignation, and his underling Schmid, who kept chewing at his lips as though an unspoken question was itching to tear off his nicotine-stained tongue: *The White Rose 'wanted' poster said I'd get three thousand marks' reward; well, where is it?*

With a stir of distaste in his stomach, Mohr ignored Schmid's impatient shifting from one foot to another.

"What are you doing with this suitcase?" He turned to the girl again, his tone softening for a reason he couldn't quite explain to himself.

Mohr had been a policeman in Bavaria ever since he had received his discharge papers when the Great War was so gloriously lost some twenty years ago. He'd always prided himself on being an excellent judge of character. His colleagues wondered at his ability to sort the criminal types from the innocent ones after mere moments in the interrogation room. And now, the instinct honed by years and years of police work told him, in no uncertain terms, that the couple before him were innocent. Their clear, noble features were free of guilt; in their eyes, not a shadow of malice.

"Our family lives in Ulm," Sophia Scholl said, looking at Mohr with those dark, frank eyes. "We were planning to catch a train home for the weekend and took the suitcase with us so that we could go to the station straight after the lectures."

"But why is it empty?" Mohr almost wished he didn't have to ask all of these idiotic questions.

"Our mother is ill." This time it was Hans Scholl who spoke. His voice was deeper than his sister's but with the same husky undertone to it. "We take laundry from Ulm and bring it here, to Munich, so that she doesn't have to exert herself laboring in the tub."

"She has a weak heart," Sophia added, matter-of-factly, not looking for any sympathy.

Mohr smiled at her and this time it was genuine. "I'm sorry to hear that."

He was ready to let them go. Return to his office; have Weltman type out a report; file the evidence and forget it all like a bad dream. But then that insufferable serpent Schmid had to go and demand that Herr Kriminalkommissar search them, *for surely they must have something incriminating in their pockets,* and Mohr didn't have an excuse not to follow the protocol of his own organization. If he had those blasted three thousand Reichsmarks on him, he would have thrown them in Schmid's face and advised him kindly to piss off back to where he had crawled from, but the ever-efficient Weltman was already reaching into Hans Scholl's pocket—

And then all hell broke loose.

As though in slow motion, Mohr watched Hans pull something out of his pocket first, tear it into pieces and stuff the bits in his mouth; Weltman lunged at him, screaming, "No! Stop resisting! Give it here!" as he tried to pry what was left of the leaflet out of Scholl's mouth.

At last, Mohr came out from under his spell and threw himself on the medical student as well. After his palms caught Hans' jaw—"Stop it, spit it out, it's over"—Scholl suddenly relaxed and allowed Weltman to retrieve whatever was left of the paper from his mouth.

Weltman's face betrayed nothing, even after he read out loud the newly assembled leaflet—different from the stack on the rector's desk. Neither did Hans' face, when he told them it was a leaflet given to him by a student he didn't know. He tried to swallow it to save the fellow from legal trouble. No wonder he did; whoever had given Scholl the handwritten affair had somehow gotten wind of the American President Roosevelt's speech at the Casablanca Conference. The speech had left no doubt concerning the Allies' plans—demanding an unconditional surrender, no less. If distributed, the leaflet would create such a panic among the German population that the SS would not be able to contain it.

... Hitler is less likely than Paulus to capitulate: there will be no escape for him. And will you be deceived like the 200,000 who defended Stalingrad in a hopeless cause, to be massacred... Roosevelt, the most powerful man in the world, said in Casablanca on January 24, 1943: "Our war of extermination is not against the common people, but against the political systems." We will also fight... Today, Germany is completely encircled just as Stalingrad was. Will all Germans be sacrificed to the forces of hatred and destruction? Sacrificed to the man who persecuted the Jews, who

eradicated half the Poles, and who wanted to annihilate Russia? Sacrificed to the man who took away your freedom, peace, domestic happiness, hope, and joy, and instead gave you soaring inflation? This will not, this must not happen! Hitler and his regime must fall so that Germany may live. Make up your minds: Stalingrad and...

The text stopped abruptly, its remnants lost to Hans Scholl's brave attempt to keep its author out of trouble.

The author, but not himself.

It took Mohr great effort to suppress a disappointed sigh as he retrieved two pairs of manacles from the pocket of his civilian suit. Once again, he looked into the girl's eyes as he placed the manacles on her slender, white wrists and saw that he wasn't mistaken: she was innocent.

Innocent and far too young to die.

Now, he only had to prove it.

ONE

ULM-MUNICH. MAY 1942

As the train was gathering speed, carrying her further away from her small hometown Ulm to bustling Munich, Sophie's childish longing for home and everything familiar was gradually transforming into excitement. The prospect of independence and adventure was slowly unraveling before her along with the endless expanse of the countryside's brown, fertile fields. Alone in her compartment, she felt rebellious, triumphant even. They had done everything in their power to stop her, to steer her onto the correct course for a German woman, to persuade her that she would be more useful to the Fatherland as a mother and wife; that she would only take up some promising young man's place at the University of Munich, instead of following her nature and having sons for the Führer.

But Sophie was her father's daughter; the father who still spoke his mind against the regime even after having his share of run-ins with the Gestapo. Independence ran deep in Robert Scholl's blood. Personal convictions had served as his infallible moral compass ever since the Great War, when he, risking execution, refused to shoot at people he personally had nothing against. When accused of cowardice, he had set off for the front after all—but in a medic's uniform, to heal the ones his compa-

triots maimed and gassed. It was little wonder he fell in love
with and married a Red Cross nurse, Magdalena, whose heart
was just as big and full of compassion as his. It was just as little
wonder that their oldest son, Hans, Sophie's brother, had chosen
the same path for himself some twenty years later, also choosing
to become a healer instead of a killer, Wehrmacht uniform
or not.

For Sophie, it had been a long game, far longer than the mere
150 kilometers separating Ulm from Munich. It had been a long
game of three intolerably long years, during which she had been
forced into field work and then a kindergarten, and even her
father's tax office, where she had worked as a bookkeeper. Though
that last "office position" Sophie didn't mind one bit, much like
Robert Scholl himself didn't mind trading the office of a mayor for
one of a lowly tax consultant back in 1933.

Robert Scholl had never stood a chance with his new Nazi
superiors. Too outspoken, too liberal, too tolerant to the non-Aryan
minorities, too friendly with the Jews. It mattered not that the
people loved him; he had still been dismissed from his mayoral post
as politically unreliable, replaced by a rabid nationalist who knew
nothing about governing the city and cared not one whit about its
inhabitants, but slammed his heels obediently to each order from
those above and never questioned his higher-ups.

Sophie didn't remember her father being too upset about losing
the well-cushioned post. If anything, he had released a breath of
relief, announced that he rather preferred being an independent
consultant who reported to no one and was in charge of his own
schedule now and could spend more time with his lovely wife and
five children... and with his Jewish friends too, whom he began
inviting for dinners even more often than before. The Nazis and
their opinions could very well go and hang themselves, as far as he
was concerned.

Just as they tried to hold her father back, the Nazis did everything in their powers to keep Sophie away from pursuing a career
of any sort. But Sophie had clawed her way out of that Nazi-

imposed slavery and into the measly, state-rationed pitiful ten percent of the university's female student population.

She had won.

She was officially a student.

On her lap, a diary lay forgotten, its pages rippling softly as though caressed by the breeze of the half-opened window. Too restless to write, Sophie was gazing at the silvery ribbon of the Danube river sailing slowly past, without quite seeing it in her dreamlike state. She should have occupied herself with something useful; she thought of starting a letter to Fritz, her fiancé, but with the best will in the world, Sophie couldn't assemble her thoughts into anything coherent just yet. They buzzed and twirled inside her mind and each time she brought her pen to an empty piece of paper, they scattered like ants and there was no recalling what it was precisely that she wanted to share with her beloved. How selfish of her; Sophie chastised herself. He was missing her terribly there, on the front, fighting Hitler's cursed war, and she couldn't even manage—

A sharp rap on the compartment's door startled her momentarily. Before she could voice her permission, it slid open, revealing two men—one uniformed and one dressed inconspicuously in civilian clothing.

"Passport control." The uniformed one held his palm out for Sophie's papers.

The lingering, gaunt shadow behind his back—*Gestapo, of course, who else?* Sophie forced herself to conceal a smirk—sniffed the air like a well-trained hound.

"The aim of your trip?" The uniform held her passport to the light, his eyes scrutinizing it for signs of possible forgery.

"I'm beginning my first summer semester at the University of Munich," Sophie announced, tasting the delicious sound of every word. "My admission letter is attached to the back of the passport."

The uniform grimaced slightly after the papers checked out. From over his shoulder, the pallid specter from the secret police dungeons narrowed his colorless eyes at the bag next to Sophie.

"Is that wine?" An accusatory tone in his voice was scarcely veiled, as though it was a crime to celebrate while the brave German soldiers were giving their ultimate sacrifice on the front.

It was idiotic, of course, to push her luck, but that day Sophie felt particularly defiant.

"And cake," she said sweetly and viciously, smiling at the pair with extraordinary charm. "My mother baked it for me."

The Gestapo bristled slightly. *There was a war going on, in case she wasn't aware; everything was strictly rationed and here she sat like some countess,* his eyes read. "What's the occasion, Fräulein?"

"I'm twenty-one today. And I'm going to Munich to study philosophy."

The Gestapo eyed Sophie's boyish haircut—the same exact one her brother Hans wore, with a long forelock falling into her eyes and the back clipped closely to the skin—with visible disapproval, chewed on one insult or the other but must have decided that it was beneath him to dignify such an attitude with a remark and retreated back into the shadow-shrouded corridor.

"Safe travels," the uniform said, returning her passport.

Just before he left, he threw a last glance full of unspeakable longing at Sophie's cake. Her poor mother would be terrified to learn that it had almost landed Sophie in trouble, but her father would grin gleefully instead, much like she was doing now.

The rest of the trip was uneventful. The train slowed down once, tentatively probing its way along the tracks damaged by bombs and hastily patched up by slave labor workers. Skeletal, in tattered clothes with wide crosses painted on their backs or armbands with different letters signifying their nationality, they were clearing the remaining rubble with primitive tools and bare hands. Sophie's first instinct was to avert her gaze, much like the rest of her compatriots did whenever another pitiful troop of concentration-camp inmates or forced foreign laborers was being marched through their towns and cities. Instead, she kneeled on her seat and stuck her head through the crack in the window. Satisfied that the only uniformed foreman was smoking with his back to the train, Sophie threw all four of her sandwiches, lovingly wrapped by her *Mutti* in waxed paper, toward the nearest worker's feet.

He startled for a fraction of a moment, but then snatched the food and concealed it under his threadbare shirt, searching the windows of the passing train for the face of his benefactor. Sophie's eyes met his for the shortest instant; an instant during which the emaciated man's face was transformed by a radiant, grateful smile; an instant during which Sophie's hand pressed against the thick glass in a gesture of sympathy and solidarity. And then the train made a sharp bend and instead of the begrimed prisoners, small picketed gardens in full bloom sailed past the windows, but Sophie was no longer interested. It was then that she began writing in her diary, furiously and accusatorily, words flowing in angry torrents from her pen as though from a vein sliced open.

She was still writing when the gray industrial sights of Munich's outskirts, smeared with smog, replaced the idyll of the countryside. She was still writing when the train crawled toward the station and screeched to a stop. Only when someone knocked on the window from the other side and her brother's grinning face appeared did Sophie return to reality.

Swiftly gathering her suitcase and the bag with her birthday cake, she pushed her way through the carriage and onto the platform—straight into Hans' awaiting arms. Smart and impossibly handsome in his medic's uniform, he lifted her easily off the ground and kissed Sophie's cheeks, rosy with sun and happiness.

Only after her feet touched the ground again did Sophie notice a pretty blond girl holding out a small bouquet of spring flowers to her.

"Welcome to Munich," the girl said and smiled so widely that Sophie instantly felt welcome.

"Sophie, meet Traute," Hans said. "Traute, this is my Sophie."

As it always was with him, there was no formality about the introduction, no explanation. Brother and sister with only a three-year difference between them, they had grown so attuned to each other over the years, everything was understood after a mere exchange of a half-glance and a conspiratorial grin. And now they would live together, in the same rented apartment, about which Hans had bragged to her in his letters while she had still been toiling "for the glory of the Fatherland" in fields or changing toddlers' nappies. His friends would become her friends, hopefully, just like his new lady friend, Traute.

Sophie smiled at the girl as they shook hands. Her exhilaration knew no bounds.

An entire life lay ahead of them.

They would make every day count.

Hans rented an apartment in Schwabing—a bohemian neighborhood of Munich that had, by some miracle, managed to survive and thrive in the Brownshirt-infested Bavarian capital. As they jumped off the tram trolley that hadn't quite stopped but had slowed down by a dingy *Lokal* with a faded Luftwaffe recruitment poster plastered crookedly next to its door, Sophie felt instantly, oddly at home. Even the disheveled drunkard, who dozed rather comfortably by the *Lokal*'s closed door as he waited for the seedy haunt's opening, added color to the neighborhood's refreshingly diverse look.

The rest of the city—despite being more Austrian than German, with its Catholic cathedrals on every corner and a certain Viennese or even Italian flavor contrasting with the usual Prussian austerity of Northern Germany —was still much too strangled by the bondage of crimson Nazi banners, trampled under the feet of constantly marching *Hitlerjugend* troops and their older SS counterparts.

But here in Schwabing even the air was different, tinged with the smell of cheap ersatz coffee sold in open cafés; old, leather-bound editions in the bookstores standing with their doors thrown open as though welcoming the youth that still valued independent thought; and the sound of the carefree laughter of students walking in pairs in their fencing uniforms.

The apartment itself was on the second floor of an old building bearing the baroque accents of the past century. A creaking wooden staircase, high vaulted ceilings with plasterwork adorning their corners, mismatched furniture and books, books everywhere —Sophie roved her gaze around in wonder and, in a rush of excitement, threw her arms around Hans' neck.

"I take it you like your new home," he said, grinning slyly. "Now, pop that bottle open, birthday girl. We ought to celebrate properly today."

Traute was rummaging through the kitchen cabinets in search of a corkscrew when someone knocked on the door in a peculiar manner.

"That would be Shurik," Traute said without looking up, a knowing grin curling the corners of her mouth upward.

"I hope you don't mind?" Hans paused on his way to open the door, a sudden shadow of concern creasing his dark brow as he looked at Sophie. "I invited him to celebrate with us. Though, knowing Shurik, that aspiring Soviet Picasso could have brought an entourage with him." Hans cringed further.

"Do I mind? What sort of question is that at any rate?" Sophie stared at him in frank wonder. "I've been dying to meet your friends! Well, don't just stand there like a Reichstag sentry on leave —open the door!"

Even though she'd never met him in person, Sophie knew of Alexander Schmorell—Shurik for short—her brother's best friend, from Hans' letters and countless stories he'd told her in person. Born in Russia to a Russian mother and a German father, Alex was a wandering soul lost somewhere between east and west, his mind always at war with itself, unsure where he belonged. Without knowing him, Sophie felt an inexplicable kinship with the young man trapped into military service he loathed instead of becoming an artist, much like she had been trapped into the state-imposed gender constraints before her sheer willpower and persistence triumphed over Hitler's ideas of where a woman's place was—somewhere between the kitchen and the nursery, far below her husband.

"That fellow will end up with the gypsies," Hans had professed, only half in jest, on multiple occasions, shaking his head with fondness. "Or as an alcoholic; whichever comes first."

Now, peering from behind the heavy velvet curtain adorning the hallway entrance, Sophie saw three young men in medics' uniforms enclosing Hans in a brotherly embrace, but she instantly guessed which one was Alex.

He wasn't blond like the other two of his comrades, and neither did he possess the broad, wide features that would betray his Slavic roots. He was tall and dark, all sharp angles and brooding, deep eyes. It was in them that Sophie could see the tearing fabric of his soul splitting itself in two: the eyes were the mirrors reflecting all the sorrow of an artist forced to become a medic, a pacifist stuffed into a Wehrmacht uniform, someone without a home.

Sophie's cheeks flushed when he caught her shamelessly staring, but instead of saying something to that effect—something Hans would have done with a teasing grin—Alex advanced towards her with the ease of an old friend, momentarily wiping away all traces of Sophie's discomfort.

"Shurik. It's a Russian nickname for Alexander." Removing the pipe from the corner of his mouth, he outstretched his hand and gave Sophie the warmest of smiles.

"I know. Hans has explained it to me," Sophie said, shaking his narrow, cool palm smelling faintly of plaster. There were specks of it in his dark hair too; it dusted his long eyelashes. "He has told me a lot about you."

"Has he now?" Alex shot a glance full of mischief at his friend. "Let me guess: he told you that I smoke like a chimney, that I have the talent to be a great physician but I never take my studies seriously, that I skip lectures to spend an afternoon in my studio instead and that I bring all sorts of vagabonds into his apartment, and that I'll end up as one of them one day."

"Why, is any of that not true?" His comrade, with longish, sandy hair and smiling blue eyes, winked at Alex as he held out his hand to Sophie. "Christoph Probst."

"Christoph?" Sophie gave his hand a thorough shake, her eyes widening in recognition.

She'd heard of him too. Hans simply adored him—sunny Christoph Probst seemed to have that effect on people. Unlike Alex who was pushed into the medical profession by his father, Christoph was a born healer, always ready to help, unconditional love and sympathy radiating through his blue eyes that had a net of wrinkles about them. He was a man who laughed often and in earnest. It was no surprise that he had married before anyone else in the group and was already a father to two young sons.

"The very same." Christoph beamed at her and gestured to the third friend, who'd been lingering in the background. "And this is our Willi."

"We call him Father Willi," Alex added with a wry glance at his comrade, pulling him into the living room.

"Because he's very pious and very Catholic," Traute commented playfully, brandishing the corkscrew she had unearthed from a mountain of disorganized silverware.

"Everyone in Munich is Catholic," Willi mumbled in his defense, his color mounting. "It's a pleasure to make your acquaintance." His palm in Sophie's was warm and clammy.

"So formal." Alex rolled his eyes and took the bottle out of Traute's hands without further ceremony. "Don't be so tense. You won't go to hell for being friendly with a girl."

He was prone to occasional barbs and cool irony, Sophie was already beginning to notice, but there was no malice to Alex's jests. Effortlessly, he uncorked the bottle and began pouring its contents into the glasses—also mismatched—that Hans was holding in front of him.

"To our birthday girl!" Hans lifted his glass.

"Who's the birthday girl?" Alex stopped pouring momentarily.

"Sophie is the birthday girl!" Hans laughed.

"Why didn't you tell us, you cast-iron limb of Satan?"

Sophie exploded into giggles in spite of herself. Even Alex's insults had a wonderfully artistic, imaginative flavor to them.

"Shurik," Willi muttered in reproach.

His half-hearted reprimand swiftly drowned in everyone's laughter and the shower of congratulations.

Sophie's head was soon swimming—with wine, with the exhilaration of being in the company of people she felt she belonged with, and with an intoxicating feeling of freedom that had swept her and carried her away. It took her away from Germany outside the window, from the war, and from everything she despised with every fiber of her soul.

In the evening, the scattered notes of live music from the nearby café invaded the room through the windows that had been thrown open, blackout curtains hanging grimly by the sides. It wasn't their time yet; the young people inside still had a few precious hours of twilight that belonged only to them.

"You ought to take Professor Huber's class." Her fingers grasping Sophie's wrist, Traute was trying to speak over the men's loud chatter. "He's such an old fox; he says all sorts of unimaginable things against the regime, masking it with supposedly ancient history."

"Who, Huber?" Suddenly interested, Alex ceased cleaning his pipe and looked up. "Oh, yes. He's a crafty old bird. Very Prussian but very anti-Nazi."

"Which is rather strange, since the Nazis based their ideals on Prussian militarism," Christoph said, cleaning the cake crumbs off his plate until it was immaculate.

"Nah, he likes Bismarck and all that rot that came with him." Alex waved him off, returning his attention to his pipe. "I gather it's a regular case of psychological overcompensation. He suffered from diphtheria as a child," he explained to Sophie, "which has left him crippled and limping and therefore unfit for front-line service.

And that was during the time when all the *conscientious* young Germans—" he said the word "conscientious" in a very peculiar, mocking way—"were volunteering for the front in droves."

"Just to be shipped back in wooden boxes or missing a few limbs," Traute inserted, pondering the red wine in her glass. "One would think he'd consider himself fortunate to avoid such a fate."

"He still thinks himself less than a man because of that." Christoph shrugged, somewhat sympathetically. "I bet his wife gives him a hard time about that."

"It didn't prevent her having two children with him." Alex lifted a lively brow, looking directly at Sophie.

He was flirting with her, it occurred to Sophie just then, but she was too cozy, too warm and lightheaded to consider such a possibility properly. Instead, she leaned her head on Hans' shoulder and let the descending evening envelop her in its warm, fragrant embrace.

Closer to the night, when the blackout drapes had to be drawn and voices lowered, the subject of the conversation turned to war once again.

"Shurik, you're the gypsy among us." Hans gave his best friend a teasing prod with his foot. "Tell us our fortune. Shall they ship us off to the front any time soon or not?"

"Show me your palm," Alex said in a deadpan tone. "I'll read it for you."

As soon as Hans offered it to him, Alex slapped it hard.

"Naturally, they'll ship us off, give or take a couple of months."

"Whatever is the slap for?" Hans shook his injured hand in mock indignation.

"For asking idiotic questions."

"But, Shurik, really?" It was Traute this time, her gaze imploring. "Your father treats those Party Golden Pheasants." Instinctively, her lip curled in disdain at the mention of the overfed and overdressed Nazi bigwigs. "Has he heard anything from them? Rumors, perhaps?"

"One doesn't need rumors when cold facts rain down on our

poor heads from the sky." Alex tossed his dark head toward the window. The night was moonless; good flying weather for enemy bombers. "The Allies have already leveled Cologne. I imagine it's only a matter of time and raw war materials till they lay a few of their RAF eggs on our little nest in Munich. Do you imagine the war is going well for us?" He arched a mocking brow before shaking his head and lifting a match to his pipe once again. "And, you know, I *want* them to annihilate us. We deserve the entire blasted business."

"Shurik!" Willi regarded him in horror. "I agree with you when it comes to regular soldiers; the SS even more so... But women? Children? The elderly? Innocent people—"

All of a sudden, Alex narrowed his eyes and struck out like a snake. "No one is innocent in Hitler's Germany! We're all complicit. Isn't it 'innocent children' that march daily around one church or the other, beating their drums and bellowing their songs, just to disrupt the mass? Your Catholic mass, I should add."

Willi averted his eyes.

"And as for women"—Alex snorted and released two streams of smoke through his nostrils—"Only a few normal women are left. The rest have been turned into walking incubators for the Führer. They turn on their own kind as soon as they detect revolt among their ranks. Weren't you, Traute, denounced by some BDM broad for refusing to donate for the winter front relief out of conviction?"

Traute nodded sagely, proudly.

"Innocent. No one is innocent," Alex repeated, his voice hissing like hot coals. "We, as people, deserve this government and everything it has done. If we're too weak to stand up, to resist—"

"Shurik." Hans called his name very softly, but some undertone in his voice, an unspoken warning in his brown eyes, stopped Alex right in his tracks.

All at once, Alex's demeanor changed. He turned back to Sophie, all playfulness once again. "Have you ever been denounced by a BDM broad, Sophie?"

"No," she acknowledged, feeling her cheeks grow warm from those penetrating eyes on her.

"Sophie, you disappoint me." He pressed his hand to his chest, feigning being wounded.

"I had to be an exemplary worker." Sophie tried not to grin in response and couldn't. "I needed excellent recommendations from my superiors to be admitted into the university."

"Shurik, leave my sister alone." Hans dealt his friend a half-hearted kick in the shin. "She's engaged."

"Are you?" Alex pulled forward, studying her with unconcealed interest. "You never said you were."

Sophie made no reply, only smiled mysteriously. The room was much too warm, the couch far too comfortable, the company too welcoming, too like-minded... Somehow, she had forgotten all about Fritz. She felt a pang of shame at the realization; tossed her head to clear it from the alcohol and the spell she had seemed to have fallen under, and headed to the kitchen. There, in relative silence, picking at the chipped green paint next to the window, Sophie swore to herself that she would write to Fritz first thing in the morning, the longest letter she could possibly compose, to make up for all her radio silence lately... and particularly for today.

"Are you really engaged?" Traute's voice behind her back made Sophie jump. "Sorry. I didn't mean to startle you. I thought you heard me come in." Her expression unreadable, Traute brought a cigarette to her lips, struck a match and lit up.

"Yes, very much engaged." Sophie shook her head when Traute offered her the crumpled pack and a matchbox. "Why?"

Traute pretended to be unbothered as she inhaled deeply. "Nothing. I just thought..." She quickly waved the assumption off.

Sophie, however, only pulled forward instead. "What did you think?"

"Nothing. I just thought Hans only said it to make Shurik leave off."

Stunned into silence, Sophie blinked at her with her mouth

slightly open. "Hans never mentioned Fritz to you?" she finally asked Traute after recovering herself.

"Not really, no," Traute admitted, offering Sophie a somewhat guilty smile. "But you know how men are," she rushed to add, waving the cigarette in the air. "They aren't like us girls. They don't gossip about amorous affairs all that much."

Sophie only grinned crookedly to Traute's forced laughter. "And yet I know that you're from Hamburg and that you don't eat meat because of that one summer you spent on the farm tending to the little lambs and ever since couldn't take a single bit of their flesh in your mouth after you saw them slaughtered by the farmer."

A blush of pleasure at the thought of Hans speaking to his sister of her in such intimate terms rose in Traute's cheeks, only to be replaced by yet another look of guilt right after. She had just opened her mouth to say something, to offer a suitable explanation, to remedy the situation somehow, when Sophie stopped her in her tracks by placing a hand on top of Traute's wrist.

"Don't. Hans has never liked Fritz, is all. He thinks this entire engagement was a mistake. I suppose that's why he never mentioned Fritz to you. Hans hopes I'll break it off sooner rather than later."

Traute's eyes snapped wide open. "Why would Hans be so against the poor fellow?"

Sophie was quiet a moment, searching for the explanation. "Fritz is in the army."

Obviously confused, Traute arched a questioning brow.

"Yes, yes, I know, Hans is in the army too." Sophie laughed softly. "But Fritz is a career officer. Hans was forced into the service and, even then, he chose to become a medic—someone who saves lives instead of taking them. Hans doesn't think we make a good couple."

"Well, stiff luck for Hans then. He's not the one who's marrying the guy."

Sophie smiled in gratitude for Traute's unexpected sisterly support, but the grin slipped off her face before long as she lost herself in thought. Just her luck, Traute noticed the passing shadow of doubt on Sophie's face.

"Sophie?" The gentle touch of her fingers only added to Sophie's inner torment. "You *do* want to marry this Fritz fellow, don't you?"

"Of course I do!" The words were out of her mouth before Sophie had a chance to even think about her answer. "We've known each other for five years..." Judging by Traute's look, she had expected to hear a different reason for marriage. "He proposed to me right before he went to the front, back in 1939..." Once again, her voice trailed off.

"Chose some moment, too; knew that Soph would feel too guilty to say no to a soldier leaving for the front."

Swinging round, Sophie came face to face with Hans. How long he'd been standing there listening, with his arms crossed over his chest and that conceited grin on his face, was anyone's guess.

"I said yes because I loved him," Sophie hissed back, thrusting her chin forward in defiance. "Not out of some demented sense of duty, as you have assumed."

"You've never loved him."

"What do you know about it?"

"You were infatuated with him." Hans turned to Traute, who was watching the exchange between siblings with an amused grin growing slowly on her face. "To be frank, he did look very dashing in his uniform. Even had a new, shining sword after graduating from the officers' school." His tone was thoroughly mocking now.

"It was never about any blasted swords!" Sophie exploded, much to Hans' delight.

"No, of course not. It was all about you being just the sort of a girl who dreams of becoming a career officer's wife. Brushing his uniforms and shining his boots and being a dedicated wife and a mother to a brood of fourteen children."

"Go hang yourself, Hans," Sophie said with an overly sweet smile, swatting her brother when he had the nerve to laugh, and storming out of the kitchen and back into the safety of the living room. The discussion going on there had nothing to do with her personal life, which, Sophie realized that very moment, she couldn't make heads nor tails of with the best will in the world.

From across the table, Alex continued to observe her subtly as he spoke to Christoph about the types of shrapnel-inflicted wounds they were presently studying, and Sophie continued to pretend that Hans was still wrong about her engagement and that her very life hadn't just turned upside down.

TWO

The weeks that followed were crisp with novelty and a vague sense of excitement. Concentrating on her studies, Sophie couldn't quite recall how the entire thing started. At first, there were whispers near the auditorium entrance, students throwing looks over their shoulders and growing silent as soon as she approached them as though they were a part of a conspiracy she wasn't trusted with. Then, in a university canteen, she saw a student in steel-rimmed glasses pass something to a girl in a checkered vest—a love note, Sophie had assumed. Bored, she almost returned to her textbook that lay open next to an unfinished plate of roast potatoes when the girl's frantic scrambling riveted her attention back to the couple. Pale as death, the girl was stuffing the note under the band of her skirt, her hand trembling violently.

By sheer chance, Sophie encountered the same girl later in the ladies' room. Alone in a locked stall, Sophie was fixing the clip on her stocking when she heard rushed steps, the banging of the door two stalls down, the unmistakable sound of tearing paper and the flushing of the toilet. When Sophie emerged from her stall, she came face to face with the girl from the canteen, who turned an even ghostlier shade of white, looking like a criminal caught red-handed next to a butchered body.

"Hello," Sophie said, deciding to politely ignore the girl's odd state.

"Hello," the girl barely managed in a hoarse voice. The piece of soap slipped from her hands a few times before she abandoned her futile attempts and all but ran out of the bathroom, away from Sophie.

Immersed in Huber's lecture—today was dedicated to Socrates —Sophie had all but forgotten about the girl's puzzling behavior and the general tension that seemed to hang in the air along with the scent of the blooming lilacs, when a crumpled ball of paper hit her in the back and landed at her feet.

Annoyed with the interruption, Sophie swung round in the hope of identifying the perpetrator, but not a single student betrayed themselves with as much as a glance in her direction. Blank faces, keen eyes trained on their professor, pencils scribbling furiously in their notebooks—they were a picture of rapt attention.

Only a scarcely audible whisper—"Read it"—so soft that Sophie wondered for a moment if she had imagined it, prompted her to pick up the small paper-ball and smooth it over her lap, under the cover of her desk.

All at once, she couldn't hear what Huber was saying. Neither could she see the auditorium's walls around herself with Hitler's likeness looking at her sternly from his usual place at the front of the room. All that existed was this leaflet, signed simply, White Rose. The leaflet and the dangerous, treasonous words swam before Sophie's widening eyes:

Nothing is more unworthy of a cultured people than to allow itself, without resistance, to be 'governed' by an irresponsible ruling clique motivated by the darkest of instincts. It is certainly the case today that every honest German is ashamed of his government. Who among us has any conception of the enormous shame that we and our children will feel when eventually the veil drops from our eyes and the most horrible of crimes—crimes that eclipse all atrocities throughout history—are exposed to the full light of day?

Shaken to the core, her wet palm covering the wrinkled sheet protectively, Sophie roved her gaze around once again, wondering who had the courage to not only preserve, but pass along, to prompt to read what she could only describe as a one-way ticket to a concentration camp, if not the gallows.

If the German people are already so corrupted and spiritually crushed that they do not raise a hand, unquestioningly trusting in the dubious legitimacy of historical order; if they surrender man's highest principle: his free will; if they abandon the will to take decisive action and turn the wheel of history and thus subject it to their own rational decision; if they are so devoid of any individuality, have already gone so far along the road toward becoming a spiritless and cowardly mass—then, yes, they deserve their downfall.

Adopt passive resistance wherever you are, and block the functioning of this aesthetic war machine before it is too late, before the last city is a heap of rubble, like Cologne, and before the last youth of our nation bleeds to death on some battlefield because of the hubris of a subhuman. Don't forget that every people gets the government it deserves!

From Friedrich Schiller's The Lawgiving of Lycurgus and Solon...

Lapsed into paralyzed, blood-chilling thought, Sophie sat and stared with unseeing eyes at the small figure of Professor Huber writing something on the chalkboard. She was still torn, undecided as to what to make of this pamphlet, of the feelings it had stirred in her. Waves, hot and cold, were rippling through her—her mind was previously a still lake into which someone had gone and hurled a huge rock.

Her first instinct was to follow the canteen girl's steps, tear the dangerous thing up, flush it down the drain and forget it like a bad dream. *But that was fear speaking*, it occurred to her after she had stilled her breath a little, allowed herself to think rationally. *The fear that they wanted them all to feel. Fear of thinking for oneself. Fear of going against the government. Fear to read, as ridiculous as it sounded.*

When had they become such a nation of cowards?

Slowly, gradually, the auditorium came back into focus. Uncovering the leaflet once again, Sophie reread it, deliberately this time, soaking up every word, every emotion, feeling them in her own soul as though the words belonged to her, as though someone had expressed precisely what had been brewing inside her this entire time—this desire for revolt, this resistance to the present-day order, this loathing of the war and everything that came with it: violence, death, devastation.

Yes, the safe thing would be to throw the pamphlet away.

But Sophie had never followed the safe way.

She followed the right way, just like Hans, just like their father before them.

And so, she slipped the leaflet discreetly between the pages of her textbook and placed her hand atop it, her eyes burning with newborn, fiery determination.

She wasn't alone in her rebellion. There were others. And she would find them. And she would join them. And she would fight along with them, no matter the cost.

Sophie returned to their room in Schwabing in great agitation. Just her misfortune, Hans was still out, either at a lecture with Traute or at one of his troop drills. Just like his comrades, he'd been fortunate enough to have been "furloughed" from active service to continue his medical studies in Munich, but the Wehrmacht still refused to release their grip on the healthy German youth that could hold weapons and fight "the Bolshevist threat." Hans' uniform and mandatory daily roll calls were a grim reminder of his involuntary service.

He would love the leaflet, Sophie thought as she paced the deserted rooms, sitting down and getting up momentarily, unable to find anything to do with her hands. She considered going out, getting herself a coffee in one of the student haunts on the corner, but then there was the question of the leaflet again.

Take it with her? No, far too dangerous. She'd been risking so much by keeping it in the first place.

Leave it here, in the apartment? Looking around, Sophie drummed her fingers on the textbook in which the dangerous pamphlet was concealed. But where? And just how reliable was the landlady? What if the seemingly harmless, birdlike elderly woman Sophie politely greeted in the hallway whenever the former stopped to gather her mail happened to be one of the Gestapo informers? She did have a spare key; what if it was her habit to snoop around when Hans was away?

Sophie was new to Munich. She was still learning who to trust and who not to. But staying put was entirely beyond her powers. She was too excited to remain within four walls, too eager to share her discovery with her brother. In a surge of relentless, nervous energy, she threw open all the windows, letting the fragrant June air in. Unable to resist the temptation, Sophie perched on the sun-warmed windowsill and began rereading the pamphlet.

Now that she could study it in the full light of the sun without fretting about being uncovered, she saw that it was well-read, bearing smudges of multiple fingers, ink stains and what appeared to be tiny drops of fat—someone must have read it in the canteen. She also saw that the pamphlet wasn't handwritten but mimeographed, so there must have been more of them floating around, being passed from student to student and—who knows—from professor to professor?

Jumping to her feet once again, Sophie began to bounce around the apartment, lifting cushions off the sofa and prodding at the bottoms of the desk drawers in search of a suitable hiding place. Her eyes glinted in triumph when she stopped in front of the bookshelf filled from top to bottom with books. There was no rhyme or reason to them; medical encyclopedias were shoved next to German classics and cheap penny dreadfuls; histories of the Orient and Middle East bordered travel journals from all over the world; yoga atlases rolled into tubes lay upon similar atlases of poisonous weeds and human anatomy; philosophy textbooks were piled upon French fashion magazines—Traute's, as Sophie had assumed. It was the oddest assortment of volumes, which reflected, with amazing precision, Hans' personality. That bookshelf was Hans in a nutshell—his sharp intellect always questioning everything, his versatile interests, his fascination with world cultures and their histories. But it was his love of humanity threading through that disorganized library that brought a fond, proud smile to Sophie's face. *After the war is over, he'll make an excellent physician,* she thought, carefully rearranging the tomes in order to squeeze in her textbook with the leaflet still inside.

She had all but succeeded in jamming the thick volume in between a Russian dictionary and an Agatha Christie mystery when, preceded by the rustling of the pages, something dropped on her head. Issuing a curse and rubbing the place where the offending book hit her, Sophie bent down and froze, her hand not quite reaching the volume.

It was a collection of Schiller's works—one of the first German poets rallying for brotherhood and equality for all mankind, who, therefore, fell out of favor with the Nazis for that very reason. It had spilled its pages that wavered with uncertainty in the breeze for a couple of seconds before resting at last on the page that had been smoothed open with a forceful finger far too many times, its borders crawling with Hans' slanted handwriting right next to the underlined text:

> "At the price of all moral feeling, a political system was set up, and the resources of the state were mobilized to that end. In Sparta, there was no conjugal love, no mother love, no filial devotion, no friendships; all men were merely citizens, and all virtue was civic virtue. A law of the state made it the duty of Spartans to be inhumane to their slaves; in these unhappy victims of war, humanity itself was insulted and mistreated. What an admirable sight it is, in contrast, to see the rough soldier Gaius Marcius in his camp before Rome, when he renounced vengeance and victory because he could not endure the sight of a mother's tears!"

Slowly, on shaky legs, Sophie straightened, pulled her textbook with the pamphlet hidden in it back from the shelf and lowered herself to the worn carpet, clasping the textbook to her chest. She dared not extract the leaflet and compare the words; she dared not even touch it, for touching it would make it real and she refused to believe that it was.

With the best will in the world, Sophie couldn't tell how long she remained in the same paralyzed state. The day stretched along the floor in golden rays, pooling at her feet, igniting the pages she refused to look at. There was a labored whizzing coming from the ancient wall clock; a headless cuckoo bird flew out, leaning precariously to the left, croaking twice in its hoarse voice.

It was a quarter to three when Sophie finally began comparing the text line by line, analyzing the tone of the leaflet, reading it inside her mind in her brother's voice.

It was three fifteen when she had finally surrendered, wiped her hands down her face, came to terms with it.

Naturally, it was Hans. She should have known, should have realized that he would attempt something of this sort.

For the hundredth time, her fingers traced the lines she felt like she knew by heart: *"Don't forget that every people gets the government it deserves!"*

A knowing grin tugged at the corners of her lips as recognition ignited in her eyes. She vividly remembered Alex saying this very thing at her birthday party: there are no innocents among us; we deserve the annihilation that is coming to us.

No wonder they were thick as thieves. They had to be, with such a secret between them.

As though on cue, there was the sound of the lock turning and the creaking of the front door. Hans was trying to prove something to Alex, his words somewhat muffled by the traffic coming from outside. Sophie heard Alex laugh, cynically yet good-naturedly, and call her brother a pitiful idealist.

"He is a militarist of the deepest conviction; he shall never agree to—" Alex had stopped abruptly as soon as he saw Sophie, causing Hans to almost stumble into him.

"Soph! You're home already! Why didn't you—"

Sophie cut him off mid-word by holding up the leaflet in one hand and Schiller, with Hans' markings in it, in the other.

She was still sitting on the floor, all skinny legs, sharp elbows, and boyishly short hair, but both men suddenly shrank, cowered somewhat before her accusatory glare, not even their uniforms providing any comfort at the threat of the veritable storm emerging.

"What in Hades were you two thinking?!" Sophie's shout echoed around the room, startling the pigeons from the plaster ledge outside.

Hans was silent for a moment, before he wetted his lips and began explaining something about freedom and war and his trip to the Nuremberg rally and something about the flag they wouldn't let him carry and the importance of self-expression.

It was Alex who stepped forward and interrupted his best

friend's embarrassed ramblings with a bright and unconcerned, "Did you like it though?" He was beaming down on Sophie, childishly proud, as though craving encouragement. "You oughtn't be too hard on us. It was our very first effort, after all. We're still experimenting, finding our voices, so to speak, but what's important is that it seems to be getting the message out and—"

"That's not the issue, you pair of muttons!" Sophie rose swiftly to her feet, waving Schiller menacingly in front of Alex's bemused face. "What I'm asking is what in the blue hell you were thinking, keeping this book here with all the notes in the margins and text underlined for anyone to find?"

Hans blinked once, twice. Alex also stood still as a statue before he exploded. "Hans, we shall indeed be a pair of muttons if we don't involve Sophie in our little affair! It is rather obvious—no matter how embarrassing—that she has more brains than the two of us put together. Just look how fast she has uncovered us!" He was looking at her with unconcealed admiration.

Hans appeared to be less than enthused with the idea. "Sophie's here to study, not get involved with all sorts of—"

"I'm already involved, Hans," she said calmly. "Is it just the two of you or someone else? Christoph? Traute? Willi?"

"Just the two of us," Hans replied hastily.

Alex regarded him with reproach.

Rolling his eyes, Hans released a voluminous breath. "Just the two of us writing and printing it. But yes; Christoph, Willi, and Traute all know about it and support the idea."

"Anyone else?" Sophie demanded, her arms folded across her chest.

The men exchanged glances. "Just you," Alex said with a wink and that playful grin of his that made professors forgive his missed deadlines and forgotten assignments, and Sophie's heart skip a beat no matter how hard she tried to keep it under control.

"Welcome to the White Rose," Hans said and smiled wistfully, the protective older brother who didn't mind dying himself for his convictions but loathed to imagine his little sister losing her life over them.

"Thank you," Sophie said and meant it. "It'll be my honor to fight alongside you."

THREE

Dear Fritz...

Stuck on the same line for over twenty minutes, Sophie turned her gaze to an opened window in search of inspiration. It shouldn't have been such a chore, writing to one's fiancé. She never suffered from lack of words whenever she sat down to write to her parents or her best friend Lisa, but when it came to Fritz, her hand suddenly turned to lead and all her thoughts scattered like the pages of old, torn newspapers carried by the wind along deserted Munich streets.

Sophie blamed the war. They had scarcely seen each other in three years after his leaving for the front back in 1939. Faithfully, she carried his photograph wherever she went, in which he stood in his officer's uniform, clasping the handle of his sword with his gloved hand, tall and handsome in that poster-perfect Aryan way, all blond hair and strong jawline and slightly furrowed, light brow. Sophie couldn't quite imagine him in civilian life, as that perfectly tailored uniform was just as much a part of him as his obsession with order and intolerance of anyone being even two minutes late. His love of horseback riding was just as innate as his hunting and commanding skills, for which he received promotions and commendations with envious regularity. She still remembered these vague bits about him, but all at once it occurred to Sophie that she could no longer remember how his arms felt around her or the sound of his laughter. But what was even worse, she could no longer feel the fire that used to ignite in her at his slightest touch, at only the mention of his name, at the sight of his familiar hand-writing she used to kiss whenever she discovered those longed-for letters among her mail.

Yes, it was that cursed war's fault. Things would be back to normal as soon as it was over, as soon as he could gather her in his arms again. Setting her jaw, Sophie willed her hand to pick up the pen once more.

"The weather has been splendid here," she wrote, forcing the meaningless words onto the paper. "Hans and I spend most of our weekends hiking. To my great disappointment, my bicycle is still being held hostage by the postal service and I have to make do with streetcars and my two feet. The lectures are most interesting, and particularly anatomy and philosophy..."

She stared blankly at the page, words mocking, avoiding her once again. To be sure, she couldn't write anything about her joining the White Rose—censors would report the letter before it had a chance to make it to the front line—but when Sophie imag-ined standing face to face with Fritz just then, reunited at long last after such a long separation, she realized that she still wouldn't confess to it. Something that she would announce with pride to her father was suddenly a taboo subject of when it came to her own fiancé. Hans was right all along, it had dawned on Sophie. Fritz *was* a career officer, with a sense of military duty dominating his entire life. He was born into the life of unquestionable loyalty, raised to salute and obey whoever was in charge and it mattered not if the orders went against his own conscience. Fritz could despise his superiors but die on the battlefield, fighting their idiotic wars, all the same. Almost physically, Sophie felt the already thin fabric tying them together tear even further as her hand crumpled the unfinished letter of its own volition.

Annoyed with herself, preparing a fresh sheet of paper with

yet another *Dear Fritz* staring at her with accusation from its top, Sophie didn't notice someone calling her name at first. Only after a small pebble, with a daisy tied around it by a string, landed on her desk and startled her did she look out the window to discover Alex standing on the sidewalk. Dark shades concealing his eyes made a startling contrast with his Wehrmacht uniform, which he wore with the first two buttons undone against all army regulations.

"Are you busy?" he inquired without any preamble.

Painfully aware of the unfinished letter that was long overdue, Sophie tossed her head. "Not really, no. Why?"

"Want to take a ride to the countryside?" He jerked his thumb over his shoulder, indicating a shiny black convertible parked near the curb.

"Is it yours?" Sophie regarded the vehicle dubiously. Nazi Party bigwigs rode around in similar models, with little red flags mounted above the headlights.

"What do you think?" Alex grinned at her wryly.

"I think not, hence the question."

"Of course it's not mine. I don't indulge in such bourgeois luxuries out of personal convictions. I borrowed it for the day."

"From whom?" Sophie scowled further.

"Get in the car; I'll explain on the way."

"I'm not getting into a stolen car!"

A couple of passers-by slowed their steps, observing Alex closely.

"A *borrowed* car!" he said intentionally loudly for their benefit, swiftly putting both hands up in mock surrender. "Borrowed, not stolen. Borrowed from my own father." He turned back to Sophie's window. "Now, will you kindly climb inside or would you rather have me arrested first?"

Shame flushing her cheeks, Sophie pushed the unfinished letter into the desk drawer, slammed it shut, alongside her thoughts of Fritz and her guilt over this entire blasted situation, and headed for the door.

Outside, the asphalt was hot and pliable under her sandaled feet; not a tree stirred in the oppressive, balmy air.

"It looks like we'll get a storm," Sophie said, her eyes directed upward.

Without Hans' presence, she felt unnerved somewhat and particularly after Alex leaned forward—intentionally slowly, as though asking for silent permission—and planted a kiss on her burning cheek. Sophie couldn't explain to herself why she hadn't turned her head away. He was a friend, after all, and this was a perfectly innocent gesture, Sophie tried to persuade herself, struggling with a guilty conscience once again.

"If it rains, we'll put the top on," Alex said, holding the door for her.

Inside the car, it was hotter still. From the long, obsidian hood, heat was rising in waves, distorting the air. Even the upholstery under Sophie's bare legs was warm. She felt beads of sweat breaking on her temples, sliding down her back.

"Are we picking up Hans?" she asked when Alex expertly pulled away from the curb and merged with the light afternoon traffic.

"Hans will meet us there," Alex replied, purposely mysterious.

"Where?"

"You'll see."

"I hate surprises, you know."

"Why did you get in the car with me then?" He looked away from the road just to arch his lively brow at her.

"I wish I knew," Sophie grumbled, more to herself than him.

Before long, the outskirts of Munich replaced its busy streets. Warm wind in her hair, Sophie closed her eyes against the sun, soaking up the delicious day. Rather to her surprise, the ride was mostly silent aside from Alex's occasional, "Are you comfortable?", "Want my sunglasses?", "Am I going too fast?", "Is the wind too strong for you?", "Want me to put the top up?". However, next to him, even the silence was comfortable, companionable; Sophie didn't feel pressured to fill in awkward pauses with irrelevant remarks and, instead, she let her shoulders drop and relaxed, giving herself fully to the crisp air of mountains, pines, and freshly turned earth.

"Will you tell me now where we're heading, or would you prefer me to think that you've shamelessly kidnapped me?" Sophie asked, only half in jest.

In profile, Alex's features were angular and sharp, as though cut by a sculptor from a hard stone. During his troop exercises with Hans, he had acquired a bronze tan and, in contrast, his already dark hair seemed almost raven-black.

"Which one would you prefer?" he asked instead of a reply, but, glimpsing a look of mild reproach on Sophie's face, he broke into soft laughter and finally answered, "We're on the way to my parents' house."

"And where would that be?"

"In the suburbs." Alex made an evasive gesture.

"Are they training you as a medic or an Abwehr intelligence agent?" Sophie couldn't contain herself any longer and exploded in laughter. "Why are you making me pull the answers out of you as though in an interrogation?"

He was silent a moment before he finally said, so softly that Sophie had trouble making it out, "Harlaching."

Now the expensive convertible began to make sense. From hiking with Hans, Sophie was familiar with the affluent suburban area they passed on their way. Harlaching was populated with villas and mansions built by architects hired for exorbitant prices, even for prewar times, with spacious emerald lawns and meticulously maintained orchards where the owners of those mansions held luncheons and wine tastings for their wealthy neighbors and friends. In Munich, there were blackout regulations and lines in front of butchers and grocery stores; in Harlaching, men in hunting boots toasted champagne to their elegantly dressed women while a manservant carved freshly killed venison near tables covered with pristine white tablecloths.

"Shurik!" Sophie nudged him playfully with her elbow. "It is my profound conviction that you're taking me to a castle, not a simple house."

She laughed, but Alex didn't smile, as though the subject was painful for him for some unimaginable reason.

"They're rich," he countered with an odd undertone to his voice. "I'm just a poor student."

"In a convertible."

This time, Alex grinned, but changed the subject all the same. "Hans invited that actor, von Radecki, to a reading. My father doesn't really approve of our literary luncheons, but we came to an agreement a long time ago, he and I."

A shadow passed over his face, clouding his features once again. Sophie searched it for clues and gently probed when Alex didn't elaborate further, "You don't get along, the two of you?"

Alex grimaced slightly. "We do and we don't. It's difficult to explain."

There was nothing difficult about Sophie and Robert Scholl's relationship. The door of his study was always open for her and her siblings. He had never silenced their opinions and only encouraged their questioning minds. And Sophie's mother, even though she wasn't as outspoken as her husband, made up for her lack of rebelliousness with unconditional love and devotion to her husband and children. A politically unreliable family, frequented by the Gestapo with their searches whenever it struck the agents' fancy, Sophie wouldn't trade them for all the prestige and riches in the world.

"You can try." She stole a glance at Alex.

He was silent for over a minute, as though searching for a place to start.

"You know that I was born in Russia, don't you?"

Sophie nodded.

"My father was born there too. His father—my grandfather— settled there and became a successful fur merchant, but he never gave up his German nationality, so my father was technically born a German. He made use of it; went here, to Munich, to study medicine, but then returned to Russia; married my mother. When the Great War broke out, he was assigned to a hospital for German prisoners of war in the Urals. I was born there in 1917—the Revolution year. I don't really remember my mother. She died when I was two." His voice was cool, detached, as if he was merely reciting facts of someone else's biography that bored him to tears. "I was raised by a Russian nanny, whom my father brought here, to Germany, when he left soon after the Revolution. Didn't fancy the Bolshevist ideas, as you can well imagine." Grinning cynically, he patted the gleaming, polished wheel of the convertible. "I grew up here, in Germany, but on Russian folk songs and Russian fairy tales my nanny told me each night before sleep. She taught me how to pray to a Russian God; my father taught me how to love the Fatherland. As long as I remember, I've been constantly torn between east and west, between Gogol and Goethe, between balalaika and piano, between art and science. I wanted to become an artist or a sculptor, but my father explained to me in plain terms that he'd disown me if I followed that path."

"Something tells me you wouldn't mind being a traveling artist," Sophie remarked, also growing serious.

"No, I wouldn't," Alex agreed. The wind muted it, but Sophie saw a heavy sigh escape his chest all the same. "It's just... we need money, and particularly now."

"We?"

He looked at her pointedly. "We. The White Rose."

Sophie's breath caught in her throat. It was the first time they'd spoken about it since the day she had confronted him and Hans.

"When Hans and I first came up with the idea of printing pamphlets, we realized that it would come at a price. And I don't just mean our poor heads." He was back to his jokes and Sophie was inwardly glad of it. "The mimeograph to print the copies on, the stencils, the paper, the ink, the stamps and envelopes—everything costs money and I just happen to be the one with most of it in our little circle. So, my dream life will just have to wait until we sort out this war and the Nazi business."

That was also meant as a joke but came out much too wistfully for Sophie's liking.

Before she could think it over, she reached across the seat and pressed Alex's hand lightly. "Do you think we will?"

"We have to." He shrugged with a sort of melancholy resignation about him. "Else, we might as well hang ourselves right now and save us the misery of such a life."

Sophie turned out to be right: the "house" was a veritable familial estate, imposing, with an immaculately maintained garden and stables next to which a young man of Alex's age was washing a magnificent black horse. As soon as they pulled to a stop, the groom greeted Alex with a wide smile and a hand raised in the air, a soap-soaked brush still enclosed in it.

"Good afternoon, Alexander Hugovich!" he called in his strongly accented German. "You ride today?"

It suddenly occurred to Sophie that he was either a prisoner of war or a foreign laborer dragged to Germany against his will. However, it was only his Eastern accent that betrayed him, and the odd manner in which he had addressed Alex; unlike most slave laborers, he wasn't dressed in the begrimed remnants of the attire in which he had arrived and neither did he appear to be half-starved. On the contrary, muscle and flesh was visible under the rolled sleeves of a clean cotton shirt, and in the man's eyes, genuine emotion gleamed at the sight of the young master of the house.

"Not today, Sash," Alex replied with a grin, holding the door open for Sophie. "Important guests today."

The groom nodded knowingly and deeply.

"Come, say hello." Before Sophie could fix her hair, all tousled after a drive despite being short, Alex had gripped her hand and pulled her toward the young man. "His name is Alexander too; fancy that? Not to cause any confusion, we address him as Sasha. It's also a diminutive, like Shurik. But we already have one Shurik, so he has to make do with Sasha."

In another instant, Alex scooped the groom into a tight embrace, getting soap and water all over his uniform. Sasha tried to protest something in Russian, pointing at the stains and holding his brush as far away from Alex's tunic as possible, but the latter paid no heed to such trifles.

"Sasha is my brother!" He turned to Sophie, positively beaming. "My soul brother; he's from Russia too! Also a soldier. He was in a cavalry and loves horses as much as I do. They brought him here to work as a farmhand, but as soon as I learned that he's a cavalry officer, I went straight to my father and gave him an ultimatum: either Sasha works only at the stables and lives with our own domestics, or I'll quit my studies and will become a sculptor like I have threatened him before. Well," he tousled his friend's hair, "here we are! Sash," he said, clapping the Russian on his shoulder, "what do you say to that?"

"Germany is a good country," Sasha announced, his head inclined to one side. "But Hitler is an *Arschloch*."

In spite of herself, Sophie snorted at the crude German curse that the Russian pronounced with such relish.

"Have you taught him that?" she demanded, turning to Alex.

"Naturally." He acknowledged it with pride. "I taught him all the curse words but, more importantly, when and in front of whom he may say them in order not to get shot."

After a final wink, Alex left his "soul brother" to his duties and led Sophie along the neatly manicured path toward the back of the house, from where distant voices and notes of music carried along with the warm summer breeze.

"Do you have many prisoners of war working here?" Sophie asked.

Alex cringed visibly. "Most of our former hired farmhands have been replaced by them after the farmhands were shipped off to the front. Poor devils."

He didn't specify whom precisely he meant—the farmhands or the POWs—and Sophie didn't ask. Both, most likely. It was obvious that under the lightheartedness of Alex's playful manner, a deep-seated shame for the actions of the German army, to which he himself ironically belonged, was brewing.

"Your family seems to treat them well," Sophie noted in the hope of cheering him up a bit.

He took a deep breath, as if he thought of saying something—how wrong it was that his family had those prisoners of war slaving away for them in the first place, how wrong the entire filthy business of war was, together with Hitler's imperial ambitions, how infinitely guilty he felt just for being half-German before this Russian man—but he ended up saying nothing.

Sophie still saw it all, hidden deep in his eyes, and once again pressed his palm ever so slightly, in a much-needed gesture of support.

As was often the case with Alex, the jolly mask had slipped without him noticing it, replaced by one of dark melancholy. His bouts of clowning about were invariably short-lived, an act performed for the sake of others. But as soon as he forgot himself, the same dim veil glazed over his eyes, robbing them of any light; the same brooding look knitted his dark brows together, set his sharp jaw as if he were battling some invisible foe within himself. His German half perhaps; the one confined to the prison of his uniform, Sophie pondered, gazing at him subtly from under her lowered lashes.

But then a tremendous white canopy came into view, under which several pulled-together tables were brimming with beer and fruit, and Alex's expression brightened at once, as though someone had flicked a light switch within him, and before long he was laughing and shaking hands and clapping friendly shoulders—"Hans, you old crow, your sister is much better company than you! Sigi, look at you, you performer of arts! Golden cufflinks, during the rationing? Someone has made himself up swell! I ought to report you for strutting about dressed in such finery!"

While Alex transferred his attention to his guest of honor, Hans, his uniform collar also undone and sleeves rolled up to his elbows, greeted Sophie with a kiss on her temple and offered her his own chair. Tucked between Christoph with his guitar and a raven-haired beauty clad in a man's tailcoat, Sophie gazed around in stunned wonder. Having never attended any such literary luncheons, she wasn't quite sure what to expect. Some reading, acting perhaps—

"Hitler has only got one ball..."

Straightening bolt upright in her chair, Sophie stared at Christoph Probst, a glass with lemonade frozen inches away from her open mouth. Christoph's guitar sounded slightly slurred, just like his English, as his fingers stroked the strings lazily.

"Göring has two but very small..." He continued to sing, some highly treasonous affair he must have heard on the BBC.

Rather to her surprise, the entire table picked up the song in an instant: "Himmler is rather sim'lar..."

"...but poor old Goebbels has no balls at all!" Alex finished just above Sophie's ear, making her clasp her mouth with her hand to stifle her hysterical laughter.

Sophie certainly hadn't expected *this*. The entire setting had a quality of a drug-induced dream about it, a Mad Hatter's party with Alex presiding. Schnapps-spiced lemonade sweated next to Oriental hookahs and a faint scent of something intoxicating and dangerous collected in vaporous clouds under the white canopy along with the notes of allied army repertoire mocking the highest hierarchy of the Reich.

"Sigi, are you planning to delight us with your interpretation of Mann or have you come here with the sole purpose to stuff your guts at my expense?" Alex set upon his guest in the most undignified of manners.

It only prompted more laughter from his tipsy audience. There were no ranks or privileged classes here, it suddenly occurred to Sophie. In Alex's world—his fictional, ideal world he was able to recreate in the privacy of his estate for a few short hours—everyone was equal, everyone was a good comrade, everyone was welcome—unlike the rest of Germany that surrounded this little paradise-like island like a leaden, hostile ocean.

"My esteemed host"—Sigismund von Radecki, a man in his thirties who truly belonged on the stage, or the screen, with his well-modulated voice and features not unlike those of classic Greek sculptures, pressed his hand to his heart in a theatrical gesture—"allow me a few more minutes. I'm not quite there yet."

"Where? Under the table?" His fists butting his hips, Alex proceeded to mock him savagely.

"Shurik, leave off." Sophie's neighbor, the black-haired beauty, waved Alex off languidly. "You know that unlike me he needs liquid courage to perform banned stuff."

"Why don't you go up first then?" Sigi narrowed his eyes at her in mock contempt.

The tails-clad beauty only shrugged, unconcerned, and rose from her chair with that innate elegance Sophie always admired in women who were so unlike her, with her tomboyish ways.

"Shurik, my record," she demanded over her shoulder as she strode onto the lawn in front of the canopy.

While Alex fumbled with the gramophone, she produced a mask of sorts from under her tuxedo jacket and, having turned her back to her audience, began to tie black silk ribbons behind her immaculately coiffured head.

"*War and Peace*, interpretive dance," she announced in a low, husky voice that carried far and seeped under the skin at the same time. "Part one: War."

Next, she flung her shoes—also men's—off her feet and onto the grass and froze in an elaborate pose, waiting for the first notes of music to strike.

When they did—Wagner's "Ride of the Valkyries"—a rush of something inexplicable broke all over Sophie's skin.

"You've never met Lilo, have you?"

She hadn't even noticed when Alex lowered himself into the empty chair next to her, his gaze also riveted to the woman.

"She's my very old friend. She's not only a dancer, but a successful sculptress. We rent a studio together." His explanation seemed a bit rushed, as though he didn't want Sophie to assume anything untoward about his and Lilo's friendship.

"She's amazing," Sophie whispered, following Lilo's movements with sheer admiration.

Her entire body seemingly boneless, Lilo was leaping forward one instant and falling in a heap, as though cut down by an invisible scythe, the next. All by herself, without a single prop, she was re-enacting men fighting, suffering, and dying with a frightening realism in her agonized death throes.

"Where did she learn..." Sophie desperately groped for the right word.

"What the front-line death looks like?" Alex finished for her. "From the front."

When Sophie turned to look at him in surprise, he only grinned sadly in response.

"Lilo managed to get permission to go to the front from the local *Promi* office, 'to entertain the troops.' Of course, she dances rather different stuff for them. But those experiences, whatever she sees there, she brings back here and shows it all to those who despise the war as much as she does. We all revolt in our own ways. Lilo does it by dancing and by sculpting amputees and death masks of the soldiers she saw and still has nightmares about."

Now, Lilo's brooding silence and disdain of small talk, which Sophie, rather to her shame, had taken for arrogance at first, made a whole lot of sense. Just like the dance that soon consumed Sophie entirely, transporting her straight onto the battlefield under the blinding spotlight of the sun.

Now fluid and animalistic, Lilo's next movement was harsh and broken, almost ugly in the realism of the emotion she managed to deliver to her audience with the sole power of her body, her face hidden behind the terrifying mask that would fit the Grim Reaper himself.

"She hides her face for a reason—doesn't want people to get distracted by it," Alex explained in a respectful whisper, so as not to disturb the perfect silence that had befallen those who had gathered in his garden that golden afternoon. "She thinks her beauty to be her curse. She thinks people never take her seriously because of it, hence the clothes, hence the absence of makeup—"

"Hence the mask," Sophie finished, nodding knowingly. "She wants her art to speak for her, not her face."

"Precisely." Alex beamed at her, delighted that she understood everything not only about him, but about the friends he cherished —his entire world—with such ease.

After Lilo's performance ended with wild applause, Hans took to the improvised stage to read some poetry, old Weimar stuff that they were too young to remember but the freedoms of which they shared an inexplicable longing for.

Sigismund von Radecki, who was introduced to Sophie in a very informal manner, which seemed to be the custom among Alex's friends, turned out to be a wonderful actor indeed, liquid courage or not. As soon as he began reading—Thomas Mann's latest book, *The Coming Victory of Democracy*, banned and condemned, just like the freedom-loving author himself, by Goebbels' Propaganda Ministry (Alex wouldn't have anything *Promi*-approved read at his literary luncheons)—everyone froze in their seats, positively transfixed, their glasses sweating in their hands, the beer forgotten and slowly going flat.

Alex's father, Hugo, came out for a minute or two, dark like a raven in his black, made-to-measure suit, with a stiff collar cutting into his neck. He listened to Sigi read a passage about fascism being an offensive child of the times and democracy being a time-less human with an impenetrable expression, and disappeared back into the house after remarking to Alex, in a hushed voice, to change his stained uniform.

When Alex returned, dressed in riding breeches, tall jackboots, and a pristinely white short-sleeved shirt—the vision of a young English lord enjoying his drink after a game of polo—it occurred to Sophie that this was his plan all along: to soil his uniform on purpose with soap and horsehair just to have a good excuse to be rid of the hateful thing.

"He refused to take an oath to Hitler, you know," Hans remarked to Sophie, his arm draped over the back of her wicker chair. In his other hand, a forgotten cigarette was slowly turning to ash. "The ceremony was under way—flags, military brass, all business as it should be—and our hero suddenly goes and announces that he would not swear his absolute loyalty to Adolf Hitler. His commanding officer goes white as a sheet, tries to plead with him through gritted teeth, but Shurik refuses to see any reason. Shakes his head like an obstinate ass; no, I'm not swearing anything," Hans recounted with barely concealed admiration and disbelief in his voice. "*Court-martial me, send me to the camp—I'm not saying this particular oath, and that's that.*"

"What happened?" Sophie whispered, holding her breath and not quite noticing it.

"Oddly, nothing." Hans looked as though he himself found it to be surprising. "The highest-ranking officer shrugged it off; said that since Shurik is a medical officer, he won't be fighting anyone anyway and, in his case, the Hippocratic oath would do. But that's Shurik for you: he always gets into trouble and gets out of it again by some miracle. I suppose the officers had simply grown used to it by then much like Shurik's family did."

The reading about democracy and fascism turned into a discussion, with Alex soon emerging as the leading voice. He was gesticulating animatedly, arguing about something with Willi.

Hans was asking her a question for the second time, but Sophie couldn't stop staring at Alex in wonder. She didn't understand him and, yet, she understood him all too well.

She, too, felt the same conflict deep inside her.

She, too, didn't know where she belonged.

Fritz did, she suddenly thought, remembering the unfinished letter she had shoved into her drawer what seemed like a lifetime ago. In Fritz's life, everything was structured and organized to the minute. He was a typical Prussian and proud of it, his love for the military running in his very blood. Just like his father and grandfather, he was born into the army and had grown into it, his roots binding him far too tightly to consider even the possibility of escape. Not that he had ever wanted it. No, Fritz wanted a regular officer's life and a family.

And with a sudden rush to her heart, Sophie realized that she no longer fit into that picture.

FOUR

GESTAPO INTERROGATION ROOM, MUNICH.
FEBRUARY 1943

Despite the shorthand pad in front of him, Robert Mohr had a most distinct feeling that it was him who was being interrogated; such was the steely, calm power radiating from Sophia Scholl's dark eyes. She was staring him down, invoking the memories of the White Rose's very last pamphlet—"we will not be silent; we are your bad conscience; the White Rose will not leave you in peace!" —and this time it was Mohr who had looked away first.

"Sophia," Mohr addressed her in the same soft voice he used with his own teenage daughter.

The Scholl girl sitting opposite him looked nothing like her and yet he couldn't help but feel something paternal stir inside of him at the sight of her smooth, clear skin, at the youthful idealism of her principles, at that untainted belief that she and her generation would change the world for the better. She had confessed to everything as soon as she had sat down across from him in this unheated, dimly lit, moldy interrogation room. Not out of fear—there was not a trace of it in her countenance—but to spare the others, no doubt. Little did she know that her brother, Hans, had just confessed to the exact same thing mere minutes ago in the exact same interrogation room. Hans' seat had been still warm when Sophie sat down in it.

Mohr didn't have anything against men dying for their ideals. There was something noble and even natural about them martyring themselves for the cause. But women—no, she wasn't even a woman, a mere slip of a girl—that went against all Mohr's instincts.

"Sophia," he repeated, softening his voice even more.

"It's Sophie," she corrected him, holding his gaze. "Nobody calls me Sophia. The name exists on my passport only."

"Sophie." Mohr inclined his head to one side, interlocking his fingers on top of the closed pad, in which he hadn't written a single line of her entire confession. "It is evident from what you've told me so far that it was your brother who dragged you into this entire rotten affair. It was him who began printing and distributing those pamphlets, long before you came to Munich."

"Not long before." Sophie corrected him calmly. "Only a month."

"A month." Once again, Mohr decided not to argue. "My point is, you would have been pursuing your studies and enjoying your student life if it hadn't been for him and his subversive actions."

Sophie broke into laughter so unexpectedly that she startled him. "Herr Kriminalkommissar, it's rather misogynistic of you to assume that women can't think for themselves whatsoever and it's always a man that propels them to action. Hans didn't *drag me* into anything, as you have put it. In fact, I have clearly told you that he was against my joining the group."

Mohr shifted in his seat, considering his next move. He had already miscalculated, it occurred to him then. Sophie Scholl turned out to be far more intelligent than he had expected from a girl her age.

Too intelligent for her own good, he thought to himself, before trying a different angle.

"Forgive me, please, Fräulein Scholl. It was never my intention to insult your intelligence. I'm confused." He threw her a probing glance. "You arrived in Munich with an excellent report from your BDM leader."

"What has that got to do with anything?"

"It tells me that you never got into any trouble in your League of German Girls' group."

Sophie's only response was a dismissive, one-shoulder shrug.

Mohr licked his lips, sensing an opening in her so far impenetrable defense.

"Is it safe to assume that you enjoyed being in the BDM?" he asked and held his breath.

But even now she saw through him without any effort. A wry grin began to tug on Sophie's lips. "Herr Kriminalkommissar, I understand where you're leading with this. You're hoping for me to say that I was an exemplary National Socialist before my brother came and turned me into an anarchist or some such." Her grin grew wider. "This is simply not the case. The BDM membership, just like the *Hitlerjugend* one, is mandatory. I had to join, whether I liked it or not. Just like Hans. Just like Inge, Elisabeth, and Werner—my two other sisters and brother. It's true, I did enjoy certain aspects of it—camping, hiking, singing, comradery among the girls—but I couldn't, for the life of me, tolerate its political facet. And if you had dug deeper, you would have come across several reports from my teachers who complained about my outspokenness on quite a few occasions. Speaking of BDM, one of the first such reports was about my questioning the racial theory itself."

"Care to elaborate?" Mohr asked, genuinely curious.

Ordinarily, the older generation that had come of age in the liberal Weimar Republic had a very problematic habit (for the authorities, at least) of questioning everything. The younger generation that had grown up in the new German Reich that had replaced Weimar was usually so indoctrinated by the time they reached their teens, they blindly followed whatever came out of their leaders' mouths. The Scholl siblings were clearly an exception to the rule; Mohr wanted to know why.

Sophie shrugged once again, almost too bored to speak, to explain the obvious. "I had a Jewish friend who was much more

Aryan-looking than me. Hair white as snow; long, beautiful braids; a perfect little upturned nose; gorgeous blue eyes. Naturally, my question was why she was banned from being admitted to the BDM and not me." With great irony, she gestured toward her short brown hair, and deep brown eyes. "So, I said it out loud in the middle of the class that the entire racial theory was rot. Before you ask, I was twelve years old." She smiled with great pleasure at ruining, with one single blow, Mohr's carefully constructed theory.

Robert Mohr fell silent, cursing inwardly at himself, at the stubborn girl who made such a surprisingly interesting conversationalist; wondering why she had set her mind on going down with the rest of the ship when he had made it obvious that he would gladly help her if she only helped him.

All of a sudden, a thought occurred to Mohr. He brightened, pulled himself up visibly.

"Can we talk about your fiancé?" he asked innocently, hiding his eyes as he consulted the Scholl file laid out in front of him. "Fritz Hartnagel; is that correct?"

A strange shadow full of melancholy passed over Sophie's features. "That is his name, yes," she said at length and quickly added, looking at Mohr almost sternly, "He has nothing to do with us, with the White Rose. He's an exemplary officer and a good patriot."

"And you aren't?"

"We are patriots too; it's just... we have different ideas of patriotism."

"What is yours?"

"You read our pamphlets. You should know."

"I'd like to hear it from you."

"Freedom," Sophie said and added, "For everyone, without exceptions."

"And what do you think is our idea?"

"War and obliteration of everyone who goes against you."

Mohr thought of protesting but suddenly realized that he had absolutely nothing to say against that blunt accusation, not a damned thing.

"Let us return to Herr Hartnagel," he said instead. "Why did you accept his proposal if you're such different people, as you claim?"

Sophie considered her answer for a while. "I fell in love with him when I was only sixteen," she said with an odd, pensive intonation in her voice. "Stupid, impressionable girl. He was four years older than me, already in the army, a dashing young man. When you're sixteen, you don't really think about whether you're compatible or not; you think of how marvelous his eyes are and how your heart flutters when he holds your waist as you dance. As I said, stupid. I wrote him ridiculous, sentimental letters and then—"

She stopped abruptly, pursing her lips into that stubborn line Mohr had grown to like and even admire.

"And then?" he pressed gently.

He sensed that there could have been another young man involved; wondered if that Russian sod, Schmorell, Hans' best friend, had something to do with setting Sophie on the wrong path, but she had already closed herself down, shut her emotions off from him.

"And then we grew apart," she said with cold finality. "I suddenly didn't know what to talk to him about any longer. I didn't know what else to write and so, I began writing less and less. I thought of breaking it off with him completely, but..." She looked away. "It's a very dastardly thing to do, to break it off with someone fighting on the front line, even if you don't love him anymore."

"That's very commendable," Mohr murmured, shuffling through the file, discarding Hartnagel as yet another dead end. "Now, let us talk about Professor Huber. I understand it was your brother who had advised you to attend his lectures? Because Professor Huber expressed certain views that—"

"Professor Huber is innocent." Sophie pulled forward, cutting Mohr off before he could complete his thought. "Strike him from your lists. It was all us. He's just a harmless old man."

"A harmless old man practicing sedition—"

"No."

"...causing pliable, young, confused minds to stray from the path of—"

"No!" Sophie's face was set. Under her tightly drawn brows, her dark eyes flashed about wrathfully. "Haven't you heard a thing I've said? He didn't work with us. He didn't like the Nazi Party, that much is true, but he would die for the blasted Wehrmacht that didn't want anything to do with him." Her voice was dripping with derision.

"He met with your brother on a few occasions."

"It was pure coincidence. They attended the same literary evenings. They both knew von Radecki, who was invited a lot to such evenings as no one could read the way he did."

"Is that so?" Mohr regarded her almost imploringly.

He had worked in the police long before the Gestapo came into being. He knew when people lied to him, and Sophie was certainly lying about Huber's involvement. In fact, he had already gathered from his sources that the last pamphlet was written by the professor. But never before had Mohr come across such a selfless, suicidal desire to protect those who weren't even her own blood, who didn't even matter in the grand scheme of things.

Who, after all, was Huber to her? No one. Just one of the professors. She scarcely mentioned him during the interview. And yet, there she sat—arms crossed, jaws set—not a girl; a warrior, and a formidable one.

"Yes, it is so. They only met in person in June. Hans said something during that evening and Huber called him an ignorant hothead. Later, in private, Hans called him an old Prussian numbskull. Now, why would those two collaborate on anything if they clearly detested one another?"

Mohr regarded her for some time, thinking that this was precisely what he would like to know.

FIVE

MUNICH. JUNE 1942

"It appears Huber is on our side!"

The excitement in Hans' voice was palpable, contagious. He had just returned from the reading evening to which he'd been invited by sheer luck and only thanks to his acquaintance with Sigi von Radecki, whose declaiming abilities were famous around Munich.

Forgetting all about her textbook, Sophie leapt to her feet. "He was there?"

Hans nodded enthusiastically. "He was quiet throughout the evening. I had almost abandoned all hope, when suddenly the hostess, Doctor Mertens—she's one of our professors—ventured into politics. That circle, they're a liberal bunch but only to a certain extent. Their idea of resistance is nothing radical; it's lots of bleating and not much wool, as Father would say."

Sophie's grin mirrored Hans'.

"But then," Hans continued, sitting down to remove his military jackboots, "I, annoyed to the point of boiling by such placid attitudes—'oh, we ought to wait it out; educate the youth using our positions as scholars; passive resistance is the only way' and other such rot—decided to say something."

"My guess is that something was almost offensively sarcastic."

Sophie arched a brow.

"It's boring telling you stories. You know me too well."

"Go ahead, healer of the brave Aryan knights."

Finally succeeding in kicking off the second boot, Hans began rubbing his throbbing feet. "I said that if education is the only way, why don't we rent ourselves an island in the Aegean and offer courses on world views."

Sophie snorted and then exploded into a full-blown fit of laughter as she imagined the astounded silence that must have fallen over the room after one big-mouthed medical student's remark.

"What did they say?"

"Most scrambled to get away, suddenly recalling that they forgot something on the stove." Hans was uncharacteristically all playfulness too now. "As I said, they're not the bravest bunch. They don't mind lamenting their fates, but only to the extent that wouldn't lead to their arrest. Now, Professor Huber, that old fox, surprised me pleasantly."

Sophie waited for her brother to continue with great impatience.

"He had scarcely spoken two words to anyone throughout the entire evening, but after I went and opened my beer trap, he suddenly slammed his fist on the table and said: 'The young fellow is right. Something must be done and it must be done now'!"

Hans stared somewhere past the blackout drape, reliving the moment.

"We walked home together," he added very softly after a pause, amazement audible in his voice. "He said he was very interested in what we had to say."

"Hans," Sophie whispered, crouching in front of him, gathering his hands in hers. "If we get professors on our side..."

He nodded passionately a few times.

Outside, the curfew was going into effect, locking everyone inside the jail cells of their homes, but here, in the darkened apartment in the Bohemian corner of Munich, hope was alive.

. . .

The cellar was damp and smelled strongly of earth and mildew. Under the layers of peeling, rotten plaster, exposed red brick was weeping moisture. In the corners, where the spiderwebs were thick as cloth, water gathered in big shimmering beads that reflected the light from the solitary bulb on the moldy ceiling like a thousand precious gemstones.

Looking around, Sophie found it difficult to believe that this dingy vault was the heart of the entire White Rose operation. But then Hans approached what appeared to be a workbench, tore the tarpaulin off its surface, sending the accumulated drops of condensation flying in the air, and Sophie couldn't help but inhale sharply at the sight of a duplicating machine, black and somewhat intimidating—solid, iron-clad proof that this was all real, that this was not an empty dream but very much a matter of freedom versus slavery for their entire people, and of life and death for them.

"Where did you get it?" The air itself was different here, in the quite literal underground, and instinctively Sophie spoke in an undertone.

"From the back of a truck." It was Alex who answered, his gaze also riveted to the machine. He, too, seemed to be under the spell of its immense power. Almost reverently, he caressed its metal surface, pausing at the corner where the black paint was chipped. "From a gentleman who takes only cash, doesn't ask any questions, and prefers not to look in the faces of his customers so that he can't identify them later."

"A black-market dealer," Sophie said, nodding, as though reassured by it.

Outside, it was a gorgeous summer day, but here hung the permanent twilight and the damp coldness of the crypt. Adding to the eerie impression, odd, misshapen structures lined the walls covered by white, paint-splattered cloth. In spite of herself, Sophie shivered and wrapped her arms around her body.

"Whose cellar is this?" she asked.

"A friend's," Hans answered evasively and began shifting papers neatly stacked next to the machine.

Alex regarded him with a faint reproach. "The fellow's name is Manfred," he said, turning to Sophie and removing his civilian, light linen jacket. "Manfred Eickemeyer," he added for Sophie's benefit, as if it clarified anything. "He's an architect. It's his studio that occupies the entire building."

"Must be some architect," Sophie said, visibly impressed. She suddenly froze when Alex draped his jacket around her shoulders. It wrapped her in a warm cloud of faint masculine scent and expensive tobacco and something else she couldn't quite place.

"He's posted at the General Government in Poland," Alex explained. "The position is very well paid; that much is true."

"It's unfortunate that the job itself is rotten," Hans said grimly.

Sophie looked at him. When he didn't elaborate, she exhaled in exasperation.

"Hans, will you stop it?"

He blinked at her, feigning ignorance.

"Will you stop shielding me from everything?" Sophie went on, growing annoyed. "Why take me on board at all if you keep having secrets and fighting me at every step? I'm not your little baby sister anymore. I'm living through the same war. I'm seeing the same atrocities perpetrated against our own people. And I want to stop it, just as much as you do. So quit your protective big brother act and out with it. Do I really have to pull every word out of you with pliers, like some Gestapo butcher?"

Next to them, Alex tried to conceal a thoroughly amused grin.

Hans glared at his best friend but, after heaving a sigh, finally surrendered to the superior force. "It is Manfred who is behind the text of our second leaflet."

"There is a second leaflet?" Sophie made a gesture with her hands that could only be translated as *unbelievable*.

Looking infinitely guilty, Hans extracted a carefully folded piece of paper from the inner pocket of his tunic. Unlike his best friend, he was dressed in uniform. Unlike his best friend, he didn't have friends in high circles who could get him out of trouble for wearing civilian clothes; only a father with a few prior arrests by the Gestapo. It would have been idiotic for Hans to run the same risks that Alex had made his habit.

Sophie snatched the paper from his hand before he could offer it to her—or change his mind altogether and tell her to forget the entire White Rose affair—and she began reading, her scowl growing deeper and deeper with every new line.

> ...we do not intend to discuss the question of the Jews, nor do we wish to offer a defense or apology here. No, instead, to demonstrate this, we want to cite the fact that since the conquest of Poland three hundred thousand Jews have been murdered in that country in a bestial manner. Here we see the most terrible crime committed against the dignity of man, a crime that has no counterpart in human history. Some may say that the Jews deserved their fate. This assertion would be a monstrous form of insolence; but let us assume that someone said it—what position has he then taken toward the fact that the entire Polish aristocratic youth is being anni-hilated?
>
> Why are the German people so apathetic in the face of all these abominable crimes—crimes so unworthy of the human race? Hardly anyone thinks about that. It is accepted as fact and put out of mind. The German people slumber on in their dull, stupid sleep and thereby encourage these fascist criminals; they give them the opportunity to carry on their depredations...

It was almost all Hans; Sophie could almost hear his voice as she followed the lines burning with accusation and righteous anger without the softening, pacifistic influence of Alex to smooth out its edges.

But that anger was nothing compared to Manfred's, as it soon turned out.

Manfred burst into their apartment the following day, nearly knocking Sophie off her feet and apologizing in passing, his stern, handsome face flushed and pinched into a severe mask of a man who had been mortally betrayed.

"How could you do this?!" Waving a freshly printed leaflet in the air, he shouted at a startled Hans, who sat, half-turned, at his desk littered with textbooks and notebooks. "I spilled my guts before you! I entrusted you with the nightmares that I witnessed firsthand; nightmares that won't let me sleep at night; that had all but turned me into an alcoholic and morphine addict and you, you —" he gasped, choked on his emotion and, completely and utterly drained, fell in a heap onto the sofa as if shot.

Pale and frightened by such an outburst, Sophie nevertheless had the presence of mind to rush to the window and pull it closed before hurrying to the front door and turning the key in the lock.

"Manfred," Hans' voice, shaky with confusion, reached her from the living room, "whatever are you talking about? I wrote precisely the things that you told me about—"

"Did you?" Manfred retorted bitterly, not even noticing Sophie, who had entered the room once again. "Let us see." Deliberately, he slammed the pamphlet onto the coffee table and smoothed out its crinkled edges. "Two lines. I described to you in detail how men and women were herded onto the trucks with cudgels and rifle butts, like cattle. I told you how they were told to dig ditches as their crying children looked on. I told you how they were stripped naked—men and women together—and shot without further ceremony, without an ounce of remorse, some still holding infants close to their chest; how they begged for mercy from the bottom of that ditch, wounded but not yet dead, when more and more bodies fell down onto them, how they suffocated under the weight of their husbands, mothers, sisters, brothers, and children—

and you go and summarize all this horror in three pitiful lines? Before heaping Polish aristocracy into the same pile? Before going into philosophizing and quoting blasted Lao Tzu?"

In the silence that followed, only Manfred's heavy breathing could be heard. He was not much older than Hans, but there was something dreadful and already dead in the heavy shadows that lay beneath his pale gray eyes. Sophie had imagined him a prosperous, fleshy Golden Pheasant but instead came face to face with a man whose features were drawn and almost hollowed out from the inside and so utterly devoid of color, as if the sun itself couldn't save him from whatever was eating him alive any longer. Even his tailored clothes were wrinkled as though he'd slept in them, much like his dark hair that was a wild, tangled mess.

"I gave you details: exact names of the villages, names of the SS commanders, names of some victims even—all verifiable and available for people to actually look into them and you..." Manfred whispered in the broken voice of a man whose life had gone to pieces and who had reconciled himself with it and only lived for the tiny sliver of the hope still burning for the others.

"But I did it only to protect you." Finally recovering himself from such an assault, Hans was on his feet, kneeling in front of his friend, searching his face in desperation. "If I had given all the details in the leaflet, it would have been all too easy for the Gestapo to deduce precisely who it was that had witnessed these things and reported them. They would have come for you and—" Hans' voice broke off.

"And what?" Manfred looked at him, suddenly sounding horribly tired. "Executed me for treason? Together with the next batch of Jews, as Wehrmacht soldiers like you stand helplessly and look on? I'd thank them for doing the dirty work. I, myself, am too much of a coward to put a gun to my own temple. Trust me, I tried."

The image was soon swimming in front of Sophie's eyes. Together with the two men in front of her, she cried silently, without a single muscle moving on her face, for the Germany that couldn't be saved anymore, for all the souls lost, and for the collective guilt they would forever share because they hadn't started this earlier, because they had allowed this to go on for so long, because they began revolting when it was much too late for the others.

Manfred left after giving Hans a few hundred Reichsmarks—for paper, envelopes, and stamps—but his ghost still lingered in the apartment long after he'd stepped out of the door and into the blazing sunshine, haunting its dark corners, together with his words that Sophie would never forget for as long as she would live.

Something else stirred in her that evening, some dark suspicion that prompted her to put away the shorthand pad from the last lecture she was transcribing and pick up a clean sheet of paper.

"Dear Fritz," she began writing, almost tasting the falseness of her words on her tongue, "how are things on the front? How is the weather by you? Not too hot, I hope? I'm writing to you in part because I had the silliest argument with Anneliese when she came visiting on the weekend. You know that she's always had some mad imagination; well, now she has invented the story that on the Eastern Front both the SS and the Wehrmacht use Jewish children as target practice. I told her to shut it, of course, and not to spread such idiotic rumors about our noble troops. I know for a fact that you, personally, would be appalled to even think of such a thing, but won't you be so kind as to write to me in a clear language that it is rot through and through so that I could shove it into her silly mug and shut her up once and for all? Unless, of course..."

She stopped there, a sudden chill settling over her. She had to know and she didn't. She thought of finishing the letter and sending it, and the very next instant, she wondered if she should better tear it apart and forget all about it. The censors wouldn't let it through at any rate. But some of them weren't always diligent.

That night, she fell asleep to those what-ifs haunting her mind and the next morning, when she awoke to a splitting headache and a head still full of ghosts from her nightmares, Sophie felt a sudden kinship to Manfred, whom she scarcely knew but all at once understood all too well.

SIX

On Friday, after classes had been dismissed, Sophie met Hans at their appointed place—the bottom of the grand staircase. Immersed in an animated discussion with Alex and Willi, he hadn't noticed her at first; only after Traute pulled on his sleeve and motioned her head toward Sophie did he stop mid-word and break into a wide smile.

"Soph!" Hans pulled her into a quick embrace. "You always listen to the news in the morning; what did they say about the weather for the weekend? I'm saying that it'll be perfect for the hike we've been planning for what seems like forever and Alex insists there's going to be a storm." He gave his best friend a dirty look.

"There is though. I spent my entire childhood surrounded by nature. You city lot don't understand these subtle things one grows attuned to at the farm." Unimpressed, Alex shrugged with all the nonchalance in the world and gave Sophie a friendly peck on the cheek. Innocent as it was, Sophie felt a rush of heat shoot through her and spread in a delicious glow under her skin, intoxicating like liquor.

"Farm?" Hans didn't appear to notice anything. "You mean, an estate bigger than Göring's."

Alex ignored the jab. "If you refuse to see reason, I can't help you here. Let's set off, but don't nag me like an old wife when the storm breaks in the middle of the night and you wake up in a puddle. I rather don't mind it, but you will quite certainly have a regular fit."

Christoph, weighed down by books as he descended the stairs, saved Sophie from the uncomfortable position of a referee between her brother and her...

...*His best friend,* she swiftly corrected herself, feeling guilty for no apparent reason.

"Christoph!"

He appeared startled by Sophie's unexpectedly enthusiastic greeting, but smiled warmly, albeit tiredly, in return. "How goes it, Soph? Sorry I'm late. The blasted autopsy dragged on for hours and I scarcely slept last night. Our youngest one is teething." He rolled his eyes, with telling purple shadows lining them, to the ornate ceiling.

Sophie barely heard him. Alex had tugged on the handle of her book-laden bag while Christoph was speaking and, for a brisk moment, their fingers touched, separating almost instantly after Alex took the bag from her. All at once, all of her thoughts scattered like butterflies, before settling somewhere at the top of her stomach.

"Hans wants to go hiking this weekend, but Alex says it's going to be stormy. What do you think we should do?" Sophie stared at Christoph almost in desperation.

Traute looked at her curiously. She must have noticed the slightly hysterical notes in her voice, it occurred to a panicked Sophie.

"We'd better hurry with that hike or else we shall only be hiking soon together on the Eastern Front," Hans muttered, only half in jest.

The rumors about the need for medics were swelling despite Goebbels' cheerful propaganda that things were going well for the German army and Hans didn't nurse any illusions concerning their own fate. At the rate things were going, even student medics weren't safe any longer.

"Christoph, don't take the children with you in case there is a storm," Traute said, instantly attracting a look of mock betrayal from Hans. "What?" She stared back at him, her blue eyes open wide in play innocence. "I said, in case."

"I can't make it at any rate," Christoph said, dropping his bag at his feet and rubbing his face with his hands, seemingly to wake himself up. "Herta and I are going to Ruhpolding to stay with my stepmother. I didn't like how she sounded last time we spoke on the phone. Far too depressed for my liking. Almost like *Vati* just before his suicide. We should have never moved away from her," he added very softly, rubbing at his bloodshot eyes, and descended to the bottom step.

"We ought to go with Christoph," Alex said when Sophie, Hans, and Traute parted ways with Christoph and Willi. "I'd rather visit Frau Probst than hike as though nothing is the matter."

The day was still young and the wrought-iron tables at the nearest coffee house looked very inviting under the shade of the navy awning with an Old Empire design decorating it. As soon as the four of them sat down, they ordered iced coffee and beer. The waitress—all the male staff had been long dead and buried at the front—didn't even raise a brow when they asked her to bring it all at the same time. Students were known to be a peculiar lot and she had clearly long lost the habit to be surprised at such orders. So she only took their ration cards and left, tucking her notepad into the pocket of her apron.

"Won't we be disturbing them?" Sophie asked, risking a glance at Alex. He was concentrated on stuffing his exquisitely made pipe; she didn't have to be afraid of him looking up, meeting her gaze with his piercing, beautiful eyes and making her heart falter. But he did. In fact, Alex looked at her even longer than Sophie could possibly bear. "I mean, they're taking the children there; no?

Won't we be a hindrance? Taking up Frau Probst's time and attention she'd rather spend on her grandchildren?" She was rambling and realized it and yet couldn't stop for the life of her.

"Frau Probst could use some distraction. And friendly support." It was Traute who spoke, in a very soft voice and with a careful, over-the-shoulder look that had become a sad custom in Nazi Germany.

"Christoph's stepmother is half-Jewish," Hans explained just as quietly, nodding his thanks to Alex for passing him his expensive tobacco. "After Christoph's father committed suicide—he suffered from depression, the poor devil—she was left without the protection of a German husband. And you know how it is with the Nuremberg Laws."

Sophie did know. In 1939, only Polish Jews were subjected to the humiliation of wearing a white armband with a blue star on it. Now, in all of the Reich territories, including Germany itself, Jews had been proclaimed stateless people and subject to immediate deportation. Only spouses of Aryan Germans were somewhat safe from the persecution that kept gaining force like a rock hurtling down from the Alps, sweeping everything off its path, destroying and crushing. But still even those Jews living with Aryan German spouses had their fates hanging by a thread; Hans hardly needed to explain just how precarious Christoph's stepmother's situation was now that her husband was dead.

"Oh..." Sophie said after the pause that followed. There was nothing much one could say in such a damned sad situation. "Is she... in trouble of any sort?"

"No, not in trouble per se," Hans ventured, exhaling a cloud of gray smoke away from the table. "It's a small provincial town, a village almost, like our Ulm, only even smaller. All the neighbors know each other."

"People loved their family back when the father was alive, and they take care of his widow now, rather to their credit," Alex finished.

There was something defiant about his tone, as though he

threw the words directly at the swastika flag mounted directly above the awning. It didn't sway proudly in the wind though, as one would expect, but rather was wrapped around the staff as if tangled by a powerful wind. He was still looking at it curiously when the waitress reappeared with their order and followed his gaze to the offending object. Sophie noticed a silent exchange between them: his expressive, dark brow arched in silent question; her chin thrust slightly forward, challenge in her eyes—"*yes, that was my doing; are you going to report me?*" And then, a familiar leaflet peeking discreetly from between the banknotes Alex slipped into the waitress's hand with his sincerest thanks—"for your excellent service."

Alarmed, Sophie stared at him in silence, but Alex simply winked at her in the way that only he could and leaned back in his chair, folding his arms behind his head.

"What do you say, Soph?" he asked her, his voice full of velvet. "What do you want to do: hike or visit Frau Probst?"

Sophie knew that despite the innocence of the question, he meant something entirely different; that he posed the same question perhaps to tens of fellow students every day: what you would rather do—continue living your life as though nothing is happening or do something, anything, to help the ones who suffer at the hands of the regime he loathed with all his being.

"I think we ought to visit Frau Probst." Sophie didn't need time to contemplate it. "Let's bring her whatever she might need. It has to be difficult for her, getting things that she can't grow on her farm. Let's pool our money, ration cards, and buy her whatever she may use."

"Soap, tea, chicory coffee, dried meat, flour, some wool to knit something for the winter perhaps." Traute began counting on her fingers, the same enthusiasm burning in her eyes.

"You girls, go," Hans agreed, already emptying his wallet, "before the grocer's closes for the day. And tomorrow morning, we'll catch a train. I have the address."

. . .

Instead of Frau Probst, Christoph's wife, Herta, met them on the porch of her mother-in-law's house.

"She asks you to forgive her, but Frau Probst doesn't come out much these days," she said by way of greeting as she bounced a beautiful, cherubic child on her hip, away from her newly pregnant belly. The boy kept whimpering pitifully, his small fist at his mouth. "I also hope you'll excuse the inconvenience," she added with a smile, meaning the child. "He's teething."

"I suppose it's fortunate that we brought this." With an air of a magician, Traute produced a tube of numbing cream from her purse.

At the sight of it, Herta nearly threw herself into Traute's embrace. "Oh, you're a savior, Traute, dear, you don't have the faintest idea..."

Following Herta inside, Sophie soon lost the thread of their conversation. The terrace, despite being draped in greenery, betrayed the first signs of neglect that invariably follow a sudden death or a departure of someone who used to mind such affairs. On the posts of the ornate balustrade, the white paint was chipping, revealing the gray wood underneath; some of the floorboards had begun to sag, undoubtedly after the heavy rains and snowdrifts of the past few winters that no one had cleared in time. The entire house gave off the impression of a property one could rent for summer but not live in properly all year round. There was something abandoned and infinitely sad about the living-room furniture draped in white cloth, the grand golden chandelier that had long lost its luster under layers of dust, the bare floors stripped of carpets that Frau Probst most likely had sold to pay at least some of her bills, too guilty to live on her stepson's handouts, no matter how generously and willingly given. It was just as well—moths would have eaten them all the same.

Immersed in Frau Probst's imaginary reasoning, Sophie had failed to notice Frau Probst herself, who had materialized silently and discreetly from the depths of the house too enormous for her alone. However, it was no wonder; the woman, dressed in black from head to toe and ghostly pale despite the summer raging outside, had the quality of a shadow about her as she stood against the dark oak paneling of the wall, only her blond hair, streaked visibly with gray, betraying her presence.

Her tiny, narrow palm, delicate like an ancient parchment, all but drowned in Sophie's own small hand. Frau Probst greeted everyone in a voice so soft it was almost a whisper and trembled imperceptibly—she was obviously overwhelmed with attention and gratitude. Sophie noticed how, from time to time, Frau Probst's light blue eyes, always alert and on guard, flickered toward the young men's uniforms until Hans noticed it as well and, after clearing his throat with a meaningful look toward Alex and Willi, suggested that they should all go and change now that the train with all of its insufferable inspections was behind them.

At lunch, most of it supplied by whatever Sophie and Traute had bought at the grocer's and Christoph had brought with him, Frau Probst jumped at every noise and threw frightened gazes at the window each time someone bicycled too close to her fence. She sat much too straight, always at the edge of her seat as though ready for flight at a moment's notice, and she constantly appeared to listen to something inaudible to everyone else.

"Would you believe that she's only thirty-eight?" Alex whispered in Sophie's ear when they sat down on the terrace to have their iced lemonade—also made of an artificial concentrate, also begged from the grocer by Traute and her impossibly blue eyes.

Sophie started somewhat and peered closer at Frau Probst. Sophie had assumed that Herr Probst's widow, with her frail frame and drawn, pallid face, had to be at least in her late fifties.

"She looked nothing like that just a couple of years ago." Alex sighed, shaking his head at the whole damn sad business. "The Nazis did it to her. The poor thing is afraid of her own shadow. Have you seen the garden? She could have become rich letting it to her neighbors, or farming it herself, but she's too fearful to come out of the house. The terrace is as far as she will go, and only when Christoph or we are here."

"Whatever happened to Father's Sanskrit books?" Christoph asked his stepmother, fishing in an intricate bowl with Oriental motifs. Concentrated on a piece of fruit that kept escaping his dessert fork, he didn't notice Frau Probst's terrified look. "I wanted to take them home. It's drier there and they won't get damaged—" He stopped himself abruptly after finally lifting his gaze and seeing how deathly pale his stepmother had grown. "You sold them?" he asked then, as softly as he would talk to a child who had just broken an expensive crystal vase. "It's all right if you did," he rushed to assure her, already reaching for her hand before she broke into guilty tears. "They're yours. Father left them to you. Everything in this house belongs to you. I just meant... I only wanted to help, so that they don't get ruined. But no matter now. I'm glad you sold them. No one, except Father, could read them anyway." He broke into forced laughter. "Whoever even bought them from you?"

Frau Probst, her lips trembling, was smiling too through a film of tears. Next to Alex, whose face was still as a stone, Sophie felt the bitterness of her own tears rising in her throat.

The sun had only just dipped its toes in the lake at the edge of the darkening woods, and Alex was already writing something, his pencil scribbling with a hateful, ferocious force, when Sophie found him in the late Herr Probst's study. It was a room that had obviously belonged to a great intellect and a man of the world, beautifully paneled and decorated with artifacts from across the globe. But, on closer inspection, Sophie noticed empty spaces in between African masks and intricate ivory netsuke statues; behind the glass, leather-bound books now leaned on each other, instead of standing in neat, proud rows, half of their comrades missing in action and leaving them to fend for themselves.

"*Our present state is the dictatorship of evil,*" Sophie read, bending over Alex's shoulder.

He didn't even pause to greet her, only kept pouring the pain he felt for his hostess and his friend Christoph and all of them, the doomed generation, onto the paper.

Why do you allow these men in power to rob you step by step, both openly and in secret, of one of your rights after another, until one day nothing—nothing at all—will be left but a mechanized state system presided over by criminals and drunkards? Is your spirit already so crushed by abuse that you forget that it is your right—or rather, your moral duty—to eradicate this system? Many, perhaps most, of the readers of these leaflets cannot see clearly how they can mount an effective opposition. We want to try to show them that everyone is in a position to contribute to the overthrow of this system.

Breathlessly, Sophie kept reading the words bleeding from his pencil when Alex stopped suddenly and swung round on his seat. "I've got this far. Any ideas as to how exactly we're going to overthrow the system, Soph?"

Caught off guard at first, Sophie was prepared with her answer. After all, she'd been brooding and obsessing over it night after night, for what felt like an eternity.

"Sabotage armament industries," she began dictating in a steady, resolute voice. "Sabotage every assembly, rally, ceremony, and organization sponsored by the National Socialist Party. Obstruct the smooth functioning of the war machine."

She felt like a traitor to Fritz to speak such words, and yet when she saw them on paper, they filled her with such immense fire. Sophie suddenly realized that this was bigger than any individuals, bigger than Fritz and herself, and even Hans or Alex—this was a war against the most formidable enemy, and in war, just like in love, there could be no just methods.

Sabotage the scientific and intellectual fields involved in contin-
uing this war—whether it be universities, technical colleges, labo-
ratories, research stations, or technical agencies.

Sophie read her own words from the freshly printed leaflet that
had just come from under their makeshift printing press, two days
later in Munich.

Sabotage all cultural institutions that could enhance the prestige
of the fascists among the people. Sabotage all branches of the arts
that have even the slightest dependence on National Socialism or
serve it in any way. Sabotage all publications, all newspapers that
are in the pay of the government and that defend its ideology and
help disseminate the brown lie.

She folded the paper carefully with her gloved hands—thank
heavens for her brother and his friends being medics and having
wagon loads of gloves—put it into the envelope and, an hour later,
dropped it, unnoticed, into Professor Huber's mailbox along with
the invitation to the cultural evening at the Schmorells'. It was a
risky enterprise to be sure, but Alex, Hans, and Sophie had
decided that the risk was well worth it.

Do not contribute to the collections of metal, textile and the like.

Sophie grinned, watching her fellow students read the leaflet
under their desks.

Try to convince all your acquaintances, including those in the lower social classes, of the senselessness of continuing, of the senselessness of this war, of our spiritual and economic enslavement at the hands of the National Socialists; of the destructions of all moral and spiritual values.

Please, make copies and pass them on.

SEVEN

Fritz's letter caught Sophie off guard. For some time, she stood in front of the mailbox dumbfounded, turning the envelope this way and that, as though puzzled by the fact that a part of her former life had somehow reached her here in Munich. The letter itself, lightly torn at the corners, having been opened and resealed, lay heavy in her hand, an archaeological artifact, a relic of the past that was no more. Her heart at war with itself, Sophie dragged her bag filled with books and shorthand notepads up the rickety stairs and fumbled with the lock longer than usual, the key suddenly refusing to fit.

Just when she needed the company the most, the apartment met her with silence. There was only a dull thud when her schoolbag dropped onto the floor, spilling the books onto the worn rug, and a hushed whisper of Sophie's dress against the faded yellow wallpaper as she slid down to the floor. She sat without motion for a very long time, her legs crossed, eyeing the letter with a mixture of painful remnants of some girlish exuberance and a poisonous dose of harsh reality. After a few torturous minutes of self-doubt, Sophie picked at the corner at long last and felt her very soul tear as a thin strip of paper uncovered the truth. Avoiding it was no longer an option.

After Hans' confrontation with Manfred, she had mailed her letter peppered with questions after all. To hell with the censors and whichever authorities they could report it to—Sophie had to know where the man she had promised to marry stood in all this. However, Fritz's answer was not an answer at all. A bunch of useless, watered-down lines, half of them redacted with a black censor's ink, stating that everything was fine, just fine, on the front: there was hard work in the officers' quarters to be sure, but in between there were sandy beaches of the Russian rivers, fishing, sunbathing, beer for the officer staff... Annaliese heard what rumors? Mass murder? Jews? What silliness! He hadn't met a single Jew in these parts, only the local Russians and even they loved Germans; simply *loved* them! They were glad to be free of the oppressive Bolshevist regime. They welcomed their German liberators with open arms; if Sophie had only seen it! At any rate, she oughtn't worry her head about the war. The war was men's business. It was all for the Fatherland's sake and no matter how much he enjoyed word-fencing with Sophie about politics, she simply didn't understand the big picture—

With a bitter, sarcastic smirk, Sophie shook her head in disdain. She might as well have been reading a *Beobachter* issue. Instead of Fritz's voice, Propaganda Minister Goebbels' smooth lies dripped like poisoned honey from every line unmarred by the black ink.

But what if Fritz couldn't spell the truth out? What if he witnessed it all but couldn't put it into words for her to see? Leaping to her feet, Sophie began to pace the rooms, bumping into things, biting her nails to the quick. She was grasping at straws, but what did it matter if an image of the man she thought she loved so selflessly, so devotedly, was rapidly fading, disintegrating into nothing?

How come you could pose all the dangerous questions in your letter without fearing retributions? Another voice, of an adult Sophie, chimed in, ruthlessly shattering whatever illusions her old self still tried to salvage.

Before she could think it through, Sophie grabbed a pen, tore a fresh sheet of paper out of one of Hans' medical notebooks that lay in a pile on his desk, and began writing her response, harsh words scratching the paper and leaving angry slashes, almost cutting the paper through.

Dear Fritz,

How long is it since I last wrote to you? Meanwhile, another of your letters has turned up. However much I always enjoy answering your latest letter, I find it very difficult because it's hard to say things in writing that can only be resolved by conversational toing and froing. I'm perfectly prepared to believe that you simply argue with me for argument's sake when we get onto ideological and political subjects—the two go hand in hand. Personally, though, I've never argued for argument's sake, as you may secretly believe. On the contrary, I've always unconsciously made certain allowances for the profession you're tied to, in the hope that you'll weigh these things more carefully and perhaps make concessions here and there. It keeps me silent when I ought to speak out— when I ought to admit to you what concerns us both, I put it off till later. How I wish I could live awhile on an island where I could do and say what I want, instead of having to be patient indefinitely.

I'm sure you find it unfeminine, the way I write to you. It must seem absurd for a girl to worry her head about politics. She's supposed to let her feminine emotions rule her thoughts. But I find that thoughts take precedence and that emotions often lead you astray because you can't see big things for the little things that may concern you more directly—personally, perhaps. I'm sure your attitude to all that's happening today is quite unlike mine. You and your men have plenty to do now. I just can't grasp that people's lives are now under constant threat from other people. I'll never understand it and I find it terrible—don't go telling me it's for the Fatherland's sake.

Forgive me if you find this letter puzzling, but I can't always show myself the way I'm not. Don't think I'm good, that's all I ask, because I'm bad. Don't do it for my sake, so I needn't always be afraid of disillusioning you badly someday.

This letter may leave you completely cold and seem alien to you, but I don't propose to rhapsodize unnecessarily. That would surely be unwholesome. But I assure you I often think of you, and of our times together, and of what we've embarked on, whether rightly or wrongly.

All the best,

Sophie.

Without rereading it lest she lose her nerve, Sophie folded the letter in two, shoved it into an envelope, and headed for the post office. There, after mailing it, she purchased more envelopes—for the White Rose's next leaflet distribution.

"Writing to your beau so often?" A round-faced post office worker smiled at Sophie as she handed her the change. "Commendable."

Sophie smiled back at her. "Anything to support the troops' morale."

"More girls ought to be like you."

Sophie looked at the woman. "Yes. Indeed they should," she said, swiping the change into the pocket of her dress, meaning something quite different.

"What time did Hans say he's meeting Professor Huber?"

It was the third time Christoph had asked Sophie that same very question.

"Five," she answered patiently. "Traute and Hans will meet Professor Huber at five at the nearest streetcar stop to his building and bring him here."

"Did he say anything about the leaflet when Hans asked him if he was coming to Alex's?" This time, it was Willi who distracted Sophie from helping Alex set the table.

Alex himself was unusually quiet and tense. By four o'clock, he'd changed his clothes three times, switching from a uniform to a formal suit and, finally, to a more relaxed attire of linen trousers, a shirt and a light pullover draped over his shoulders. At four thirty, it had suddenly occurred to him that the china was much too casual, and, after a quick raid of his stepmother's cupboards, he'd re-emerged with armfuls of familial silverware and crystal goblets, which Sophie was presently arranging atop the starched white tablecloth.

"He only said that he received it when Hans asked him," Sophie replied to Willi over the immense, five-arm silver candelabra towering over the table. "They couldn't quite talk about it openly; Hans caught him on his way out of the auditorium after the lecture was over."

At the chiming of the grandfather clock, tucked in the same corner where a gilded Russian Orthodox icon gleamed dimly in the light of two thick candles, Alex dropped a butter knife on the chair, cursed under his breath, and polished it on his sleeve before placing it with utmost care in its place.

"Anytime now," Christoph said breathlessly, his eyes riveted to the clock that had just struck six.

They had the villa to themselves: Alex's parents had gone to one Austrian inn or the other for the vacation—a vacation from what, was anyone's guess—and the maid was also promptly dismissed after cooking a veritable feast for the young Herr Schmorell and his guests, leaving it in the kitchen covered by silver cloche domes to keep it warm.

Their nervousness was contagious. Sophie wished Willi would sit down already instead of pacing the living room and getting under her and Alex's feet as they were bringing the heavy dishes from the kitchen. She wished Christoph would put his pipe away as her eyes were beginning to smart with the ringlets of smoke hanging over the room like a cloud. She wished her hands were steadier and the silver didn't betray her state by the tiny clinking noises no one else noticed but yet annoyed her no end.

By the time Hans' voice, accompanied by Traute's silver laughter, echoed around the open veranda outside, they all were as tense as springs ready to be released, their nerves strained to the utmost.

Alex was the first one to rush to greet his guests.

"Herr Professor!"

Sophie heard his unnaturally cheerful voice from the hallway, followed by the shuffling of feet and murmured greetings. With the sharp, effortless elegance of a young English squire, Alex escorted his esteemed guest into the living room, where Sophie, Christoph, and Willi were anxiously waiting, their faces frozen with exaggerated smiles plastered on them.

Nodding their greetings stiffly, Professor Huber came to a halt as though taken aback by the unexpected extravagance and luxury he'd encountered. He'd only seen these students in his auditoriums —a uniformed mass with the Wehrmacht insignia—and now, he appeared to be suddenly self-conscious of his tweed jacket that was several years old, very carefully worn but with slightly frayed cuffs nevertheless and elbows where the material was wearing much too thin; of his thoroughly cleaned shoes, the heels of which were scuffed too much to go unnoticed; of his tattered leather belt, which he hiked up with one hand as if in the hope of recovering his status somewhat. All at once, Sophie felt sorry for him—a lone authority figure suddenly stripped of his position and faced with a group of towering youths, all eyes on him, smoldering with an unspoken question: are you with us or not?

They sat down to eat, still wary of each other, still exchanging occasional glances and meaningless phrases, only prolonging the agonizing, growing tension spreading over the room with the rays of the setting sun. Their shadows grew longer; grotesquely, they quivered in the light of the candles; danced macabrely among the barely poked-at dishes and blood-red goblets of wine.

"I have a fine ten-year-old Riesling, nice and cold from Father's cellar, if you don't like Chianti," Alex offered Professor Huber, seeing that he had barely touched his glass.

"Oh no, the wine is fine." Professor Huber dabbed at his lips ceremoniously without meeting Alex's searching eyes.

"Are you quite sure? Please, do tell me if it's not to your liking. I only served it because it goes well with red meat, but it's no trouble at all for me to get—"

"No, no; I assure you, everything is perfectly splendid." Professor Huber sank even further into himself, visibly uncomfortable under such close inspection. "I'm afraid I have lost the habit for wine, with the rationing... It goes straight to my head now and I wish to remain sober."

"Naturally." Alex nodded and went silent again.

They had overdone it, it suddenly dawned on Sophie. Professor Huber hadn't only lost the habit for wine, but for the red meat that most Germans hadn't seen in years. He seemed miserable and out of place among these healthy young men with his handicap and even more out of place with all this familial porcelain and silver and starched napkins like in the best Munich restaurants. Each time Traute or Sophie ventured into politics, he stared at them mutely, obviously suspicious of the young women who were much too outspoken for his traditional tastes, and invariably responded with a doubtful "hmm" to every question they attempted to probe him with.

It was Hans who tried the most to make Huber speak. However, all of his inquiries broke on the rocks of Huber's silence. The professor hid behind his much-too-tiny coffee cup, grumbled something general about the decline of academic standards until Hans' patience ran out and he demanded: "Herr Professor, do you agree or not with what we suggested in the leaflet concerning the resistance and sabotage?"

Startled, Huber sat bolt upright in his chair, all the blood instantly draining from his face. "So, it was you, who..." He swallowed the rest of the sentence, too afraid to even utter it.

Hans exhaled tiredly. "Of course it was us. We're the White Rose. We've been printing the leaflets all along, but you already knew it; else, you would have never agreed to come here in the first place. Whatever do you have in common with a bunch of students?"

"Perhaps I came to eat," Professor Huber suggested, his expression impenetrable.

"No, you didn't." Hans refused it flat out. "You're much too proud for that."

At last, a hint of a smile appeared on the professor's drawn face. "Why me?" he asked, his tone much softer than before. "There are plenty of sympathetic people out there, people with means and..."

Hans was already shaking his head. "Those people with means, they have too much to lose. You've heard what they were suggesting at Dr. Mertens': passive resistance and all that rot; let's wait it all out; we ought to preserve our own integrity and the war shall resolve itself someday. As long as we're not personally involved, all is peachy." Hans' tone turned outright mocking.

Professor Huber pulled slightly forward, listening.

"Herr Professor, you said something that night that struck a note with me," Hans continued, inching closer across the table, his intense, dark eyes never leaving the older man. "You said that something had to be done and done soon. Well, we happen to be of the same opinion. I know that due to your unfortunate illness, you missed your chance to fight for your Fatherland."

Huber reddened slightly in embarrassment, but Hans waved it off as if the past mattered not.

"Forget that war. Think of this one. Perhaps, this is your war. Perhaps, you were born to fight it not on the front line, but from inside. Perhaps, this is your chance to prove yourself to your fellow Germans and all of humanity to be the hero I know you are. Herr Professor, we all here admire you greatly as our intellectual leader. We cherish your lectures because you're not afraid to inspire the spark of resistance in us. But perhaps you would be willing to inspire the same spark in a much wider audience?"

In the pause that followed, only the ticking of the clock and the crackling of the fire could be heard.

"What exactly are you suggesting?" Huber finally asked. "That I write pamphlets with you?"

"Write and distribute them among your fellow educators," Hans confirmed plainly as though it weren't a question of life and death for either of them.

Huber nodded as he thought, steepled his fingers together. "What makes you so certain that I won't report you to the authorities?" he suddenly asked.

"Because you won't," Hans answered simply.

Once again, Professor Huber lapsed into silence.

"Such matters require thinking over," he concluded after another interminably long pause. Sophie's coffee had gone cold and the milk in it acquired a spidery film that quivered whenever she crossed and uncrossed legs under the table. "I have a wife and daughter; surely, you understand."

"I have a wife and two sons also," Christoph inserted, his voice uncharacteristically cool. "And a Jewish stepmother who is only alive because I happen to wear a Wehrmacht uniform."

Huber averted his eyes, mumbled yet another promise to think it over, and rose from his seat, thanking Alex and everyone present for the excellent and very productive dinner.

"He hasn't the guts to do it," Christoph announced blankly as soon as the professor was out of the door, saying his goodbyes to Alex, who'd followed him to the veranda to see him off.

"He's just afraid," Willi protested softly.

"It's the same thing." Christoph snorted with disdain, lighting his pipe.

"Not the same in the slightest!" Traute turned to him, her dessert spoon poised as if in attack. "Don't forget, he's not a young idealistic man anymore. He's old and frail and is afraid for his family, for which he is the only provider. Don't judge him."

Lifting his hands up in the air in mock surrender, Christoph busied himself with his pipe.

"He'll do it," Hans said, emerging from his brooding.

"You think?" Sophie asked her brother, her head tilted doubtfully to one side.

"He will. I feel it."

At that moment, Alex walked in, cleaning his hands with a towel and grinning.

"What are you so happy about?" Hans looked at his best friend suspiciously.

"I wrapped up the second duck we hadn't even started for him and some sweets to take home to his wife and daughter."

"Bribing the officials?" Hans arched his brow.

"Did he take it?" Willi asked incredulously.

"Sure he did." Alex beamed wider. "The war is going on, if that notion is new to you."

"He'll surely do it then!" Hans slammed his palm on the table in triumph, his eyes shining about excitedly. "He's exactly the sort of a man we need: very cautious, but ready to take action when no one sees it."

"I don't know about that," Christoph said, his eyes narrowed through the haze of his pipe smoke. "Duck is one thing, but leaflets are a different matter entirely."

"Shall we rename ourselves the White Duck perhaps?" Alex suggested, perfectly serious. "So that Herr Professor is more comfortable."

Out of nowhere, a suppressed snort came; then Traute spat her coffee back into the cup, and soon, the entire living room was in an uproar, thunderous and basking in waves of relief like a sky that had finally broken into a cleansing spring storm.

EIGHT

GESTAPO INTERROGATION ROOM, MUNICH.
FEBRUARY 1943

Robert Mohr studied his young opponent from the corner of his eye, deciding on his strategy. She'd been perfectly cool and composed so far, fending off his probing questions with a wonderful bravery about her that Mohr had never before encountered in a woman, let alone a girl as young as Sophia Scholl.

Sophie, he reminded himself. She'd asked to be addressed as Sophie.

That martyr-like fearlessness of hers drove Mohr to distraction; after all, who in their right mind would treat a Gestapo official's obvious desire to let them off the hook with a mere slap on the wrist with equally obvious contempt? And yet, no matter how many times Mohr carefully tried to steer her toward her brother— his influence and his guilt—Sophie kept turning the subject back onto herself with a marvelous obstinacy.

No, Herr Kriminalkommissar; Hans only wrote the very first leaflet. The second was already a joint effort and the third was almost all her, Sophie, just as she'd told him. Alex's fault was only in writing her subversive thoughts down. She even printed the entire affair all by herself and mailed it to Professor Huber, the poor unsuspecting, innocent soul, just like her comrades, her poor boys seduced by her sweet, serpent's tongue.

She even smiled charmingly at that, her dark eyes turning almost black—a biblical Eve who had lured several naïve Teutonic Adams into biting the apple of sedition, which, according to her, was so contradictory to their noble nature.

But Mohr knew better. His daughter was a first-rate liar too, despite her tender age. There were no rivals to her skill of presenting her beau in the most innocent of lights whenever Mohr caught them leaving a cinema hand in hand instead of checking their assigned streets' windows for blackout drapes as they ought to have been. *But,* Vati, *Paul didn't want to go; it was me who dragged him to the movies*—the same excuses, accompanied by the same half-coy, half-disarming smile that was presently playing on Sophie's lips.

Mohr sighed, rubbing his forehead in desperation.

"All right. Supposing you did write the second and the third leaflet." Mohr pretended to accept Sophie's claims for now. "But what about the fourth one?" After fumbling among the papers in the thick, swastika-stamped binder, he finally fished out a well-read, wrinkled copy of a pamphlet. "*Who has counted the dead— Hitler or Goebbels? Neither of them!*" he began to read. "*In Russia, thousands of German lives are lost daily. It is the time of the harvest and the reaper cuts into the ripe grain with wide strokes* '"

He looked up from the paper bearing the fingerprints of hundreds of people, only to find Sophie regarding him almost with amusement.

"A bit Biblical; won't you say that?"

After she moved her shoulder, feigning indifference, Mohr continued: "'*Every word that comes out of Hitler's mouth is a lie.*'"

"It is."

Mohr ignored the interruption. "'*When he says peace, he means war—*'"

"He does."

She was provoking him on purpose, but Mohr wouldn't have any of that. "'*...And when he blasphemously uses the name of the Almighty, he means the power of evil, the fallen angel, Satan.*'" He paused only to give Sophie another pointed look. "'*His mouth is the foul-smelling maw of hell. Everywhere and at all times, demons have been lurking in the dark, waiting for the moment when man is weak; when he yields to the force of evil and, after voluntarily taking the first step, is driven on to the next and the next at a furiously accelerating pace.*'" Mohr dropped the paper, bursting into chuckles. "Come now, Sophie. I may buy your writing the second and the third leaflet, but this? You didn't write this religious nonsense."

"Who did then? Hans, most certainly." Sophie cocked her head in mock reproach, still smiling faintly, seeing through all of his maneuvers, much to Mohr's dismay.

"No, it wasn't your brother either."

That got her attention.

"Who then?" she asked, looking almost bored but on guard now.

"Willi Graf did." Mohr shrugged as though stating the obvious. "Among you, he's the only fiercely devout Catholic."

"We all believe in God," Sophie countered coolly.

"Oh, I have no doubt about that," Mohr agreed at once and folded his hands atop the table, smiling benevolently. "Say a Hail Mary with me, please."

Sophie's dark eyes narrowed with resentment in them. However, she swiftly recovered herself. "I'm a Protestant."

Mohr compressed his lips to hide a smile of a small victory. "That's perfectly fine. Let's say Our Father together then."

Sophie was staring at him silently.

"No? You know who would most certainly say Our Father with me? Willi Graf." Mohr extracted the young man's file from the binder and laid it out neatly next to the fourth White Rose leaflet. "Willi Graf, a former member of the now-banned Gray Order—it's a Catholic version of Hitler Youth, in case he didn't tell you," he clarified, looking through Willi's file with interest. "Arrested in 1938 when he was a student of the University of Bonn for participation in illegal gatherings of his disbanded Order and released shortly after. Among his possessions was discovered a diary in which he'd apparently made an entry around..." Mohr checked his records. "As early as 1933!" He raised his brows, almost impressed. "In the entry, in which he listed all of his friends, he wrote HJ next to the names of the boys who'd joined *Hitlerjugend*, crossed them out and, according to witnesses, never associated with them again. A rather strong anti-regime position, as far as I'm concerned." Clasping his hands atop the papers, he looked at Sophie once again. "Still claiming you wrote all this Catholic rot?"

"Yes."

Mohr almost laughed, astounded at such incredible pigheadedness.

"No. I'll tell you what you wrote." He picked up the pamphlet. "*We will not be silent. We are your bad conscience. The White Rose will not leave you in peace!*" In spite of himself, he felt chills rush along his skin, thankfully concealed by his civilian suit. For some reason, the force—or was it the message?—behind these words made him squirm uncomfortably in his chair. "Now this is something you or Hans would say. But all those hellhounds and Grim Reaper metaphors? With all due respect, Sophie, that is not you."

Mohr was smiling genuinely now. It was all coming together. Sophie hadn't authored any of the leaflets. She was in love with that half Russian sod Schmorell, who must have written the third leaflet in Probst's house and whose crime she was ready to confess to because of her feelings for him. Naturally, she protected Hans, whom she also loved and was fiercely devoted to; in fact, devoted to such an extent that she was ready to go to the gallows all by herself just so he would live.

Mohr was rubbing his hands together gleefully, already imagining how excellently such a theory would play out in court when he presented the Scholls' case to the judge, when, suddenly, Sophie gathered herself together and struck out at him when he was least expecting it.

"I have proof that I wrote the fourth leaflet."

For a few moments, Mohr just sat there in stunned silence. It was impossible, surely. The girl was lying.

When he finally squeezed a strangled, "What?" out of himself, Sophie only grinned wryly and tossed her head in the direction of the door.

"Your agents must have seized all of the papers from our apartment. Why don't you go through them, find my diaries, and go through the very recent one? You'll find so much religion in there, you'll be able to write a few sermons to add to your prayer collection."

For the first time in his career, Mohr found himself at a loss for words. Just when he had it all lined up so finely, this twig of a girl, who reminded him so painfully of his daughter, went and knocked him squarely onto his behind.

A worthy opponent indeed.

In spite of himself, Mohr regarded her with respect before slamming the binder shut.

"I think we both can use a break."

"As you wish, Herr Kriminalkommissar."

"I'll instruct a guard to bring you something to eat."

"Thank you."

He was almost out of the door when he heard her say, "Enjoy your reading, Herr Kriminalkommissar; I wrote a lot of interesting thoughts in those diaries," and Mohr could only shake his head in helpless surrender.

NINE

MUNICH. JULY 1942

The news, no matter how anticipated, still came as an unbearable blow. It was Hans who had first announced it to Sophie, in a deliberately nonchalant tone but still looking a bit at a loss as he fumbled with the official paper in his hand.

"We're being sent to Russia."

A few simple words that had turned Sophie's world upside down in a matter of seconds.

"When?" she could scarcely hear herself say.

"July the twenty-second," Hans had responded, staring at the paper as though in the hope of discovering a mistake.

Two weeks, Sophie had thought. *Only two weeks...*

"You and Alex?" Her voice was a mere pitiful whisper now.

"Me, Alex, and Willi. Christoph was granted permission to stay, on account of his pregnant wife and his children."

Moving as though under water, Hans had lowered himself heavily onto the sofa, his eyes turning glassy, already haunted with the images of death and devastation he would shortly be calling his life. Sitting next to him, Sophie had taken his lifeless hand but said nothing, because there was nothing one could say to someone heading into the maw of hell itself.

Now, the day before the fateful departure date, Sophie kept

replaying the scene before her eyes as her hands moved of their own volition, mechanically scattering pillows about and placing candles right on the bare floor of Manfred Eickemeyer's studio. Manfred had generously permitted them to use it for a farewell evening, just as he had allowed them to commandeer his cellar for printing their leaflets. A crushing wave of terrible loss washed over Sophie at the memory of helping to dismantle the entire operation —Traute sobbing openly, Hans' tightly set jaw, Alex's eyes swimming with unshed, bitter tears as they destroyed the very traces of the White Rose's existence from the memory of the cellar's damp walls. They had felt robbed, with unnecessary cruelty, by fate itself; robbed of their chance to stir their fellow Germans to resistance, to create a wave that would eventually sweep away that hateful regime before it was too late.

"How are you not crying?" Traute's question brought Sophie back to the present moment, to the balmy, plaster-tinged atmosphere of the light-filled studio.

Sophie looked at her. Though pale and sleep-deprived, Traute was particularly beautiful that day, in her bright yellow dress and with her lustrous blond hair pinned up in rolls—for Hans, no doubt, so he'd remember her this way, the last vision of Munich's summer in bloom before he would head to the blood-soaked Russian battlefields. Her eyes were rimmed with red, as were her thin, pale nostrils, which no amount of powder could conceal.

They would both bid their farewells to their beloved men that evening; only Sophie would have to swallow her feelings and shake Alex's hand instead of throwing herself onto his neck and covering his handsome, brooding face with kisses like she imagined she would so many times. She would feign cheerfulness for a good comrade and promise to write. Just thinking of it tore Sophie's heart in pieces.

"I am," Sophie replied, slicing into cake and imagining it was Hitler's neck. "Only you can't see it."

· · ·

The warm, starry night descended upon the city, painting the cobbled streets navy in the faint blue anti-aircraft light of the streetlamps. Outside, not a leaf stirred in the still, fragrant air. Undisturbed by the bombers, Munich slept serenely, tucked in on all sides by blackout drapes, but inside architect Eickemeyer's studio, life was bursting through, bubbling like the champagne Manfred had procured by some undoubtedly illegal means on the black market.

"I want to raise this toast to life." The host, attired sharply in a black tailored suit, rose from his chair, a champagne flute in hand. "So that all of you return from the front safely. That's the thing of paramount importance. All else, we shall sort out later."

They drank to that and lapsed into funereal silence in spite of the music playing loudly in the corner, some banned jazz record Alex had brought in his duffel bag—there were no neighbors to disturb. His chestnut hair freshly cut, Hans was staring at his empty champagne flute as though searching for answers in its crystal depths. Seated on the pillow next to him, with her legs tucked underneath her, Traute kept gazing at him lovingly as if to imprint every feature of his into her memory before he would be gone—who knew for how long. Perhaps, forever...

Chasing the terrible, chilling thought away, Sophie turned to Alex to ask something, only to notice a dreamy, blissful expression on his clean-shaven face. Gone was the bohemian air and the devil-may-care attitude of a rich troublemaker. With his long hair now trimmed to an appropriate length, in a starched uniform, in boots shined to mirror-like perfection, Alex had the excited air of a young man in love setting off for a date with the object of his passion. Studying him from the corner of her eye, Sophie smiled softly to herself at this walking contradiction: Alex, the half-Russian Alex, was finally going home.

In the center of the vast room, Christoph was reciting something from Goethe as Professor Huber, occupying one of the four chairs as a cherished guest, listened attentively while he balanced a plate of cake precariously on his lap, picking at it from time to time.

Slightly removed from everyone else, half-concealed by the shadows thrown by the candles, Willi sat with a rosary uncon-cealed in his hands, moving the beads with a faint, serene smile playing on his lips. Always the quiet one, always a bit of a loner, an outsider even among friends, Willi had poured his heart and soul into their very last, fourth leaflet and now had the air about him of a man who was ready to die a good, honest death after completing the mission of his life. Sophie couldn't help envying him, just a little. It must have been nice, having some higher power to rely on instead of just oneself.

"Soph?"

Alex's lips, much too near to her ear, startled Sophie and caused her to shiver against his warm breath at the same time.

"Yes?"

"Don't fret about us." He was looking straight into her eyes, into her very soul, it seemed. "We're medics. We won't be fighting, only patching some poor bastards up behind the lines."

"Sometimes bombs fall behind the lines."

"They won't."

"How do you know?"

"I just do. I'm a gypsy at heart, remember." He grinned at her, his eyes full of mischief. "I know these things."

The record had ended with the last soulful tunes of the saxo-phone. In the silence that had fallen, Christoph's voice sounded profoundly clear, reaching for the very heartstrings with his verses of Eden and Hades and the fates of the men who sold their souls to the devil.

"Do you think we did the right thing?" Sophie asked Alex quietly. "Dismantling the entire business, I mean. With you gone, Traute and I could have—"

"No," Alex interrupted her, sharper than Sophie had expected, and seized her hand at once, sending yet another electric pulse through her skin to the very ends of her tiptoes. "It's not that we don't trust you," he continued in a much milder voice, "it's just... we wouldn't be here to protect you in case something happened."

"Perhaps, when you come back, it shall be the other way round?" Sophie said, aware of his fingers interlocking with hers. "Perhaps, it will be us who shall be protecting you."

Alex scowled as a shadow of something primal, savage almost, passed over his face and he suddenly pulled Sophie to her feet.

"Help me bring that crate of beer from the stairs?"

"I can help you," Hans called to him, making a motion to rise.

"Don't you dare move and let your sister do what she wants." Alex pointed a finger at him. "Have you not heard of women's emancipation? It was all the rage in Germany before that sod Hitler came to power, when our mothers unanimously cut their hair and skirts and began dressing in suits and joined trade unions."

"Not my mother," Willi protested from his corner. After his latest contribution, he'd begun to come out of his shell more and more, much to everyone's delight.

"Of course not." Alex waved off his protest with a negligent sweep of the hand. "You are the second person born through immaculate conception."

While the studio was immersed in laughter and the torrent of witty remarks that followed, Alex quickly grasped Sophie's hand and slipped along with her into the darkness of the staircase, pulling the door closed after himself. There, obscured from everyone's sight, with her back against the wall, Sophie instantly opened her lips to his hot, hungry mouth and lost herself to his hands that roamed all over her body, caressing and squeezing and lighting a thousand fires under her hot, sweaty skin. It was pitch-black even with her eyes open; she couldn't see but only feel his tongue tracing the outline of her neck, her collarbone; his fingertips climbing, along with her skirt, higher and higher up her thighs; his breathing just as shallow and frantic with desire as hers. He pushed his knee between her legs and she parted them more than willingly, arching her back just to press her breasts even closer against his chest, to feel his heart beat wildly against her own.

He asked her something one last time; she only nodded impatiently, breathlessly—*yes, yes, take it all, it's all yours, has always been; don't waste any time; God only knows how much we have left*—and clutched onto his stiff collar, so perfectly starched; it would be ruined, but to hell with it now. This way, he wouldn't forget her, wouldn't escape to some partisans in one Russian steppe or another, because she would be waiting for him at home. He would have to come back because, after this, there was no going back to remaining just good comrades.

No one seemed to notice their absence and their slightly disheveled, flushed appearance once they were back; the group only cheered the crate of beer that had finally arrived. In place of Christoph, Hans now occupied the center of the room, arguing about something with Professor Huber.

"With all due respect," Huber was saying, "I disagree with your position. I understand that you are young and idealistic—"

"My position has nothing to do with my age or so-called idealism!" Hans protested. His face was flushed. Once again, he was in his element.

Huber raised a conciliatory hand. "However, I don't see any possible path for an active resistance. We aren't workers who can strike, after all. We're intellectuals and what we ought to do is to silently boycott Nazi functions and perhaps wait for the regime to die on its own."

"To die on its own?" Hans repeated, incredulous. In the heat of the debate, he appeared to have entirely forgotten that it was his professor he was arguing with and not his fellow student. "Surely you can't be serious. It may take years; years, during which hundreds and thousands of innocents will be annihilated in cold blood!"

"And all German cities razed to the ground by the Allies,"

Willi added wistfully. "Just imagine, Munich's beautiful cathedrals—"

"To the devil with the cathedrals!" Manfred roared, suddenly leaping to his feet and slamming his fist into his palm. "It's human lives we shall concern ourselves with, not some bloody stone and glass! It's all replaceable; human beings are not, you pitiful pup!"

"I wasn't saying anything about humans not being replaceable," Willi mumbled in his defense, retreating to the safety of his corner. "My heart aches for every life lost, naturally; I was only saying—"

"Once you get to the Eastern Front, you shall understand what I'm saying," Manfred cut him off coldly and savagely. "Until then, don't you dare even mention some bloody monuments to me."

"No rows on our last night together." Traute stood between the men, giving each a pointed look. "Let's go back to reciting poetry, singing and dancing; shall we? Alex, put on Benny Goodman for us. Hans, if you don't shut your mug and dance with me right this instant, I swear to God I'll report you to the Gestapo personally."

A smile finally warmed Hans' face, uncertain at first, but then blossoming into one of deepest affection. With a ceremonious bow, he offered Traute his hand, which she took, also grinning now.

After putting the Benny Goodman record on, Alex turned to Sophie.

"Fräulein Scholl, will you do me the honor?"

"Most certainly, Herr Schmorell."

The beat was low and sensual, weaving threads of the silvery saxophone through the fragrant night. As they danced, closer than friends ordinarily would, Alex leaned and whispered in Sophie's ear, "Please, don't do anything stupid while we're away."

"Why?" she whispered back, feeling the palm of his hand singing through the thin material of her dress.

"Because I won't be able to live if anything happens to you."

"Neither will I, so you'd better survive. And bring my brother back, too."

"I promise if you promise."

"I swear."

"Till death do us part?"

Sophie grinned against his lips but didn't reply. There was something eternally romantic but incredibly ominous in those words and, all of a sudden, the night outside began to seep into the studio through the folds of the blackout drapes and there was no escaping that all-consuming darkness.

TEN

AUGUST 1942

It was as though with the young men's departure for the front, life itself was rapidly disintegrating, falling apart piece by piece and turning into the bare skeleton of an intolerable, dull existence. With unavoidable mail delays, meeting at the corner café and asking each other for the news from the front had become a regular pastime for Sophie and Traute until the summer semester ended and Traute was summoned back to her native Hamburg for field work. Sophie felt her absence sharply, as though with Traute's departure the last thread connecting Sophie to her brother had been severed.

The week that followed, with its stifling heat and suffocating, lonely nights, brought more bad news. First came the papers requesting Sophie to register with an armaments factory, where she would have to toil for the next two months—*a fine summer break,* she thought to herself, struggling with the desire to crumple the paper in her hand and tell them all to go hang themselves with their "duty to the Fatherland." Next, came a letter from her mother, tear-stained and written with an unsteady, trembling hand: Sophie's father had just been arrested. Again. *I told him; I warned him a thousand times to keep his opinions to himself,* Magdalena Scholl wrote, *but would he listen, that obstinate man? He just had*

to go and open his mouth and speak his mind, and about whom? The
Führer himself. Naturally, someone conscientious *reported him.*

Sophie couldn't help but break into a lopsided grin at that
remark, pride swelling in her chest. She loved her mother dearly,
but she was her father's daughter still. She understood him, his
freedom-loving, unrestrained, wild nature, like Magdalena Scholl
never could. However, the feeling of pride soon turned into
concern. Fearing the censors, her mother never explained just how
grave the anti-Hitler remark was. An image of Dachau—the very
first Nazi concentration camp, lying just outside Munich—rose,
grew before Sophie's eyes, slowly drowning out all else with its tall
gates, guard towers, and emaciated political prisoners shuffling
every day inside that hell on earth.

The very next morning, but not until she had ensured that she
had swept the apartment clean of anything remotely incriminating,
Sophie set off to Ulm, spending the entire train journey on the
edge of her seat, countless scenarios, one more depressing than the
other, flicking before her eyes like some terrible motion picture.

Upon arrival, she encountered her mother in bed, with all signs
of nervous collapse about her. Chalk-white and clammy,
Magdalena only sobbed and wrung her hands when Sophie sat on
the side of her bed and tried to pry at least some morsels of information out of the inconsolable woman.

"I don't know where they're holding him..." Magdalena's sobs
turned into hiccups. "I wrote to Hans and to Werner too; they're
both stationed somewhere near Gzhatsk..."

Sophie nodded, making a mental note to herself. At least now
she knew where Hans was.

"I think it's Gzhatsk; I copied the spelling from the envelope I
received from Hans and only then realized that your other brother
is stationed there too, but with a regular unit, not medical troops
like Hans and Alex."

Sophie scarcely kept herself from making an impatient gesture
with her hand. In her distress, Magdalena's thoughts kept scat-

tering in all possible directions, focusing on irrelevant details when all Sophie wanted was simple, unadorned facts—the kind that would allow her to act, to do something about it.

"I thought that if they pleaded for him, the court would give Robert a milder sentence," Magdalena continued, sniffling and glassy-eyed. "If the judges took into account that both of his sons are fighting currently on the front..."

Fat chance Werner will beg, Sophie thought but wisely kept that idea to herself, so as not to upset her mother even further. *Even fatter chance Hans will. He'll drop dead before he begs the Nazi regime for anything, even his father's life.*

And their father would likely disown Hans in turn for any semblance of groveling before the people he so actively despised, even if it meant serving life within Dachau's walls.

But instead of saying all this, Sophie only smiled at her mother and patted her hand with exaggerated cheerfulness. "Good thinking, *Mutti.* I'm certain it would help."

"You think?" Magdalena lifted herself feebly on one elbow, searching Sophie's face as though craving even further confirmation of her hopes.

"Of course." Sophie helped her lie down and wrapped her feet —ice-cold despite the sweltering heat pouring into the house through opened windows—with the blanket. "You rest now, and I'll be back soon and fix us something for dinner."

But Magdalena wasn't listening to her any longer. Her purple eyelids fluttered nervously and closed atop her ghostly face, as if the conversation had robbed her of all force. Sophie watched her mother's chest rise and fall unevenly in her troubled sleep and then slipped silently out of her bedroom, pulling the door shut after herself.

"You wish to be released from your duties?" The armaments factory official stared at Sophie as though she was a mental institu-

tion patient when she submitted her written request to him the
following day. "On the grounds of your father's arrest."

That wasn't a question. He raised a mocking brow above his
steel-rimmed spectacles and suddenly broke into belly-shaking
laughter.

"I thought I'd heard all sorts of excuses by now, but you,
Fräulein Scholl, have just snatched the main prize."

Taking a long breath, Sophie willed her temper under control,
even if it took all her effort to do so.

"Not on the grounds of my father's arrest, but on the grounds
of my mother's illness. She can't take care of herself or the house.
Her heart is very weak and if she—"

"Well then, perhaps your father should have taken his wife's
weak heart into consideration before he decided to badmouth our
Führer," the official continued scornfully before throwing a look of
sheer adoration at the portrait of Hitler that occupied a big part of
the wall next to lines and lines of file cabinets.

Sophie glared at the NSDAP pin on his lapel and averted her
eyes in a mixture of disgust and resignation. This Herr Müller
wasn't the kind prone to sympathy. A typical bureaucrat to the
marrow of his bones, smug and superior before others and
subservient before his higher-ups, devoid of any humanity whatsoever, he was the perfect product of the Nazi Party.

Dropping her act, Sophie snatched her registration papers
from his desk. "When do I start?"

Not without pleasure, she noticed how Herr Müller started at
her unexpected, swiping gesture, pulling back in his chair as
though afraid that she would slap him.

"Don't fret; I'm not going to hurt you," she said sweetly, unable
to stop herself.

"What else to expect from an enemy-of-the-state's daughter?"
Müller grumbled, covering a letter opener, shaped as a sword, with
his pudgy palm just in case. "Next Monday, seven sharp. Report to
the foreman as soon as you arrive. Goodbye now."

"Drop dead," Sophie grumbled under her breath, already at the door.

Judging by Müller's nod, he had assumed she wished him a good day. Smirking to herself at that last rebellious act, no matter how childish, Sophie walked out of his office and into the dying afternoon.

They will remember the Scholls yet, she swore to herself as she was marching across the street, ignoring the military car blaring its horn at her. *They will remember our name for years to come. I shall see to it, if that's the last thing I do on this earth.*

For the next two months, Sophie's life dragged like that of a prisoner. Each morning, with the first rays of sun, she trudged toward the towering, gray beast of a building where girls like her worked side by side with the Soviet slave labor workers. Each day, from dawn till dusk, she stood before the conveyor belt creating more arms for the men on both sides to slaughter each other. And with each passing day, Sophie was growing purposely more sloppy with her work, damaging the precious parts, ruining the meticulous assembly, sending the foreman into a frenzy of curses over the ruined production numbers he'd have to present at the end of the week to his superior.

"What am I to tell him then?!" he screamed, clutching at his own wild red hair at the sight of yet another ruined detail.

"That I'm clumsy and make a lousy factory worker and that it would cost him much less to dismiss me right this instant." Sophie invariably shrugged with all the nonchalance in the world.

"You wait, Scholl; I shall report you for sabotage and then you shall see!"

Just like he never finished his sentence to explain what it was precisely that Sophie would see, the foreman never went through with his threat either. Despite all of his shouting and swiping at the Russian workers, he was a decent enough fellow and knew to avert his eyes each time Sophie split her sandwich with her Soviet counterpart, who would never survive on the meager rations assigned to her.

"My two brothers are at the front; I wouldn't even consider sabotaging!" Sophie would bat her innocent eyelashes at him. "I really am clumsy. Just like the Führer says: a woman's place is at home, watching the children, minding the kitchen. Women and weapons, we just don't mix."

As though to prove her point, she'd press the button and drop the press atop a perfectly fine shell, destroying it in a second and sending the foreman into yet another hysterical fit. In the end, he banished her to the furthest corner of the factory, where women with slender fingers were polishing the shells with oil rags. Little did he know that Sophie carried a long, sharp nail with her and, rather to the delight of the Russian women, would drag its business end across the inside of the shell, virtually ruining it as well.

The White Rose might have taken a pause in the production of leaflets, but it was alive and well, in Sophie's small, fearless hands.

Nothing was more disheartening and unsettling than the silence of the authorities. No matter how many inquiries Sophie and Magdalena wrote, they were ignored with an icy scorn reserved by the Reich officials for the families of those accused of "subversive activities." As Magdalena was growing progressively more desperate, refusing to leave her bed altogether, as if set on sleeping through the heartache until the matter was resolved one way or another, the embers of Sophie's indignation were gradually turning into a veritable wrathful fire.

"Just how difficult is it to write a few short lines to the family?" she hissed under her breath as she scrubbed her hands raw doing laundry and waxing the floors after her long shifts at the factory. Exhausted to the bone, anger still wouldn't let her sleep and so she attacked the chores, neglected by her mother, with the helpless fury that could find no other outlet.

Eventually, a secretary of one of the officials, whose office

Sophie staked out on her days off, took pity on her. On the pretext of blocking Sophie's entrance to the anteroom, the young woman whispered hastily to her: "Your father was denounced by a Gestapo informant he had hired, unwittingly, a few months ago as a typist. Apparently, when she asked your father about the war, he said something to the extent that the war was already lost and that Hitler was God's scourge on mankind. He said that if the war didn't end soon, the Russians would be sitting in the Reichstag."

"Is it bad?"

The secretary gave a one-shoulder shrug. "To be frank, I have typed out denunciations that were much worse."

"But will they—" Sophie's breath caught in spite of herself. "Execute him?"

"For blurting out the truth?" The girl, hardly older than Sophie, suppressed a budding grin. "Unlikely. Go home and wait. You'll hear from your father sooner rather than later. And now," she said in the entirely different, official tone, pulling herself up for her boss's benefit, no doubt, "I will ask you to stop wasting Herr Bittner's time. He has duties to attend to."

Whispering her ardent thanks, Sophie slipped out of the office, feeling as if she'd grown wings.

Before long, a dreary autumn chill settled over the town. The sky hung low, heavy with icy rains; after some time, it was difficult to believe that the sun had ever existed. The already-gray days grew shorter, with dawns always late and cold. On their way to school, boys in *Hitlerjugend* uniform crushed crusts of ice that had settled on the puddles overnight. Old swastika banners, that were proudly displayed from windows at the outbreak of the war, now hung limp and faded like old curtains no one had the time to replace. It rained a great deal and felt all but impossible to climb out from under the warm blanket in the morning.

As Sophie was awaiting news regarding her father's fate, her factory duty days eventually merged into a bleak, loathsome routine, interrupted only by the bright, golden days on which letters from the Eastern Front arrived—invariably in twos, from

Hans and Alex. On some days, Sophie couldn't tell whose letters made her heart race faster.

Nothing from Fritz, but again, he was never good at writing letters. It had always been Sophie who kept their conversation going, always asked questions to make the chore of writing easier for him, always play-pouted or reproached him for being quiet when she had so much to say, so many things to discuss—books and paintings and nature and war and peace—just to have him laugh at her gently instead of getting into a debate. It was a grim realization, the fact that Fritz never took her seriously enough to argue with her. Unlike Hans. Unlike Alex...

She always opened Hans' letter first, leaving Alex's for the delicious "later," the evening dessert she would consume greedily under the dim light of the table lamp, already in her bed so that she could fall asleep with his words in her mind and hopefully dream of him as her hand still held onto the precious paper.

Hans' letters were sober and more to the point, just like Hans himself. He wrote of Gzhatsk, which, despite already lying in ruins, was still being shelled by the Russians. He wrote of the Russians themselves—civilians, naturally; their hosts for the most part—who had turned out to be unexpectedly hospitable and even cheerful, rather to Hans' astonishment.

I imagine having Alex with us contributes a great deal to their good disposition, Hans wrote in his elegant, quite un-medical penmanship. *He speaks only Russian to them and they, in return, only call him Shurik and bring out the samovar as soon as we return to our lodgings in the evening and sing folk songs with him, of which he knows a great number. Unlike Willi and I, he feels perfectly at home here. Frankly speaking, I don't think I've ever seen him being so openly happy, so perfectly himself... We keep calling him in jest a prodigal son, but his father isn't so thrilled with the ecstatic letters Alex keeps writing to them and is afraid that his son will run off with the partisans or some such. As for me, I still haven't quite reconciled myself with the duality of everything. It's odd to explain but... having to tend to the wounded during the day and then eating dinner with the people whose compatriots had inflicted those wounds, and singing with them, and sleeping with them under the same roof... I miss Munich.*

And I miss you, Sophie invariably thought, kissing the pages smudged with graphite and bearing the fingerprints of her brother. *Come back soon, Hansi...*

To their mother, Hans wrote something quite different, as Sophie had learned from the letters Magdalena Scholl showed her. In them, he always thanked her profusely for the parcels she'd sent, described his and Werner's health in great detail, the books he was reading—*there's really not much to do for us here, Mother, the front line is really quite far away and we scarcely hear any shooting, and even then it may be thunder and not artillery fire, one can't quite tell with these steppes*—and generally pacified her the best he could, assuring her that both sons were as far away from danger as one could imagine.

The only matter he refused to lie about was their father. As Sophie had expected, Hans invariably responded with a categorical refusal to any of his mother's pleas to beg the authorities for mercy. *I know false pride and I know real pride,* Hans wrote home in September. *Werner and I both feel that by refusing to grovel before these people, we're acting in the spirit of our father. Please, don't mistake our refusal for callousness or any absence of affection on our part. On the contrary, it is out of love and respect for him that we have decided to remain strong in our convictions and proud of our choices, just as Father has always taught us...*

Whenever Magdalena received yet another such letter, she would show it to Sophie almost with childlike helplessness in her eyes and mutter, "I don't understand them. I swear, I just don't understand..."

Sophie did though; she understood and approved of them highly and wrote to Hans and Werner even more affectionate letters, full of hidden hints that no censor would pick up on, and sealed them with kisses and sisterly love.

But it was to Alex that Sophie wrote her most personal letters, only hoping that he would have enough sense not to leave them lying around for Hans or Willi to discover and work themselves up into an apoplectic shock.

Last night I had a most wonderful dream. I went walking with you and Hans; I walked in the middle, half the time jumping so that both of you could lift me up and swing me forward a bit. Then Hans began saying, "I know the simplest proof of the existence of God"...

Alex wrote back to her that he dreamt of her too, that he saw her face in every golden sunset; her serious, black eyes in each starry night; felt her hair in every touch of a golden rye stem brushing his fingers ever so gently...

I wish you were here, Soph. You would love it just as much as I do, I just know it. The people here are fresh and young and so very brilliant, and particularly the physicians. I've made many a good friend among them. And most of them loathe this entire Bolshevism business, contrary to what the Propaganda Ministry is spewing. Among the intelligentsia, Bolshevism is good and dead; it's never coming back here after the war, that much I can tell you right now, with all certainty. And twenty years of Bolshevism has not made Russian people forget how to sing and dance. Every evening we gather outside and sing Russian songs—old and new ones—and I have rather improved my balalaika playing skills. Also, regardless of their poverty, people are so terribly hospitable here! Everything they own they instantly put on the table as soon as a new guest arrives...

Through the few phrases Alex had taught her, Sophie began to communicate with the Russian women at the factory and whenever the conversation moved, no matter how haltingly, forward, she felt herself growing closer to Alex as well, feeling the same wistful longing in her soul that he did, learning as much about these people and their different customs as she could, just so she could understand Alex better.

After all, they had a common enemy. That enemy was Nazism, and each day, Sophie headed to the factory even more determined to sabotage whatever she could, to feed as many women as she could, to teach them how to be allies against that one beast they would try to take on once her boys returned—stronger than ever, ready to continue their war, this time on their own land.

ELEVEN

OCTOBER 1942

Sophie's father was released just as unexpectedly as he'd been sentenced the month before. There were no official letters from the police or the prison in which he'd been serving his term. Robert Scholl simply appeared one gloomy, October morning, a small suitcase in hand, before Magdalena and Sophie's stunned eyes. He shrugged his shoulders when, after showering him with kisses, they asked for the reason behind such unexpected leniency. He had no insight into those people's hearts, Robert explained, adding, in his usual sardonic tone, "If they have hearts, that is."

He'd lost weight, but certainly not his spirit, Sophie noticed with relief, the bags that she was packing for her return to Munich forgotten in her old bedroom, their contents spilled around her bed.

"Maybe Hans or Werner intervened after all," Magdalena suggested, moving frantically around the kitchen, opening and closing cabinets, piling meager ingredients next to the stove in an effort to conjure up a celebratory feast for her husband who had been miraculously returned to her.

Robert glared at her from under his dark, bushy brows but softened his expression at once, not wishing to ruin the morning of their reunion. Sophie, too, couldn't help but notice an instant change in her mother's countenance: in place of a forlorn, haunted look about her, Magdalena's eyes gleamed with a girlish excitement. Faint color returned to her pale, sunken cheeks. Even her hair, which she kept fixing self-consciously as she chuckled in embarrassment—*had she known Robert was coming back, she would have washed it, pinned it into the updo he loved so much*—had reacquired its healthy shine; or was it just an illusion from an artificial source of light? Sophie wondered, regarding her parents and recognizing traces of their past, youthful flame that had kindled there just as the guns of the old war were growing silent. It burned in both of their hearts to this day.

"Hans didn't," she whispered to her father, her words hidden behind the angry hissing of the vegetable oil in the skillet. "He wouldn't."

"I know he wouldn't," Robert agreed and patted Sophie's hand with an affectionate smile. "None of you would. I raised good children; at least that much I did right in this life."

"You did everything right in this life, *Vati*," Sophie replied, catching his big, calloused palm in hers, suddenly overcome with pride for her parent.

No matter the repercussions, he had not once strayed from his chosen path. He had refused to be bullied into joining the army during the Great War and just as confidently refused to be threatened into having anything to do with this one as well, cursing the Nazis at every step with almost suicidal defiance and unafraid in the slightest to pay for his words. Or die for them, if needed.

That's why Sophie loved him so much. It was his defiant blood that flowed through her veins. It was his fire that fueled her own desire to revolt against the regime and all the evils it carried within itself.

"*Vati*," she began. She felt a sudden urge to tell him everything, to confess to her and Hans' biggest secret, to confide in him, just so he, too, would be proud of them, knowing that they were not sitting idly and watching their Fatherland go to the devil. She still had an old leaflet hidden between the pages of her biology textbook, the one written almost entirely by her. How wonderful would it be to see his eyes ignite when he saw physical proof of her resistance? "I wanted to speak to you—"

But then her mother set a steaming plate before him, piled high with gold-crusted potatoes and pieces of ham, and the conversation turned back to Robert's incarceration.

Later, he slept long and deep, right on the covers in his bedroom, and when he awoke, there was no time to chat, only a train for Sophie to catch. The moment was irreversibly lost; lost among the steam of the engine and people shouting their goodbyes and distorted announcements over the loudspeaker, either about the train schedule or more Propaganda Ministry garbage—Sophie couldn't quite tell. And so, she only hugged her mother tightly, kissed her father on both cheeks, nearly drowning in his bearlike, protective embrace, saw him nod to her words in his ear—"I have to tell you something when I return"—and hopped onto the train step, next to a Wehrmacht soldier and his crutches. The poor devil was missing a leg.

"I love you!" she shouted over the deafening whistle as the train departed and, out of the corner of her eye, saw the wounded soldier grimace ever so slightly. With a rush of color to her cheeks, it suddenly dawned on Sophie that someone must have broken it off with him and even the faintest reminder of it twisted a metaphorical blade in his gut. "Eastern Front?" she asked sympathetically.

The young fellow—he really couldn't have been older than Hans—nodded grimly, the words too heavy in his mouth to utter them.

"My two brothers are stationed there too," she continued, not quite sure why. "And my... my fiancé," she finished and bit her tongue at once, a new flood of emotions nearly knocking her over with their force.

She swayed slightly on her feet, blaming it on the train that was gaining speed. *Her fiancé, her foot.* She hadn't written to Fritz in what felt like ages after that last letter she'd sent him. In fact, she had all but erased his existence from her memory as though he had never been real at all, but a mere phantom from her innocent childhood days, a hero from the books she'd read and fallen in love with.

A few days ago, she had received a letter from him stating that he was being transferred to Stalingrad. Much to her shame, Sophie had written a lengthy reply to Alex instead.

"Where is your fiancé stationed?"

The soldier's question pulled her out of her torment-filled reverie.

"Stalingrad," she replied with a heavy exhale and closed her eyes. Facing this young man, this profoundly sad reminder of her own infidelity, pained her to the marrow.

"I'm sorry," the soldier replied and touched her arm gently, as though in an effort to express his sympathy. "The Eastern Front is hell on earth. That damned, blasted war..." he moaned, leaning against the wall with a poster of a smiling blond *Hitlerjugend* boy heading for a Luftwaffe recruitment office. "I hope he returns safe and sound to you."

"Me too," Sophie whispered, meaning someone entirely different and loathing herself even more for it.

She couldn't tell what moved her to do so, but, as discreetly as possible, she extracted her biology textbook from her bag, pulled a leaflet out of it, and slipped it, still folded, into the young soldier's pocket. He regarded her with curiosity.

"Open it when you get home," Sophie said, before adding almost in a whisper, "The Eastern Front *is* hell on earth. But together, we can do something about this blasted war."

The first thing Sophie did upon her return to Munich was write a response to Fritz.

Hans is coming back from Russia, she scribbled ferociously, making up for the lost days of her involuntary indifference. *His letter was waiting for me here—such a marvelous surprise to return to! Now I really should be happy that he is back with us,*

*and I am, and I'm already sketching out the days we'll be able to
spend together in our small flat here in Munich... and yet, I can't
be completely happy. The insecurity we live in constantly casts its
shadow; it won't allow any positive planning for tomorrow and
all the coming days... It hangs over me day and night and never
leaves me for a minute... When will the time finally come when
we won't need to clutch on with all our strength and alertness to
things that are not worth the effort? Every word, before it's
uttered, has to be considered from all sides to see if the slightest
shimmer of ambiguity exists. Trust in other people has to give way
to suspicion and watchfulness. Oh, it's exhausting and
discouraging!*

The words poured out of her, leaving a feeling of lightness and
liberation. Writing to Fritz awoke something in her, a feeling of
returning home after a long absence, even though they lived in very
different worlds now. And yet, Sophie was positive that even if
their marriage was no longer possible, they would forever remain
good friends; friends who could rely on each other and tell each
other everything. Perhaps, that was the reason they both kept
delaying the wedding? Perhaps, Fritz had been sensing it too all
along?

She wouldn't break it off with him now; that was a settled
matter. It was the most dastardly thing one could do to a lad lost in
a foreign, alien land, the ground of which had already swallowed so
many of his comrades. No; Sophie would wait for his return and
then they would sit down and talk about everything. For now, she
would pray for his safety, just like she had promised the soldier she
would, and for now, her heart felt finally settled.

That evening, Sophie went to bed with a smile on her face, just to
be stirred a few hours later by an earthquake that shook the entire
building. Instantly awake, she sat bolt upright, her eyes staring at
the faint glow growing gradually outside the window. In a few
seconds, the shrill scream of the air-raid sirens pierced the night—

too late for those caught unawares in their beds by the RAF bombers.

So here it was. The British air force got to their distant, southern city, after all.

Outside Sophie's window, another fiery flower bloomed, closer this time, ghastly fascinating in its destructive, all-consuming force. The glass rang but withstood. From the ceiling, thin strings of plaster dust began to fall. Shaking it off her hair, Sophie padded toward the window, ignoring the frantic pounding of the air-raid warden on her door, screaming for everyone to get down into the cellar. She could hear, as though in a dream, the distant drumming of feet on the staircase, a child wailing, someone calling for some Josef to hurry up, a dog barking madly outside. There was a nightmarish quality of unreality to the scene of utter annihilation unraveling before her eyes. With a chilling lack of concern for herself, Sophie absorbed it all like a sponge—a broken line of a horizon on fire, shadows darting in all directions, the ground reverberating and sending tremors through the building as though it, too, was trembling with terror, just like every inhabitant of Munich that ghastly night.

Every single one, except for Sophie.

Oddly unafraid, Sophie pulled up a chair and propped her elbows on the windowsill, gazing at the night sky slowly turning infernal orange as though lapsed into the serenest of reveries. But it wasn't shock and neither was it an unhealthy, childish curiosity. Sophie stared at the columns of fire rising ominously against the backdrop of Gothic cathedrals with their gargoyles looking merrily on, imprinting this hellish destruction of everything living and breathing into her memory on purpose.

Unlike the others, she had no right to avert her eyes.

Unlike the others, she had to witness it to write about it in all its grisly detail.

Unlike the others, Sophie firmly believed that people were born for more than obliterating one another with showers of fire and shrapnel.

Unlike the others, she was ready to die so that others could live; so that no bomb would ever again fall on Munich; so that no soldier would lose another limb in the war he had no business fighting; so that pacifists like her father would rule the world, instead of the madman and his Brownshirts.

TWELVE

NOVEMBER 1942

Sophie considered it nothing short of a miracle that the Wehrmacht High Command had permitted Munich medical students to resume their studies after three months of front-line service. Yes, there was the letter from Hans confirming it, but it wasn't until Sophie arrived at the train station, flooded with women just like her, wrapped her arms around her brother and covered Alex's and even blushing Willi's faces in kisses, that she allowed herself to believe something so good to be true.

"Too many of us ignoramuses must have amputated the wrong limbs so they had to ship us all back," Alex said with a laugh, kissing Sophie back in front of everyone as though it was the most natural thing to do.

She gathered that close quarters and the proximity of combat with all the terrors it had brought had erased all the secrets among the men. Suddenly, without any officialities, Sophie and Alex were a couple. With Alex's arm wrapped tightly around her shoulders, she discovered that she didn't mind one bit; nor did Hans, who regarded his best friend and his sister with approval.

"Nah, too many of us were far too sympathetic to the front-line troops who wanted to make it home with all of their limbs about them," Hans protested in jest. "We signed too many waivers that their gunshot wounds were Soviet partisans' doing instead of acknowledging them to be the self-inflicted affairs that they really were."

They were still slightly out of breath after helping the Red Cross nurses and their comrades unload the stretchers with the injured from the neighboring train compartments; still smelled harshly of disinfectant; still held the packages with army rations a bit awkwardly under their arms—the same boys Sophie had seen off some three months ago, but changed somehow. Sophie searched their faces on the tram on their way home, but in vain. Whatever it was that they had witnessed, they weren't ready to share it with her yet. Sophie understood and didn't pry. After going to the maw of hell and making it back alive, they had all the right to take all the . time they wanted.

"Traute is still in Hamburg. Armament factory duty. She started two weeks later than me, so she has two more weeks to go," she told Hans as they hopped onto the tram.

"I know. She wrote to me."

"She was devastated they wouldn't let her go to meet you. Her foreman permitted her to go, but the political supervisor wouldn't sign her release papers. Said they needed all hands to complete production quotas."

Self-important pig with a Party pin, Sophie wanted to add, but didn't.

"When we just started dating, I thought I'd have to compete with other fellows for my beautiful Traute, not production quotas," Hans said, a mock-serious look on his face. "Against production quotas, I don't stand a chance."

On the neighboring bench, someone snorted with laughter. Hans' mischievous grin grew wider. Just like his two comrades, he looked utterly, ridiculously happy to be back.

After the recent air raid, the central heating wasn't working, but the samovar, which the boys had brought with them from the

Eastern Front, provided ample heat for everyone gathered around the table. Sophie kept studying it in amazement; it was a beast of a device, foreign and exotic, its silver sides and the small, intricately made nose from which aromatic tea was flowing shining marvelously in the evening light.

"Do you like it?" Alex asked, following Sophie's gaze to the tremendous Russian "teapot," as Sophie had mentally baptized it. "We bought it on our last day in Gzhatsk."

"I've never seen anything like it," Sophie replied softly, afraid to move. The entire idyllic scene of their reunion still bore a faint quality of a dream and Sophie dreaded the moment when the alarm clock would burst through its protective golden bubble and destroy it right before her eyes.

"Wait till you try the tea," Alex continued, fumbling with the top of the silver beast. "You'll never take your tea any other way after you sample it from the samovar. Nothing like a good Russian samovar..." Faint traces of dreamy memories crept into his voice. "My nanny had one just like it when I was a little boy..."

Sophie was just as aware of his leg pressing into hers under the table as she was of the strong smell of disinfectant hanging over the room. Apparently, in order not to spread Soviet lice to the local population, the Munich Wehrmacht officials had chased all of the freshly arrived soldiers through the delousing army stations installed specifically for this purpose. Their uniforms stank, too, of the vile disinfecting solution, but also—vaguely—of something else: of sweat and fear and anger and endless, fierce love that had forever bound them, stronger than any blood ties would.

Unlike Alex—a part of him still in Russia, a part of him excited to be back in Germany—Hans was puffing on his pipe with a strange, dark air about him, his eyes staring, unseeing, into the void. He started at the soft touch of Sophie's hand and heaved a voluminous sigh as though something pressed down on his conscience with the weight of the entire world.

"Forgive me, please," he muttered apologetically, catching Sophie's fingers in his and giving them a slight affectionate pressure. "I don't mean to be such a bore. Just can't get something out of my head."

"They don't know it was us." Alex dismissed whatever was gnawing on Hans' mind with a sweep of his hand. "If they did, they would have arrested us already."

"Who? The Party people or the SS?" Willi looked up from the plateful of food he'd been demolishing. Life at the front had shaved whatever youthful roundness they still carried in their cheeks and chiseled them, carving them into men—all sharp lines, lean muscles and the new fluid, almost animalistic, manner in which they moved, gliding through the space as one would through the trenches, if they didn't want to catch a bullet in their forehead, that is.

Hans threw him a glare. It was obvious to Sophie that her brother hoped to conceal whatever trouble they had gotten themselves into on the front. *Ever the protective big brother*, she thought with a shake of the head.

"Hans?"

He looked at her and, seeing that the matter could not be avoided, exhaled loudly. "We got into a little row with some Party people," he began by way of explanation.

"You should have seen their snouts after we swiped them a couple!" Alex guffawed, dealing Sophie the soft nudge of a conspirator with his shoulder.

"Well, they oughtn't have been jawing about the troops with such superiority. Self-important dungheaps with Party badges," Hans grumbled with the pipe between his teeth.

"We were sitting in a tavern," Willi explained to Sophie, seeing her growing confusion and alarm. "Our table was next to theirs. They must have had a bit too much of that vicious Soviet vodka and decided that it was their place to berate the front-line troops in the most despicable of manners."

"Hogs with epaulettes," Hans added in the same hissing tone. "Desk worms, good only for blabbering and criticizing what they don't understand."

"What did they say?" Sophie asked.

"That it was our—the Wehrmacht's—fault that the war isn't progressing the way they imagined it should," Hans said with a crooked, sardonic sneer. "That we should have been in Moscow a year ago instead of fighting off the Soviets in the middle of nowhere, some two hundred kilometers west from it. That only complete numbskulls could be losing ground with such technical superiority as ours. That our soldiers are lazy and cowardly and lack spirit." He spat out the last words as though they tasted vile on his tongue.

"Needless to say, such claims called for re-education, front-line style," Alex finished, almost beaming now. "Don't fret, Soph," he added hastily, noticing the expression on Sophie's face. "We had enough wits about us to make ourselves scarce before they could notice our rank insignia and the troops we belonged to."

"And who were the SS then?" Sophie narrowed her gaze at Hans.

"The SS..." He played with his pipe for a while, in the hope that his sister would drop it after Alex distracted her with his Russian tea, but in vain. "The SS were some sods assigned to supervising the Soviet prisoners of war who were repairing the train tracks."

"Himmler's 'elite,' who didn't make it to the front because no one would take them." Alex snorted, with yet another poisonous grin directed at the Reichsführer's black-clad love child. It had deteriorated throughout the years to such an extent that it was now admitting just about anyone as long as they could brandish a whip and curse at defenseless prisoners.

"Did they also say something to you?" Sophie asked, sipping the scalding tea. No matter how much it burned her mouth, it was indeed aromatic and delicious, flooding her with warmth.

"No, they didn't," Hans admitted with reluctance.

"But they were treating the Russians like cattle and that was enough of a reason for us to jump off the train and give them a magisterial thrashing," Alex finished for him, his expression turning stern and almost savage. Sophie had never seen any of them like this before. War indeed changed people and she wasn't quite sure to what extent it had transformed her boys. "You should have seen the Soviets cheering us."

"I bet it lifted their spirits somewhat," Willi added with the same sly grin.

He had also changed, it suddenly occurred to Sophie. Out of a shy, pensive, religious young man, he had turned into a warrior who wasn't afraid to use his fists to beat the fear of God into those who lacked the humanity that his Bible was teaching. *And good for him*, Sophie thought, a smile also growing, blossoming on her face.

"Disappointed?" Hans risked a glance in her direction.

In response, Sophie only shook her head. "Proud," she replied, pecking him impulsively on his cheek, overgrown with three-day stubble.

"That's our Soph!" Alex cried, lifting his cup in the air. "*Prost!* To our sister and the best comrade a fellow can wish for!"

Later, after Alex and Willi had gone for the night, Sophie perched on the edge of Hans' bed.

"I didn't want to pry in front of your friends," she spoke, watching him closely. "But I can see that something is tormenting you, and it's not the brawls with the SS or the Party officials."

"You've always been too perceptive for your own good." Hans chuckled softly, putting away the book in which he was trying to forget himself. Now, in the dim light of the table lamp, the purple circles under his eyes appeared even more pronounced, as though he hadn't slept for days, lost in one nightmare or another.

"Tell me." Sophie saw the words that wouldn't come in the firm line of his tightly pressed, bloodless lips but refused to leave him to his demons. "It's always better when you share it with someone."

"I'm not sure I want to burden you." He cringed slightly, painfully.

"I'm your sister. Who else can you share it with if not me?"

He must have seen the infinite love radiating from her eyes, just as dark and serious as his, and surrendered to it at last.

"Remember when Manfred came here, upset about the pamphlet I wrote? About the Jews? About what he saw in Poland?"

Sophie nodded, her brows knitting together in spite of herself. Her stomach was contracting slowly as if waiting for some terrible blow to be delivered.

"Yes, well..." Hans sighed, wiping his hands down his face. "Now I know why he was so upset with me... I saw it too, with my own two eyes."

"What did you see?" Sophie dropped her voice to a mere whisper without realizing it.

"The SS... they don't only use the Soviet prisoners of war as slave labor," Hans began with difficulty. "They also use civilians. But not like in your factory, even though those don't have it so easy either."

"They use the Jews?" Sophie prodded him gently in the pause that followed.

"The Jews, yes," Hans confirmed, looking terribly miserable all of a sudden. "They were repairing the tracks, these Jewish people —civilians, I saw it from their clothes. Big, yellow stars on their breasts... There was this one girl, sweet as a picture, far too fragile and young to be working on those tracks, doing some back-breaking work under those SS bastards' horsewhips. As soon as her guard stepped away—to use a latrine or whatnot—I jumped off the train and gave her my rations, everything that I had."

Hans grew silent again, his features clouding over. This time, Sophie waited patiently for him to gather his resolve.

"The hatred with which she threw my offering away, with which she looked at my uniform... Oh, Soph, I wished for the ground to open up and swallow me right where I stood. She had not once looked at my face, just the uniform, as though that was the only thing that mattered to her, the only reason for her to loathe me. And then it dawned on me: what a disgusting world it is, in which everything is distorted. Like Alice in the looking-glass. Our fellow folk hate the Jews for those stars on their chests and they hate us in return for our uniforms, and we're all lost, lost I tell you, in the well of hatred in which we'll eventually drown if we don't stop—" Hans gasped, choked on his own emotion that had been eating him alive for days, and covered his face with his hands.

At once, Sophie was at his side, kissing his fingers and his wet cheeks under them; stroking his hair in which a few premature silver strands shone dimly, imploring him not to lose heart, not to give up because the war—the White Rose's war—could still be won and it was up to them to cut through this knot of racial hatred once and for all, and restore peace for all children to live in and prosper.

Hans' expression softened a bit. "I was ashamed to such an extent, my entire face was burning. All I wanted was to walk away and never look back and forget about the entire affair, strike it out of my memory as though it had never existed. But then I thought of the girl, of the food that she needed much more than I needed to save face, and I picked the bag up from the ground, dusted it off, plucked a flower that was growing nearby and placed it all before her feet. As I was on my knees, I begged her, if not for forgiveness —I know that as a part of the nation for which I am forced to fight, I don't deserve that much—but to accept the food just so she would survive and avenge whoever she had lost. And the flower, that was because I wanted to give her at least some pleasure on that horrid day, I explained."

"Did she take it?" Sophie held her breath without quite realizing it.

Hans' lips pulled to a wavering, warm smile at her question. His eyes were once again lost in the memory, gazing somewhere past Sophie's shoulder, where the girl's shadow must have been standing.

"She did. When I looked back, from the train, she stood there with that flower in her hair, smiling at me."

· · ·

Despite her exhaustion, Sophie couldn't fall asleep for a long time that night. But when she did, she dreamt of the girl with the yellow star and a golden flower in her hair.

She could only hope the girl would live through this war so that she, Sophie, could ask for her forgiveness too when all this terror was finally over, when people came to their senses at long last and stopped slaughtering each other on blood principle only.

THIRTEEN

GESTAPO JAIL, MUNICH. FEBRUARY 1943

The day seemed to drag its feet like a refugee from a bombed-out city. The analogy felt suitable for Robert Mohr: there were more and more of them now, passing right under the windows of his office, weighed down by the meager possessions they could salvage from the ruins they used to call homes mere days ago. It was one tragic, unending funeral procession, only with baby prams bursting with suitcases and women, black-clad women everywhere, and no men at all, as far as the eye could see. The crumbling empire's mourners, unpaid and homeless, throwing hateful glances at the swastika flag hanging limply above the Gestapo headquarters' entrance.

With a snap, Mohr closed the shutters and drew the heavy blackout drapes across the window, blocking the pitiful view. Suddenly, he didn't want to return to the cellar and face Sophie Scholl and listen to her words—"We are your bad conscience"— and tremble inwardly at the realization that she was already winning, that her generation was winning this war and he, the calcified relic of the Reich's past, was already fading into nothing, along with the ash that seemed to hang permanently over the city of Munich like a blanket of gray, never-ending snow.

But while the Führer was still in charge and Mohr's headquarters still had all of their walls about them and he, himself, hadn't lost his head to one British RAF-supplied bomb or another, he had work to do.

Because someone had to.

Because if it wasn't him, someone else would take his place.

Because orders were orders and duty called and all that rot— disgusting, generic excuses, most of them used to justify torturing and executing people in the name of the Führer and the Reich.

With the heaviest sigh, Mohr gathered the documents he'd been perusing on his desk and pushed his chair back, rising with a groan more suited to an ancient man on the verge of death. Every step on the way shot a pain through his spine; every exposed bulb along the long corridor made him wince as though it was him who was about to be interrogated, as though he was to defend himself against some terrible crimes; as though it was that tiny slip of a girl with those all-seeing, dark eyes who was the presiding judge and the executor—all in one.

She studied him with unconcealed curiosity while Mohr arranged the files and binders around himself, as if conscious of a change that was churning his very insides under his seemingly unmoved exterior. For some reason, it unnerved him greatly, even though he understood that there was no possible way for her to see inside his soul. Still, in order to defend himself, he decided to attack from the angle Sophie couldn't possibly expect.

"The leaflets found in the University of Hamburg." Mohr looked up from his papers sharply. "Those are yours, aren't they?"

Rather to his astonishment, Sophie only nodded, undisturbed in the slightest. If anything, a little prideful grin curled a corner of her mouth upward.

Mohr cleared his throat. "Who took them there?"

"I did."

He laughed mirthlessly. "I thought this was coming."

"What?"

"Another admission of guilt on behalf of everyone else involved."

"Isn't that what you want?" She slightly cocked her head. "A signed confession from the criminal—case closed, the criminal executed—another award from the Führer?"

Mohr grimaced, unsure of what had insulted him more: the girl's ironic tone or the truth behind her words. Each of them lashed at him like a whip, leaving a burning mark in its wake.

"All I want is the truth." He tried to sound calm and unmoved, but it came out lofty and defensive instead.

It was Sophie's turn to laugh. She had a beautiful laugh—a little too hoarse and loud for a girl, but incredibly sincere and contagious.

Mohr was yet to hear Sophie's brother laugh. He wondered if Hans Scholl ever would.

"If you wanted the truth, Herr Kriminalkommissar, you wouldn't have been working for the Gestapo."

"How come?"

"Because the truth and the Gestapo are two polar opposites of the spectrum," Sophie explained patiently, as though it was self-evident. "No, Herr Kriminalkommissar. If you were on the side of the truth, you would have been tried and executed already, much like all of those brave people from the Berlin resistance circle."

Mohr pulled himself up in his chair. That got his attention.

"What Berlin circle?" he probed in a neutral voice, afraid to betray himself.

Naturally, he was well aware who Sophie was referring to. Berlin's Gestapo were still raking through the conspirators' acquaintances, arresting more and more of them after the initial wave of arrests, trials, and executions had subsided somewhat.

And what names were on the list of the accused, *Herr Gott!* Mohr had grown pale when a colleague had sent him a copy—a rare occasion of its own, but the net of the conspirators was so wide that the entire territory of the Reich had been alerted and ordered to follow up on the leads to cut as many loose ends as possible. The entire affair was a matter of the strictest secrecy, of course; heads would roll if any of this got out of the dusty offices of the Gestapo and flooded the general public with rumors of the highest-ranking officials and diplomats turning on Hitler and his clique. Harro Schulze-Boysen, before his execution that is, had served in the personal quarters of Reichsmarschall Göring himself. Schulze-Boysen's wife, Libertas, had worked for Goebbels' Ministry of Propaganda; her familial estate neighbored Göring's; their families had hunted together, for heaven's sake!

And the Harnacks, also husband and wife, Mohr continued to recall the names and faces, all black and white, staring straight at the camera in their mugshots with the same triumphant looks that Sophie presently displayed... Diplomatic attachés supplying both the Soviets and Americans with the most sensitive information right under their superiors' unsuspecting noses.

The infamous Red Orchestra, the Gestapo had dubbed them. Traitors of the Reich.

"Heroes who gave their lives for their country." Sophie's unexpected remark cut into the stream of Mohr's thoughts. "You know who I'm talking about." And as if to mock him even further, she proceeded to recite the names from her memory: "Harro and Libertas Schulze-Boysen. Arvid and Mildred Harnack. Hans Coppi..."

All the blood seemed to drain from Mohr's face. He stared at Sophie, wide-eyed.

"You must be wondering how I know their names." Sophie smiled at him as one would at a child. "Foreign radio."

"Impossible. The trial has never been made public."

Sophie's soft chuckles sent a chill through his spine.

"People talk, Herr Kriminalkommissar, whether you like it or not. You have multiple leaks everywhere—among your secretaries and typists, among the guards in your cellars, in your own Gestapo offices. There are many more people sympathetic to our cause than you wish to admit. And these leaks, these little innocent trickles—they're only the beginning, Herr Kriminalkommissar." Her voice turned steely and shudder-inducingly cold. "We're everywhere. You will never arrest and execute all of us. The White Rose was only the beginning. Now, the real resistance movement shall pick up where we have left off."

Mohr clasped the pen in his hand just to conceal the trembling of his fingers.

"There are more of you then?" He sounded marvelously calm and professional even to himself. Only inside everything was stirring and ready to crumble, fall apart, much like the Reich itself. Despite the façade still holding on, the cracks of the nationalist foundation were growing, spreading with each new Soviet offensive lost, with each new city bombed, with more and more citizens going hungry, homeless, and destitute. Outside the thick walls of the official buildings, people's indignant murmurs were slowly turning into wrathful thunder. It was only a question of when the storm would break and annihilate them all. "I want the names."

Sophie lifted her expressive, dark brows as though he'd just said something terribly funny, grinned and gestured around herself. "Franzes and Hanses and Hertas and Sophies and Martas and Magdas and Wilhelms and Harros and Arvids and Alexes and Roberts—"

Unwittingly, she called his name and Mohr felt his hand twitch above the empty sheet of paper.

"You haven't been listening to me, Herr Kriminalkommissar. I have told you, we are everywhere. The movement has spread far beyond the original cell. I couldn't give you the names even if I wanted to. I can only tell you that I did a lot of traveling last year. To Hamburg and to Ulm, to Berlin and to Linz. And in every single city, I discovered people sympathetic to the cause. Not just among the students, but among the military as well. Wounded soldiers discharged from the front are particularly set against you, not that anyone can blame them. And after your Führer had doomed the entire Sixth Army in Stalingrad, together with Feldmarschall Paulus, choosing to sacrifice hundreds of thousands of men instead of allowing them to retreat while it was still possible, while they could still break out of the Soviet encirclement, they truly have no more faith in him."

In the pause that followed, Mohr could hear himself breathing.

"The question is, Herr Kriminalkommissar, do you still have faith?" Her black eyes were boring a hole through him. "Because it is not too late to take up the right side, you know," she added so very softly and, for an instant, Mohr thought he had only imagined it.

FOURTEEN

MUNICH, NOVEMBER 1942

Despite death raining down on Germany—a hail of fiery bombs—
life in Munich, surprisingly, went on as it always did, war or
famine, plague or revolutions. Emboldened by his recent Eastern
Front experiences, Willi surprised everyone by joining the fencing
club and now arrived at their scheduled meetings in his white
fencing uniform, his hair wet with sweat and a new sharpness in
his gaze. Homesick for Russia and personal freedom, Alex all but
confined himself to his art studio, where he sketched, sculpted, and
drew—in tormented, fiery colors—everything that tore at his heart,
pulling it in opposite directions. His art included a Soviet peasant
woman with a rosy-cheeked infant at her ample breast; an abandoned gypsy tent in the middle of a battlefield; a portrait of a
Russian doctor leaning against a birch tree; and a blue, velvet night
in watercolor with horses running wild, their bodies glistening in
the moonlight. Even at the clinic he had gotten himself in trouble
for sketching dissected corpses in some tragic, odd manner instead
of making notes. It had become an obsession of his, the constant
need to do something with his hands, to lose himself in the troubled dreamworld as though reality was altogether too much for
Alex to bear. Only with Sophie did he seem to relax a bit, whenever they had a few precious hours together in the unheated apart-

ment of the Scholls or at Alex's studio, where they kept warm by burning coal and copies of Hitler's recent speeches in a small iron stove Alex had procured from the black market. Only under Sophie's gentle fingers did his stiff shoulders soften; only on her chest could he close his eyes and rest while she threaded her fingertips through his tousled hair—at last, at home. At peace.

Hans' and Sophie's landlady had gathered her bags after the very first bombing and taken off for the countryside, forgetting to collect the rent in advance.

"It is my profound conviction that she has already buried and mourned you and was too ashamed to ask for the money considering that either you or the apartment may perish any day now," Alex jested darkly on that recent development, giving Sophie a playful wink.

"Shurik, really?" She tilted her head in reproach, balancing on the edge of the sill with a piece of soap and a roll of tape in hand. So far, the bombings had spared their part of the city; the windows shuddered threateningly but withstood.

"You're just a fountain of optimism, aren't you?" Hans grumbled as well, but even through his scowl, a hint of a smile broke through now and then.

"Not optimism. Realism." Alex shrugged, undisturbed, all the while skeptically eyeing Sophie gluing the tape to the glass. On his lap, an opened drawing album lay forgotten with some unfinished sketch in it. "Do you truly believe it will save the window from the direct hit?"

"Certainly," Sophie replied in the same mock-serious tone. "Have you not read the latest issue of the *Völkischer Beobachter*? Tape is the best defense against the bombs, just like 'shortening the front' is the newest offensive technique used against the Soviets. The further our troops retreat," she said, tearing the tape off with her teeth, "the better the chance we shall win this war. The closer the Soviets to Berlin, the closer our ultimate victory."

"Very funny," Hans muttered, his ear glued to the radio, set on the lowest volume.

It wasn't the officially issued "people's radio"—Goebbels' propaganda mouthpiece almost forcefully installed into each household in the early 1930s—but the kind that caught signals from all over the world. A neighbor had given it to Hans and Alex for a bottle of brandy, jesting grimly that he had been expecting the Gestapo any day now and that he'd be damned before they confiscated the very thing that was still giving him hope when the entire country around him was slowly going to hell.

"Funny or not, some people believe everything the *Promi* force-feeds them," Sophie countered. "No matter how idiotic it sounds."

Leaping off the sill, she padded, barefoot, past Alex to the bathroom to put the remaining sliver of the soap in its place. With winter approaching, the bathroom was the coldest place in the entire apartment and particularly now that hot water was once again a luxury due to the damage caused by the bombs. At once, sharp icy needles began to prickle Sophie's bare soles. Icy tiles, icy water—so cold, it almost burned her hands as she was washing them. Ice and fire—the entire city had been reduced to these two elements, it seemed. With a chilling lack of interest, Sophie wondered which one would claim their lives in the end.

"What's the news, Hans?" she called from the bathroom, drying her hands on the towel, gray with Alex's graphite that refused to be washed away as if it was a part of him now. She didn't want to wash the towel on purpose. "Anything about the opening of the second front?"

Both her questions were met with silence. Instantly alerted, Sophie threw the towel in the general direction of the sink and ran into the living room. Just as she'd expected, her brother and Alex were huddled next to the radio with their foreheads almost touching as they listened to some inaudible words in rapt attention. At first glance, it seemed that neither of them was breathing as their eyes locked, wide and frozen, as if such a trivial act as blinking would doom them to missing an imperative piece of information.

Moving on her tiptoes, Sophie perched close to them and

instantly froze as soon as Hans turned the volume up a bit and a torrent of English words, accented strongly with German, began pouring out, rendering her speechless as well.

...paying with their lives for the ideals that some of my compatriots still hold dear and are ready to defend to their last breath, as these heroes' example clearly shows. But it instills hope in me, the very fact that more than a hundred people have been arrested so far, which means that more than a hundred people—some of them of just as high a rank as Schulze-Boysen and Harnack—decided that enough was enough and that it was time to take Germany back from the hands of the hateful, ignorant, war-waging, xenophobic government full of crooks and thugs of the lowest rung. If such well-educated, intelligent people—I remind you once again that Arvid Harnack was a diplomat and Harro Schulze-Boysen served under Göring himself—decided that siding with the Soviets was worth it if it meant putting an end not only to this blood-shedding war but to this corrupted-to-the-core government, what does it tell us, regular citizens? Isn't it our duty to pick up where they left off? Whether you're an émigré like myself, do whatever possible to fight for our Germany, free Germany, anti-fascist Germany. Contribute to the war effort in the country that presently shelters you. Write to your local newspapers, speak on the radio of your experiences, tell your students, your neighbors, of the dangers of fascism. Donate money, metal, your wedding ring, but do something, I implore you! And if by any chance you're listening to me in Germany—

Sophie felt a shiver of excitement pricking her skin at those words, as if the man was addressing her directly in his deep, moving voice.

—first of all, I applaud you for your bravery, because in a country ruled by terror and the iron fist of the Gestapo, the very act of being

informed is resistance. But if, by any miracle, you're listening to me now, know this: over a hundred of your compatriots have been tried by the People's Court and sentenced to death for so-called treason. They were brave freedom fighters and their sacrifice hasn't been in vain. Resistance is possible. Do whatever you can, in their memory. Continue the fight, for free Germany. From Switzerland, I salute you. Your brother-in-arms, Joseph Appelbaum.

Outside, life went on as usual. A *Hitlerjugend* band passed under their windows, singing something patriotic loudly and off-key. A dog whined pitifully, tied to a lamppost while its owner was trying to procure some bread at the grocer's across the street. In the distance, a tram trolley's shrill signal was interrupted by a car horn, just as annoyed and impatient. Nothing seemingly changed, except for the lives of three people crouching by the radio, shoulder to shoulder, hands touching, eyes searching, lips quivering in uncertain, hopeful smiles.

Alex was the first one to come out of this communal stunned state.

"Harnack, Harnack," he kept repeating as he snapped his fingers, searching his memory for something that was eluding him, rather to his annoyance. "I know this name from somewhere."

"He was a diplomat, they said," Hans probed. He spoke in an undertone, as if afraid to scare off the hint of a clue from Alex's reach. "Maybe you saw his name in a paper or some such?"

Tossing his head impatiently, Alex rose to his feet and began to pace the room. "Harnack. Not Arvid though; I would have remembered such a strange name. No, it was something different. But equally rare..."

"Don't try to force it," Sophie said, following him with her gaze. "The more you think about it, the more it'll keep escaping you. Think of something different and it'll occur to you when you least expect it." She wasn't certain that he heard her.

Next to her, Hans sat with his knees drawn to his chest. "The highest echelons of the military and diplomatic service," he whispered to no one in particular, as though tasting the delicious words on his tongue. His eyes stared, unseeing, through the faded wallpaper on the opposite wall as though seeking a future where resistance was, indeed, possible, and not only possible, but triumphant. "The Wehrmacht is resisting as well. It's not just us, not only students. Professor Huber was wrong all along; it's not our youthful idealism or any such rot. The officers, the diplomats, they are with us, too..." His voice trailed off, losing itself in his delightful reverie completely.

"Harnack, Harnack..." Alex's mutterings were growing softer but no less urgent.

"Well, then," Sophie began, intentionally loudly. "What are we waiting for? If the Gestapo arrested a hundred, there must be many more of them. Let's spread our word further, to Berlin if needed, so that the remaining members of their cell know that they aren't alone. Let's print more leaflets. Let's bring more people into our ranks, from all over Germany. Let's smuggle leaflets to Werner's regiment with a parcel or some such, so he can spread them among his comrades." She saw Hans nodding enthusiastically to her idea of involving their brother as well. The Scholls' rebellious blood running thick in his veins, Werner didn't fancy the entire war business any more than they did. More than that, after speaking to Werner on a few occasions while both brothers had been stationed on the front, Hans had reported to Sophie that Werner was more than fed up with constantly seeing his comrades being blown to bits and would gladly join the resistance as well. "The Gestapo can hunt down and execute isolated cells but not the entire movement, if we mobilize enough people. What are they going to do then? Execute half of Germany?"

"Falk Harnack!" Alex cried, swinging round wildly on his heel toward Sophie. "Lilo, the sculptress who rents the studio together with me, the interpretive dancer—remember her from our literary luncheon?—she used to date him! I don't know if he's related to that Arvid fellow, but it's worth asking."

"Was he in the military?" Hans was suddenly all attention too.

"I'm quite certain he was in the Wehrmacht," Alex said, biting his graphite-stained nail in his agitation.

"If he *is* related to the arrested Harnack..." Sophie began, too afraid to finish her thought, to jinx the luck that was finally turning.

Overcome with the same exhilaration, Alex scooped her up and twirled Sophie around the room, while she laughed, delighted, with his arms around her and the promise of a new dawn for their war-ravaged Fatherland.

"If he *is* related to Harnack-the-diplomat," Hans said, watching them with a smile that was growing progressively wider, "we're in business, ladies and gentlemen."

Sophie was descending the grand university staircase with a crowd of her fellow students when, at the very bottom of it, a hand seized her by the wrist and pulled her aside with great urgency. It was Alex, and judging by his civilian attire of a cashmere coat and a felt hat obscuring his face, he had not only skipped that day's lectures entirely but was trying his utmost to remain out of his professors' sight. Annoyed with his recent antics, they had already given him notice; Alex's father's influence stretched only so far.

"What are you doing here?" In an effort to save his skin, Sophie wrapped her arms around his neck, turning him away from the crowd. Satisfied that Alex was now facing the wall, Sophie scanned the staircase from under her lowered eyelashes for any sign of his educators. "Could it not have waited for later?"

"No, it couldn't have." Alex was still slightly out of breath. It appeared he had run all the way here. Suddenly, he grasped Sophie's face in his hands and gave her a resounding kiss, prompting whistles and approving chuckles from the students. "If I hadn't kissed you right this instant, I would have certainly died."

"Shurik, quit your clowning!" Flushed, half-laughing, but annoyed all the same, Sophie pushed him off lightly. "Your professors will have your hide if they see you here after you've clearly been absent from their lectures. Do you want to be expelled and sent back to the front?"

"Yes. That's precisely my intention. Will you come with me?" He took Sophie's hand with the most solemn of expressions.

"Shurik!"

Seeing that he was in one of his moods and that there was no reasoning with him, Sophie put her arm through the crook of his and pulled him away from the student mass and watchful gaze of the new university caretaker, Jacob Schmid. With his Nazi Party badge proudly displayed on his stained overalls, he, no doubt, fancied himself a deputy to the dean. It was common knowledge among the students that Schmid, installed in the place of the old caretaker who'd been shipped to the front, had made it a point of honor to report anyone and anything remotely suspicious "to the authorities" and, therefore, they avoided him like the plague as much as they could.

"All right, all right." Alex laughed, delighted and carefree. He all but walked with a skip in his step, squeezing Sophie's waist through her thin overcoat and kissing her on her temple and cheek and the corner of her mouth every now and then. It occurred to Sophie that whatever he had uncovered was good news indeed. "Shall we wait for Hans?"

"He's still at the clinic." Sophie motioned her head in the direction of the clinic where most medical students had their practice. "They have a preliminary exam about gangrenous wounds or some such."

"Oh. Will you believe it? I entirely forgot that it was today."

Sophie came to an abrupt halt, gaping at him. "You missed an exam?"

Alex only waved her question off with his elegant, gloved hand. "Why don't you ask me where I've been instead." Mirth glimmered in his eyes, curled his lips into a mischievous, enigmatic smile.

"I don't know." Sophie sighed in surrender. "Drawing some vagabond in your studio?"

It was mostly Hans who good-naturedly mocked his best friend for the bohemian habit of befriending and dragging in whatever remaining homeless people could still be found in Munich after the Nazis had shipped most of them off to the camps for their "antisocial" behavior and bad influence on the youth. This time, however, it was Sophie who tiredly regarded this artist who positively refused to draw anything remotely "patriotic" or "lofty" and, in a sort of dark romanticism, concentrated his efforts on everything the new regime found utterly despicable and revolting.

"I was indeed in my studio, but there were no vagabonds in it this time."

"No? What happened?"

"The SS dispatched the last one to Dachau," Alex jested darkly. "I went to see Lilo before she disappeared on one of her artistic pilgrimages."

Sophie pricked her ears at once, her mind making an instant connection with the recently mentioned Harnack.

"It turns out, the two Harnacks *are* related," Alex announced triumphantly. "Falk is Arvid's younger brother. Lilo can't put us in touch directly, but she does know where he's stationed and can write a recommendation letter for us."

"Us?"

"Hans and me."

"I want to go too."

"Out of the question."

"Why not?"

"Because he's stationed at the border of the Protectorate. What business do you have there?"

"What business do you?" Sophie countered, crossing her arms over her chest in defiance. "I know you'll be traveling without any permits. It's less suspicious if two of you travel with a girl. It's always less suspicious when you have a girl with you."

"Sophie." A sudden gust of wind tore into Sophie's short hair.

Alex pulled off his leather glove with his teeth and tucked the errant strands behind her ears. "Where's your knitted hat that I like? The red one? You forgot it again? It's much too cold to walk around without a hat." Promptly removing his own hat, Alex placed it atop Sophie's head and cocked it fashionably to one side.

"Shurik, I'm not a child."

"I know you're not." His voice was full of unexpected melancholy.

"So, stop treating me like one!"

In the pause that followed, he was gazing at her like Fritz had never done, with so much unspoken emotion brimming in the corners of his eyes. They turned almost black with misery and passion, all churning and rising to the surface and barely contained by the sheer willpower of this extraordinary man she had fallen in love with.

As though reading her thoughts, Alex placed his palm on her cold cheek. "I love you, Sophie." There was not a trace of playfulness about him now. Alex was as solemn as a man ascending a scaffold. "And I would never forgive myself if something happened to you."

"What about me?" Sophie felt her lips trembling and not because of the cold. "Are you the only one to be considered?"

"I'm a lost cause, Sophie, angel." He smiled a sad smile that made Sophie's heart swell painfully in her chest. They were doomed, it had occurred to her just then. Doomed, beautiful, and damned—dead men on leave, waiting for the ax to drop. "I don't know for how much longer I'll be able to pretend that I belong to this new state. I'll crack sooner rather than later. And you—" His voice caught at those words. "You have a fiancé, a good, conscientious man who shall never get in trouble with superiors, who shall have a good career and rise in the ranks and who shall take good care of you and have a wonderful family with you—"

Sophie's little palm pressed against his mouth stopped him in his tracks, wiped the picture he was painting from existence. Despite the tears rolling down her cheeks, she was grinning at him devilishly. "I don't want any of that, you idiot. You should know that by now. I thought I made myself clear enough that evening, before you left for the front. I want you. I'm also a lost cause. And that's why you want me too." With that, she removed her hand from his mouth, wrapped her arm around his neck and pulled him close, kissing him with all the passion she felt for him.

Two days later, Sophie was seeing Hans and Alex off at the train station. In her backpack, a new batch of freshly printed leaflets snugly sat. In her hand, there was a train ticket to Hamburg. Traute would meet her there and put her in touch with the students of the University of Hamburg, Traute's hometown.

It was the women's war just as much as it was the men's, and fortunately for them, their men understood and respected it.

FIFTEEN

HAMBURG. NOVEMBER 1942

From the first moment Sophie entered Traute's friends' apartment, she was transported into a world that was completely different from everything she'd known. For both parties' sake, Traute had contacted only two of her closest friends—Greta and Heinz—with whom she'd grown up and whom she trusted with her life. However, even the absence of the rest of the Hamburg group did little to conceal the nature of the apartment's inhabitants. Shrouded in artificial twilight even in the middle of the afternoon, their dwelling resembled a gypsy tent, with its heavy red drapes, thick Oriental carpets covering every inch of the floor, and a lingering scent of some exotic incense that had seemingly penetrated every inch of the velvet duvets and sofas with pillows scattered around them.

"You do smoke, don't you?" Heinz, who reminded Sophie of Alex with his bohemian air, asked by means of the most casual of welcomes and, without waiting for the reply, disappeared into the kitchen. The sleeves of his tailored silk shirt were rolled with almost neglectful casualness, and the ringlets of longish, golden hair framed the handsome, aristocratic face that could have belonged to a nineteenth-century count. He displayed the same disdain for tradition as Alex did, rebelliousness all but dripping off his slang-tainted lips whenever he wasn't busy cursing the Nazi Party in expressions that would put any sailor to shame. Despite having just met the fellow, Sophie already approved of him immensely.

Greta, with her wintry-pallid skin, rolled her just-as-pale gray eyes expressively at her flatmate's retreating back. "Heinz, how many times..." She sighed in theatrical exasperation. "They're not here for that."

At once, her entire countenance changed. She smiled at her guests warmly and, after pouring them both tea, seated herself across from them on a divan. She wrapped herself in a lavender shawl adorned with a fringe, bearing a resemblance to the airy, dreamlike models French impressionists used to draw half a century ago.

"Forgive that airhead," she said, her long, slender fingers playing with the tassels. "I warned him not to mess about with that stuff. Makes him all confused, but, what's worse, gives him all sorts of ideas."

"I hoped that with the outbreak of the war he wouldn't be able to get it anymore," Traute muttered, sipping her tea.

Greta only moved her shoulder. To Sophie, she didn't seem to be concerned in the slightest with her flatmate's addiction to whatever illegal substance they were talking about.

"True, his former British supplier is gone, but in his place, one black-market dealer or another is now selling the goods. War or not, when one has the means to buy, there shall always be someone to sell. It's a simple matter of supply and demand, ancient as the world itself."

From the kitchen poured the sounds of an American swing tune, accompanied by Heinz's singing.

"...*today we dance, and to the devil with tomorrow...*"

Despite the record playing at a rather loud volume, the sounds were muffled somewhat, enveloping Sophie in their soft, soothing embrace. Digging her stockinged feet into the thick rug, she had finally realized the meaning behind such a puzzling number of carpets almost piled one on top of the other: Heinz and Greta must have held swing parties here for the like-minded youths.

"...*today we drink, for tomorrow we shall die*..."

As though reading her thoughts, Traute asked Greta about the neighbors downstairs.

"Some old bat who can't even hear air-raid sirens," Greta replied with a grin and a shade of something unexpectedly sly and hawkish in those innocent pale eyes of hers. "She wouldn't report anything at any rate. Heinz shares smoked ham and peach preserves with her, whenever he procures them from the same crook who sells him opium. She may be deaf, but she still knows what's good for her."

Sophie pulled forward, stealing a glance in the direction of the kitchen. "Is he reliable? I mean... with that habit of his."

"Oh yes!" Greta straightened up, unfolding her bare legs from under herself. "More reliable than anyone I know. Opium, that's just..." She appeared to be searching for the right word. "A means of a personal rebellion. Heinz has always taken everything to the extreme. When the others just began listening to the banned records, Heinz decided to host full-blown dance parties. When the others detested the Brownshirts in secret, Heinz took great pleasure in brawling with them in the open." All of a sudden, a faraway, wistful look stole across Greta's porcelain face, replacing the one of deep sorrow. "When his father—he's in the SS—tried shoving him into the Napola," she made an annoyed gesture, "you know those elite schools for the future leaders of the Reich, as they call them," another expressive roll of the eyes. "Well, Heinz shot himself with his father's own service pistol."

Sophie gasped, in spite of the fact that Heinz was very much alive and singing, right there in the kitchen. Traute, who apparently knew the story, only nodded gravely a few times. *Damned business,* her eyes read under the tightly knitted brows.

"Had the bullet passed a few millimeters to the left, it would have gone straight into his heart," Greta finished, still gazing at the kitchen entrance, concealed by a beaded curtain. "I suppose something good came out of that attempt. First, he's now exempt from military service. Second, his father has finally decided to leave him be and agreed to the University of Hamburg instead of the Napola. Not that Heinz would have made it into the Napola with his injury. Damaged material, in the Nazis' eyes," she said with a vicious smirk full of unconcealed hatred before outstretching her hand toward Sophie and Traute. "Now, let me see those leaflets. I want to see what the fuss is all about."

"The fuss?" Sophie regarded her quizzically while Traute was fumbling with the double lining of her backpack.

Greta only arched her blond brow. "Why, haven't you heard? Even the local Gestapo here are offering a handsome reward to anyone who can provide information concerning the identity of the members of the White Rose."

Suddenly cold and giddy, Sophie handed Greta her portion of leaflets and sank back into the cloud of pillows, her thoughts at war with themselves. She felt proud and important, wanted by the State Secret Police themselves, but at the same time overwhelmed and terrified—not of the Gestapo, but of the fact that she was far too small for something so grand and awesome; far too small and young and inexperienced to be a part of the spearhead of the German resistance movement.

Even her name wasn't as important-sounding as Harro Schulze-Boysen, Göring's Luftwaffe Lieutenant or his wife, Countess Libertas.

She was Sophie Scholl, and only...

Heinz's excited gasp tore her out of the spinning wheel of her own unhappy musings. He stood, a silver tray in his hands, over her shoulder, his heavily lidded eyes riveted with an awestruck, greedy fascination to the small stack of leaflets, one of which Greta was presently perusing.

"Is that what I think it is?" His voice was a mere whisper. Depositing the tray on the coffee table, he muttered something about the cocktails he'd made for his esteemed guests and instantly snatched one of the pamphlets from the top of the stack.

Sophie didn't realize that she was holding her breath while he was reading the text until Heinz fixed her with his eyes. Not a trace of his former drug-induced apathy was left in them.

"Who wrote this?" he asked.

"That particular one that you've just read—I did," Sophie acknowledged, her throat suddenly dry.

"But you're mad!" Heinz cried, breaking into the widest grin, all white teeth and fire in his eyes. "No, you're positively mad, writing things like that. I love it! Gretchen, don't you just love it? Such insolence—I could weep! Sophie, may I kiss your hands, you mad genius, you?"

Before Sophie could reply, Heinz was already covering the backs of her hands with kisses, rather to Traute and Greta's delight.

"And the rest of them?"

Sophie didn't pull her hands away but didn't betray any names either. Her life was hers to live and to lose. Her brother, Alex, Willi, and Christoph were an entirely different matter altogether.

In the pause that followed, Heinz slowly nodded his understanding and appreciation—all wrapped in one.

"Don't tell me then. The less I know, the better." He grinned like a conspirator. "Though, who's going to suspect me in dealing with resistance material at any rate? I'm a depressive, suicidal burden on the German Reich's society. They have long lost their interest in me."

From her seat, Greta was grinning like the Cheshire Cat. "As you can see, you have come to the right place. We will distribute the leaflets for you. Bring as many as you can. We'll drown the city in them."

They toasted with American cocktails—Old-Fashioneds, Sophie thought Heinz called them—and sealed the deal, to freedom and to a new Germany, no matter the cost.

Munich met them with snow and rumors of the failing Stalingrad offensive. Naturally, no one was mad enough to discuss such things openly—jokes about dentists now having to pull teeth through the nose as everyone was afraid to open their mouth were gaining more and more grim popularity in Munich. However, veiled allusions and implications accompanied by knowing looks were still there, unavoidable and self-evident, much like the bomb craters and blackened carcasses of buildings, much like the telling absence of any mail from the front. Fritz's letters had always been rare and frugal in information and emotion, always straight to the point, just like Fritz himself—*How's your health? How are your parents? Did you receive the money that I sent you?*—but now even his short one-page missives had ceased entirely. It worried Sophie more than she wanted to admit to herself. A former lover or not, she still cared for Fritz deeply, probably just as much as she cared for her brother Werner, also fighting on the front, though, thankfully, far away from doomed Stalingrad. It mattered not that her love for Fritz had turned from an infatuation of a young girl to something akin to a deep, sisterly love, it was love all the same.

Through the window of the tram carefully picking its way among the rubble-littered streets, Sophie gazed at the obliterated houses with her brows knitted tightly together. To her right, the carcass of a building crept into view, sliced in half by a bomb as though by a giant butcher knife. In one of the apartments on the second floor, a woman was gathering the surviving dishes into a plaid tablecloth as her two young children played in a mixture of brick and their neighbors' scattered belongings two stories down. At once, she called to them from the edge of what used to be her kitchen. Raising their dirty, blond heads, they shouted their military "*Jawohl*" back to her—Reich's future soldiers, at barely three and four years of age. Just across the street, not even ten meters away from the tram tracks, mangled, broken bodies had been laid out for identification, their black, blistered limbs sticking out from under the multicolored sheets as though even in death they were trying to claw their way out from under the rubble.

Something had to be done and done fast. Else, Hitler would take them all to a mass grave along with him—old and young, innocent and guilty, those who adored him and who despised him—and let God or the devil sort them all out later.

It appeared that fortune was on their side: Falk Harnack, the executed Arvid Harnack's younger brother, had promised to put them in touch with the remaining members of the resistance in Berlin.

"He wasn't all that delighted about our leaflets," Hans acknowledged with a grimace as Sophie stood, unwrapping layers of her scarf in the middle of the living room, her now-empty rucksack at her feet. "Said it was a dangerous business and precisely what had brought such a swift and unfortunate end to Schulze-Boysen's circle—"

"But he agreed to meet us in Berlin and introduce us to the people who have avoided arrest," Alex interrupted him, waving off the leaflet claim like a pesky fly.

They kept talking on top of each other and pacing the room as though they couldn't possibly sit still after they'd learned that nothing was yet lost, that the German resistance was very much alive and ready to strike at the first opportunity. But this time it had to be a deathly blow—something that would put an end to the madman himself and the war along with him.

"They have connections to the Wehrmacht," Hans whispered almost with reverence, his eyes widening in wonder as he gazed somewhere past Sophie's shoulder. "And not some petty soldiers like us, but the top brass."

"We're talking officers who have access to the top hierarchy." Alex's smile was thoroughly savage. Wild fire was burning in his eyes; the same fire Sophie felt igniting in her own chest, all-consuming, begging for release, for decisive action.

"To Hitler himself," Hans finished in a voice that was scarcely audible, but so grave and victoriously ominous, a rush of blood-chilling excitement passed through Sophie's limbs, to the very tips of her fingers.

"Did Harnack imply what I'm thinking?" she asked, almost her whole body trembling. The situation was surreal, and despite herself, she also spoke in an undertone. "An assassination?"

The word, once it had slipped off her tongue, so dangerous and delicious at the same time, enveloped the room in breathless expectation of something tremendous, something far bigger than them.

Hans and Alex nodded at the same time. They weren't smiling any longer. Neither of them took any pleasure in considering murder, let it be the most righteous, justified murder in the entire history of the world. Healers to the marrow of their bones, they were still plagued with guilt even if the man against whom they were conspiring deserved to die like no other—so that the rest of them could live. Free.

For a while, tense silence hung over the room. Each of them knew what the other was thinking, but the words were suddenly too heavy to utter, dizzying and taking one's breath away with the sheer power of such a possibility.

"How was your trip?"

Sophie was grateful for Alex's purposeful changing of the subject. She, too, hated Hitler because he had taught her how to hate at an age that was far too tender for such emotions. She would never forgive him that his mere existence had festered the gleeful feeling of joy at the prospect of that existence ending soon. That's what people like Hitler did: they contaminated everything around them and turned even the kindest of hearts into poisonous wells of resentment.

He had called Jews the cancerous growth on the body of Germany, but in truth, it was him, the Führer, who was that cancer. And just like cancer, he had to be cut out, mercilessly and without any regrets. Perhaps, it was the irony of the fate that medics like Hans and Alex were the ones to do it.

"Our Hamburg trip was also very fruitful," Sophie said, sitting down at last. All of a sudden, she felt exhausted. Her nerves were finally giving out. "We made the connection with Traute's childhood friends and they were very enthusiastic about the leaflets. We left whatever we'd brought with them. They'll copy them and distribute them around their university."

"At least someone appreciates our leaflets," Hans grumbled, seemingly offended at the neglect displayed by Harnack and Professor Huber.

Before anyone knew it, all three of them broke into loud, hysterical laughter. Tears shone in the corners of their eyes. The much-needed release had finally found its way through, like a sky pregnant with violet, threatening clouds being sliced open by a bolt of lightning and the relief of the following shower.

They were too young to carry such a burden for so long.

They were too young to be the unwitting guardians of Germany, and yet, they didn't mind it.

It was unanimously decided among them that day that if this was the way they would go, then so be it. They couldn't imagine any better, more honorable end.

SIXTEEN

MUNICH GESTAPO HEADQUARTERS.
FEBRUARY 1943

Robert Mohr had high hopes for the second day of Sophia Scholl's interrogation. She must have slept on it by now, considered all of the options Mohr had so carefully laid out before her. Whatever was there even to consider? Just point your finger in the direction Mohr had indicated, implicate your brother and his comrades, shed a few tears in front of the judge and get off with a couple of years in jail—and that was at worst. If the judge was sympathetic enough and Mohr put a few words in for her—the poor, confused child, seduced by her brother and his friends' conspiracies into treason she wanted no part of—there was a big possibility that Sophie could walk free altogether.

There was no one for her to protect anyway, Mohr mused, walking the long corridor of the Gestapo jail's cellar. On his orders, Sophie's cellmate had informed Sophie of Christoph Probst having been arrested, in addition to Willi Graf and Hans Scholl. Mohr would have given his arm to have Alex Schmorell—Sophie's carefully guarded love interest—in his hands, but so far, such luck was eluding him.

But that was all right, too. Mohr had long grown used to working with whatever he had and, besides, just this very morning he had ordered to flood Munich and all of its surrounding areas with Schmorell's "wanted" posters. Fat chance that shrewd half-Russian would be able to avoid being captured; not with his portrait gracing every wall and every tram and every train station.

Yesterday, Sophie was obstinate and brave; Mohr had to give it to her. But this was a new morning and a night spent in the Gestapo jail cells had a tendency to inspire even the most obstinate criminals to cooperate.

His spirits high, Mohr nodded his thanks to the SS man holding the door of the interrogation cell for him and stepped inside, already unbuckling his valise.

"Good morning, Sophie. How goes it?"

"Good, Herr Kriminalkommissar."

He didn't like the bright smile she gave him one bit.

"After I learned that you roped poor Christoph into all this mess, I smuggled a cigarette to his cell."

He froze where he stood, his hand still clutching the silver buckle. The girl was lying, most certainly.

Seeing the expression on his face, Sophie only grinned wider, like a feral cat. "I wrote 'freedom' on it," she added, a coup de grâce.

Mohr lowered himself into his chair heavily. All at once, his hopes evaporated. The girl was here to fight—to the victorious end, whatever that meant for her personally.

"And just how did you manage to do it?" he inquired, feigning boredom.

"That's for me to know and for you not to find out."

As soon as the interview was over, Mohr would go and personally interrogate every single guard who had access to Probst's cell. The beginning of a panic caused him to drop a binder he was extracting from the valise. Sympathetic guards, right here, in the Gestapo bastion itself! Just how far had that White Rose business spread?

"I imagine you're lying, Fräulein Scholl."

"Are we back to formal terms, Herr Kriminalkommissar? I must admit, I liked it better when you called me Sophie."

"How did you manage to smuggle it, Sophie?"

A bored half-shrug. "The same way I managed to print leaflets whenever I visited my parents in Ulm every weekend."

There was more than one printing press then. Mohr made a mental note to turn the entirety of Ulm upside down.

"It's destroyed now." Sophie shut even that hope of his down with a fascinating nonchalance about her. "That was the deal with whoever I worked with. If I didn't return to Ulm as planned, they destroy everything. It's Sunday. I have missed the trip. It's gone now."

There were White Rose people in Ulm, just like there were people in Hamburg and Berlin and even right here, in his very headquarters... Mohr's right temple began to pulse. The beginning of a migraine was creeping up.

He fumbled with his papers, momentarily forgetting what he had planned to begin with, and only regained his footing once a well-read leaflet, signed "Leaflets of the resistance movement in Germany" this time, slipped from between the pages.

Mohr held it up before Sophie. She smiled fondly at the paper as one would at an old friend.

"*Ach, A Call to All Germans.*" She evidently recognized it instantly and, closing her eyes, began reciting it, word for word, from memory. "*I will fight to the last man, says Hitler—but in the meantime, the war has already been lost. Germans! Do you and your children want to suffer the same fate that befell the Jews? Do you want to be judged by the same standards as your critics? Are we to be forever the nation which is hated and rejected by all mankind? No. Dissociate yourselves from National Socialist gangsterism. Prove by your deeds that you think otherwise. A new war of liberation is about to begin. The better part of the nation will fight on our side. Freedom of speech, freedom of religion, the protection of individual citizens from the arbitrary will of criminal regimes of violence—these will be the bases of the New Europe. Support the resistance.*" She opened her eyes and looked right at Mohr. "*Distribute the leaflets.*"

For some time, tense silence hung over the room. Mohr could hear himself breathing. It took tremendous effort to recollect himself and still his wild heartbeat under the stiff woolen jacket, right next to his Gestapo identification badge.

"I assume you'll take credit for writing this one as well?" he asked at last, just to interrupt the moment that was growing into something that was bigger than this tiny cell, bigger than Mohr and the sweaty palms he was wiping discreetly on his trousers under the table.

"Credit?" Sophie grinned at him. "Why, what a word you've chosen, Herr Kriminalkommissar. Credit. I didn't write them for fame. I wrote them to move people to action."

Again, those huge, piercing eyes of hers, fixed on him, communicating something Mohr desperately didn't wish to hear.

"Don't you think that your brother and your friends would be offended if you took all the credit—" *Blast it, again that damned word*, Mohr cringed and cursed silently to himself. "Authorship," he swiftly corrected himself, "for the leaflets? Don't you think they would like to be acknowledged as well?"

A weak attempt, he was well aware, but he had to try.

"History will judge us all, Herr Kriminalkommissar." Naturally, Sophie didn't swallow the bait. Her expression was solemn now, almost stern. She reminded Mohr of someone as she sat there with her shoulders squared proudly, with her gaze directed somewhere past him, into the future itself, it seemed.

The blindfolded justice, it occurred to him suddenly. Its statue in the People's Court had Sophie Scholl's face.

"Yes, history will judge us all," she repeated in an odd voice, clasping her hands together. "We're on the right side of it."

"You're in jail," Mohr reminded her soberly.

Sophie only smiled at him as one would at a child. "It's not too late for you, Herr Kriminalkommissar."

Mohr pulled back, breaking into incredulous laughter. Now, this was something new entirely.

"Is that an attempt to recruit me into your ranks, Fräulein Scholl?"

"Not *my* ranks. New Germany's ranks." She regarded him almost kindly. "It's not too late."

"Stop this travesty right this instant or I shall bring up additional charges against you—for sedition against a government official this time!" He was screaming and he didn't know why. It was nearly impossible to rattle him. Only his wife used to drive him to distraction and, later, his daughter, the pest he loved to death and would give his life for without any question.

As though reading his thoughts, Sophie asked, "Do you have children, Herr Kriminalkommissar?"

He made no reply, pretending to write something furiously in his notepad. He held it purposely on his lap so that Sophie wouldn't see his desperate scribbles—*Pigheaded girl, pigheaded girl, they'll hang you, why are you so obstinate? Why??*

"Christoph has three," Sophie continued, her tone softening. "His wife just had the new baby. Why don't you let him go, Herr Kriminalkommissar? He was just a comrade. He never wrote a single word for those pamphlets. It's not too late, Herr Kriminalkommissar. Let him—"

"Your philosophy professor." Mohr pretended to consult his notes, pretended not to hear her altogether. "Kurt Huber, was it not? He was present during several of your meetings. He wrote this leaflet, did he not?"

"Huber? Wrote *A Call to All Germans?*" Sophie snorted and once again transformed into what Mohr had imagined her to be— just a young girl, always ready to laugh, with her whole life before her. "I take it you haven't interviewed Professor Huber yet."

"Why is that?"

"Because he's the biggest admirer of the Prussian militaristic state after Hitler!" Sophie's shoulders were outright shaking with chuckles. "He would never write anything pacifistic of this sort!"

"But several students have already attested to the fact that he was against the National Socialist state."

"He isn't any more fond of the Nazis than most of the students. Are you planning to arrest them all?" She arched a brow.

"But he did want the war to end."

Sophie moved her shoulder, grimacing slightly. "I wouldn't say so. He was very anti-Bolshevist."

She's trying to save that old ass's skin, it suddenly dawned on Mohr.

He stared at Sophie. He could understand her attempts to take her brother's guilt on her own shoulders. He could very well understand her trying to save Alex, that tramp-loving artist. He could even understand Sophie's fondness of Graf and Probst and her desire to protect them. But Huber?

"Sophie, you can't possibly hope to confess to every single resistance member's crimes," he finally said in a mild tone. End of games. Time to talk heart to heart.

"I am the resistance, Herr Kriminalkommissar. I am them and they are me. We are all one, the White Rose, the Red Orchestra— we are one unified front. Communists, social democrats, students, Wehrmacht officers, your SS guards—we are one. You can try to cut off our limbs, but in place of one, fifteen new ones shall grow. The more you try to kill us, the more fuel you add to the fire of our resistance. But it's not too late for you, Herr Kriminalkommissar. If not for you, then for your children."

He started at those words.

"For their future, Herr Kriminalkommissar. Give it to them."

"I'm trying to give it to you, you obstinate girl." Mohr spoke through gritted teeth. "But you won't take it."

Sophie smiled at him with such kindness, Mohr felt a pinch in his unfeeling heart.

"I don't want *your* future, Herr Kriminalkommissar. I want our future. Freedom for all." She paused and added, so quietly Mohr scarcely heard her: "Either that—or death. There is no other option."

SEVENTEEN

JANUARY 1943

Their presence was announced by a little silver bell above the door. Wiping her feet carefully on the welcome mat, Sophie roved her gaze around, taking in her surroundings. The bookstore was dimly lit, quaint, and impossibly charming, with its peculiar book smell mixed with dust and leather bindings. Leaving her to roam about, Hans had already approached the counter to exchange warm handshakes with the owner, Josef Söhngen.

Hans had discovered Herr Söhngen and his bookstore sometime in late December while searching for a present that his father would actually read. When, after measuring Hans with his eyes, Herr Söhngen had asked, in a meaningful voice, what Hans' father loved to read and heard a defiant "Kafka" in response, a new and mutually profitable alliance had been formed, which had flourished into the tightest of friendships in a matter of mere weeks.

To Sophie's question whether the eccentric bachelor was reliable, Hans had replied that the man who had not only Kafka but also Mann, Remarque, Marx and virtually every single writer banned in Germany in the secret niche in his apartment just above the store couldn't have possibly been a Gestapo stool pigeon. Seeing that Sophie still wasn't convinced, Hans had added a soft and barely intelligible, "He's... not married; you understand? Not to a woman... How else should I put it? His *friend* died in the Great War and since then... It was that friend's dream to own a bookstore together. Josef opened it in his memory. You'll like him, you'll see. He's a first-rate fellow! He's always ready to listen, to offer a glass of something to soothe one's soul, so very understanding and accepting..."

Perhaps he was so understanding and accepting precisely because he'd been misunderstood and rejected his whole life, Sophie had mused. She had grown fond of the man before she even had a chance to meet him in person.

Now, standing in the middle of the store, she instantly felt at home among the rows of bookshelves assembled with meticulous love to honor the memory of someone dear's dream.

"Scholl. Haven't seen you since last year," Söhngen said with the gravest of airs. "I was beginning to think that you had abandoned me entirely for another bookseller."

"I would never."

"Or that the Gestapo had finally seized your fat tail."

"You'd like that, wouldn't you?"

"Me? I have the printing press your comrade ordered in my room upstairs. I was ready to pack my suitcases had you not showed up by the end of this week and bolt for the welcoming pastures of Switzerland." After the exchange of courtesies, Söhngen shifted the gaze of his eyes to Sophie. "And you must be Fräulein Scholl."

"Guilty as charged, Herr Söhngen." Approaching the counter, Sophie offered him her hand.

"Drop that pretentious nonsense if you intend for us to be friends. It's Josef," he said, taking her hand.

"Well, in that case, call me Sophie."

"The esteemed White Rose treasurer," Söhngen continued, studying her face.

Sophie saw that one of his eyes was green and the other one

brown, both surrounded by a net of wrinkles characteristic of someone who loved to laugh and did so often. A long scar crossed the right side of his face, slashing his eyebrow in two uneven parts. It wasn't the elegant, fencing kind of scar that some students wore with such pride, but the jagged, frightening sort—the war mark left by a shrapnel piece that had just missed his brain and spared his life. Oddly enough, instead of marring his otherwise handsome, roguish face, the same scar lifted the corner of his mouth slightly, as though fixing it into a permanent good-natured smirk.

"The fearless leaflet writer," Söhngen said, still holding her hand in his.

"Oh no. That's all Hans and Alex." She wasn't in any rush to pull it away. The man's presence and entire manner was so perfectly friendly, Sophie felt as though she'd known him for years and couldn't wait to kindle their friendship. No wonder Hans enjoyed his company so much. Now Sophie saw why.

"Don't be so modest. Your brother wouldn't stop bragging about the leaflet you composed almost entirely on your own, at your friend Probst's estate."

"Well... Alex did help me with that one," Sophie admitted, hiding a smile.

"Take credit where credit is due, Fräulein Scholl." Winking at her, Josef headed for the door, turned the lock, flipped the sign from "open" to "closed" and motioned after himself, disappearing somewhere into the maze of bookshelves. "Do you want to keep it here? The printing press?" he called to Hans.

Sophie was grateful that he did; she would have never discovered the hidden staircase leading to the second floor had they not been guided by the sound of their host's voice.

"We'll take it to the atelier tonight, if it's all right with you," Hans responded from behind her back. "We don't want to compromise you more than necessary."

Groping her way in the darkness, Sophie nearly stumbled into Josef, who was working the lock to his private quarters. "Suit yourself, but the affair is tremendous," he said, pushing the door open.

It swung inside silently. Sophie thought she detected a faint smell of oil.

Following her gaze to the heavy armoire right next to the threshold, Josef nodded at her unspoken question. "For emergency purposes."

"But for how long would it hold?" Sophie eyed the sturdy, polished oak with skepticism. "Theoretically? Do you have an escape route from here?"

"An escape route?" Josef pretended to ponder the question. "One could call it that." With those words, he produced a small caplet from the pocket of his trousers.

Sophie's expression darkened at the sight of it. "Cyanide?"

"It pays off, having doctors as friends." This time his wink was directed at Hans.

When Sophie turned to her brother, he cast his eyes around the room just to avoid her accusing look. She still couldn't stop the venomous, "I didn't know you were dispensing poison left and right," from escaping her lips.

"He doesn't." It was Josef who replied. "In fact, your brother was adamantly against it. I fear I had to blackmail him into obtaining this caplet for me by refusing to procure a printing press for him and his friend Schmorell if he didn't. Don't look so cross, Sophie. It doesn't suit you. You have to understand, I can't be caught alive if things come to that. I know too many things that I would better take to my grave rather than betray to the Gestapo."

Sophie felt her face relaxing in spite of herself. He stood before her, smiling kindly, hands in pockets, rocking slightly from toe to heel—the man who didn't mind dying just to save their lives. Suddenly, a lump lodged itself in Sophie's throat. On impulse, she reached for Josef's wrist and pressed it with all the gratitude she felt for him at that moment.

"Quit it with the sentiment." Clearly touched to the core, Josef swiped at the corner of his eye, his voice betraying him with an emotional tremor despite his attempt to laugh it all off. "We have work to do."

As Sophie followed him out of the narrow corridor and into the workroom of sorts, where Josef was likely binding old editions and restoring the leather back to life, she saw that Hans, too, had mist in his eyes.

"Told you you would like him," Hans whispered in her ear, squeezing her shoulder slightly.

"I love him," she whispered back and meant it.

In the meantime, with a dramatic gesture, Josef tore a heavy oilcloth off what Sophie had assumed to be a sculpture, revealing a printing machine that was at least twice as big as its predecessor. "Here it is. I warned you, it's rather... immense."

Hans stared at it in unconcealed awe. "How many—" His voice caught. He wetted his lips, recovering himself. "How many do you think it can handle?"

"How many leaflets?" Josef lifted his sliced brow. "Virtually an infinite number as long as you feed it paper and ink. It's a beast of a machine, if I say so myself." He patted the press with an odd emotion about him.

"How much do we owe you?" Hans asked, unable to tear his burning eyes off the formidable machine. It appeared brand new; only on closer inspection did certain parts show slight signs of wear. "Sophie, you have the money with you, don't you?"

"Naturally. I'm the treasurer, aren't I?" Sophie passed her hand over the cool metal as if caressing it.

Josef was already shaking his head in protest. "No money. I won't hear of it."

"What blooming nonsense is this?" It was Hans' turn to protest. "You paid for it out of your own pocket. We have to reimburse you—"

"I haven't paid a pfennig for it," Josef cut him off. All at once, his eyes dimmed as though someone had switched off the light. "It used to belong to a friend who is..." He released a breath. "Who is no more." It was obvious that it was still difficult to talk about it. "He perished in Dachau; brutalized and slaughtered by the SS guards for... for being who he was. An antisocial, as they call us. A homosexual. A pervert. He died, yes"—suddenly, his eyes were alight once again—"but not before he printed hundreds of passport forms and all sorts of other passes for the Jews and communists and social democrats and pacifists and other enemies of the Reich. So, no money. He will haunt me for the rest of my days if I try to be a right bastard and attempt to sell it to you."

Twenty minutes later, they were sitting in a small kitchenette drinking ersatz coffee from antique china of the finest quality. The men were deep in a heated discussion about the lost army group at Stalingrad, the imminent allied invasion, about bombing and about Hans' new contacts with Berlin and the rising hopes for the German resistance, but Sophie scarcely heard them.

Virtually an infinite number... Josef's words kept swirling in her excited mind. With Professor Huber's help, they had already written the fifth leaflet—the one that was destined to become the call to all Germans, the one with which they would flood the entire country, and hopefully all of the occupied territories. The one that would bear the signature *Leaflets of the Resistance Movement in Germany,* instead of the *White Rose.* The first leaflet of the unified, expanded front. The first of the millions to follow.

The rumbling came from the north that night, almost indiscernible behind the mechanical cranking of the printing press. Wired on pep pills—it was impossible to function without them any longer—Alex scarcely noticed it, fixated on the growing stack of papers in front of him. Sophie watched him from her position near the heating pipe, her foot tapping the concrete floor dusted with plaster that they hadn't bothered to clean after the last bombardment—a mad tattoo induced either by Pervitin or the nerves; she could no longer tell which.

"You ought to try to sleep, Soph," Alex said without taking his eyes off the crank. "You have a long trip ahead of you and you can't fall asleep on the train."

"I won't. I always take another pill right before I set off. It'll see me through to Stuttgart; don't fret."

Sophie's voice sounded odd to her own ears, as though coming from a deep well. Her glassy, bloodshot eyes burned something frightful, but all at once she found it almost impossible to blink. Sometimes, in between lectures and an interminable wait at one bombed-out station or another, Sophie wondered how long they would be able to continue this way. For the past few weeks, they had learned to function on two or three hours of sleep, plus stimulants meant for the army, which Hans and Alex stole in the most shameless of manners from the medical storage. They were fueled, too, by the sheer determination to turn the entirety of their Fatherland against the madman who had warped it into a nation of widows.

Feigning normality was of utmost importance now that their network was growing and so they showed up at the lectures and submitted their assignments in time, slept for a few hours right after and, as soon as twilight was beginning to envelop the city, they'd set off in the direction of the atelier. There they printed leaflets until they ran out of paper or ink; stacked them, already sorted into envelopes and postmarked, into their backpacks and took nerve-wracking trips to the train station, crawling with the Gestapo and regular police, who had long made it a point of honor to check every suspicious bag and person carrying it.

Even Hans' and Alex's uniforms offered no protection from such scrutiny. No matter how much Minister Goebbels' *Promi* tried to conceal the fact, the Eastern Front was bleeding deserters in appalling numbers. Now, even Wehrmacht soldiers caused suspicion, and particularly if they were alone at night, walking briskly along the ruins of the train tracks—mere shadows making use of the blackout regulations.

They had learned to avoid such patrols, hiding out in the darkness before jumping onto the train when it was already departing.

They had also learned to avoid searches on their route, storing their backpacks in one compartment and taking a seat—if one was available, that is—several compartments away from it. Only when the train slowed down as it approached the outskirts of their city of interest did they pick it up unhurriedly and inconspicuously and jump off the still-moving train to avoid the station Gestapo.

Sophie in particular had mastered this skill: small and nimble, she leapt off train steps, rolled off reinforced embankments and slipped through cordoned-off streets—a veritable street urchin, depositing her dangerous envelopes into every mailbox she would encounter on her way.

Each night, they perused the map of the Reich dividing the cities among themselves: Salzburg for Alex, Linz for Hans, Stuttgart for Sophie, Hamburg for Traute, Vienna for Willi—"he's a Catholic, he'll fit in perfectly"—a timely jest everyone appreciated in those tense, darkness-draped nights.

And every morning, they silently counted their numbers in the university as they passed one another in halls and the canteen and exhaled in great relief that everyone was accounted for.

Pervitin was eating them alive, shaving off the weight that had already been reduced greatly by rationing. It earned Hans and Alex magisterial dressings-down from their professors for their trembling hands—"Drinking again? Just what sort of medics will you make, tell me, if you'll be so kind?!"—and enhanced an already growing suspicion of being followed into an almost physical paranoia of seeing a Gestapo agent in every harmless person they encountered in the street. But it was giving them the energy to go on and that was what mattered the most. They were waging their own, invisible war—against the regime, against time itself. All else had long grown irrelevant.

"Can you get me a gun?"

Alex looked up from the press. Sophie was sitting in the same position as before. She hadn't moved for what felt like hours, her mind constantly at work, restless, oddly alert with the chemically induced drive.

"A gun?" he repeated. "Whatever for?"

"Next week, we're all supposed to go to the Deutsches Museum for the commemoration of the 470th anniversary of the university's founding."

"I thought we all agreed to boycott all Nazi gatherings of that sort."

"We did," Sophie agreed calmly. A pregnant pause filled the cellar. "They say Hitler may be coming." Her eyes seemed black in the room lit only by Alex's electric torch that was already running out of power. "They say he may give a speech before us, students, together with Gauleiter Giesler."

Alex made no reply, just turned the crank once more.

In the pause that followed, Sophie's words echoed unexpectedly loudly off the walls. "I want to shoot him."

"Giesler?"

"Him, too, if Hitler's bodyguards don't shoot me before that." She was almost fascinatingly calm. Not a trace of irony was in her voice.

This time, Alex stopped. "Do you even know how to shoot?" He regarded Sophie as he flexed his palm that must have gone numb from hours of mechanical work. "I know what you'll say—*you'll teach me*, or some such rot—so, save your breath. Even if I teach you how to cock it and how to pull the trigger, you'll still need weeks, if not months, of target practice. Else, you'll just miss the bastard and will hang for nothing."

Sophie would have grinned crookedly if her facial muscles weren't exhausted to the point where even the slightest movement was entirely beyond her powers. "I'm a girl. He's suspicious of his own soldiers after that Red Orchestra affair, but it's still inconceivable to him that women are capable of violence. That they're capable of anything at all, besides childbirth and ironing their husbands' shirts. Imagine his face when I prove him wrong."

She smiled sweetly and viciously this time. It took great effort, but she did, feeling her dry, bloodless lips cracking.

Alex shook his head before returning to the press with a

renewed vigor. "You're talking rot, Soph. You're delirious from that stuff."

"I've never been more sober in my entire life," Sophie countered calmly. "Will you get me a gun?"

"No."

"Why not?"

Alex exhaled and wiped his hands down his face before leaving the worktable abruptly. "Because I don't want you to die, you idiot." Crouching by Sophie, he gathered her face in his hands and kissed her on her eyelids, her lips, her hair and sunken cheeks.

"I don't want you to die, either," Sophie replied, feeling the warmth creeping into the tips of her fingers for the first time in days. "I don't want anyone else to die and that's why I must kill him. With him gone, this nightmare shall end. If a man can't do it, I will. I'm a perfect assassin. He loves patting his sweet German girls' cheeks. He'd never think that one of them can put a gun to his forehead while he's doing it."

"Soph—"

"I'll ask Hans, if you don't give it to me."

They both were silent for a minute, a battle of wills between two pairs of black eyes. Alex looked away first.

"I assume nothing I say will make you change your mind?"

"Nothing."

"Hans won't give it to you either." Alex called her bluff.

"Why do you think so?"

He was silent a tad before uttering, in a barely discernable whisper, "Because he doesn't want you to die either. Because he loves you too."

"Because he loves me, he'll give it to me, Shurik." Cupping his cheek, Sophie smiled at him with infinite tenderness. "Because sometimes love is sacrifice. And it is because I love you, not just you—you know that much —but all of you, my brother and Willi and Christoph and Traute and the whole of humanity. That is the reason why I must pull the trigger. Only because I love you so."

His eyes glittering with unshed tears, Alex slowly reached for his holster, pulled his service gun out and enclosed it in Sophie's hands. Unlike his, they were perfectly steady.

Perhaps, it was indeed a task for a woman.

Perhaps, to give life to millions of others, she had to take one life away.

EIGHTEEN

JANUARY 1943

The sole representative of the White Rose, Sophie patiently waited for her turn to be admitted into the main auditorium of the Deutsches Museum. The weather was deplorable. Gusts of wet wind from the Isar River tore into their exposed faces, muffled the mutterings and sardonic remarks aimed at the SS manning the doors and directing the students into their respective places according to their own logic.

"Whoever thought of holding a ceremony on a blasted island, on a blasted river, in the middle of blasted winter?" a girl of Sophie's age hissed under her breath, her eyes staring at the uniformed gatekeepers with unconcealed, icy hatred.

"The same sod who gave us orders to dress *appropriately*," another one joined in, stomping her frozen feet, derision dripping from her voice, "in skirts and stockings. No one gives a damn that the temperatures are negative outside."

"The SS look very comfortable in their jackboots," Sophie remarked casually, tossing her head toward the couple at the doors of the auditorium.

"Pigs," was the girls' unanimous verdict.

Sophie hid a grin. She'd been doing this for the past hour now as the line was slowly crawling forward: pouring gasoline into the embers of the students' discontent, fueling the fire that would soon be ripe to explode. She was one of the first ones to arrive on the island, occupied almost entirely by a mammoth of a museum dedicated to science and technology. "A typical Nazi choice," Hans had grumbled as soon as the political officer had announced the date and the location of the ceremony. "As though the university itself doesn't have enough auditoriums."

Alex had only rolled his eyes. "You ignorant bumpkin. You've lived under their rule for ten years now and still haven't grasped the basic concepts. Cozy and ornate university auditoriums are not grand enough for their rallies. They want the biggest venue they can secure, like the stadium in Nuremberg, so that they can spray more people with their saliva as they rant and rage against the Jews, Bolshevists, and whatnot. Small auditoriums simply don't produce the same effect."

Now, standing at the gaping maw of the tremendous amphitheater that dwarfed even the tall trees planted in front of it, Sophie smiled fondly at the memories of their banter. Tucked into the belt of her skirt, snug under the layers of her coat and sweater, Alex's gun pressed reassuringly against her stomach. At the last moment, he had expressed the desire to tag along, but Sophie stopped him in his tracks. It was best he didn't.

Under Hans' puzzled look, Alex had stared at her for a very long time but nodded nevertheless and let go of her hand. It was her life to live and hers to lose. He respected that right.

"You—to the balcony." A rough hand seizing her elbow tore Sophie out of her reverie. A blond SS Teutonic Knight glared at her almost with disgust. "Well? Do you need a written invitation?"

"I'm supposed to be seated with Professor Huber. I'm one of his best students."

"Who gives a damn?" He dismissed her with a smirk. "You're a girl. Girls sit on the balcony. Students in uniform sit in the front, behind the professors. The intellectuals—" he spat out the word in disgust, "those despicable bookworms shirking their military duty —" a scornful glare directed this time at the bespectacled student the SS man's comrade had just waved through—"sit in the back of the auditorium. You—to the balcony. Well? Scamper along, before I change my mind and send you home."

Not used to such attitudes—Hans and his friends had treated her and Traute as equals from the beginning—it took Sophie great effort not to bare her teeth and spill something spiteful into this smug face. But she had bigger fish to fry. The thought of it painted such a sweet, feral smile on her face that the SS man stepped back involuntarily as Sophie sauntered past him. Even he, unburdened by intellect as he was, must have sensed something predatory in the animalistic grace of her movements.

When Sophie made her way onto the balcony, to where all of the female students had been ordered, she was met with a sea of sullen, resentful faces. *They hadn't wished to be here in the first place,* their very expressions read, *the blasted political department of the university had summoned them to this circus and now—this humiliation and from whom? The SS numbskulls with nine years of school behind them?*

The air was charged with their discontent. Even their male counterparts, also pushed to the outskirts for their lack of uniform, muttered curses on account of the Nazis. The entire balcony was slowly turning into an epicenter of a brewing storm. In the very eye of it, Sophie basked in that electrified air, sniffed at it as one would at the ozone before a thunderstorm.

And a storm would come.

She was here to see to it. She would make sure of it.

Apologizing her way to the front of the balcony, Sophie peered forward, her eyes searching for Huber. It was all but impossible to discern him among the sea of black robes, but she was almost certain it was Huber's wild mop of salt-and-pepper hair that she spotted in the second row.

As nonchalantly as possible, Sophie turned to the girl to her right. "Is Hitler coming?"

The girl, who tensed up momentarily, relaxed her shoulders after hearing a reassuring "Hitler." Not "Führer," as his adoring fans called him. "Have you not heard his latest address to the nation?"

"I don't own a People's Radio," Sophie said with a shrug.

The girl measured her with even more respect this time. "Good for you. I'll fill you in then. Apparently, our fearless leader had grown mighty upset with the people of Munich after we didn't show enough enthusiasm for sending more of our brothers, boyfriends, husbands, and sons to the front for slaughter after he all but lost Stalingrad. In fact, he got his behind in such an uproar about it that he cancelled his appearance altogether and also declared that we deserve all the bombings we're getting, the insufferable cowards that we are."

Sophie's disappointment must have shown in a sudden drop of her shoulders, for the girl tensed once again next to her.

"Were you looking forward to seeing him?"

"No." Remembering herself, Sophie plastered a quick smile onto her face. "No, it's not that. Just wanted to whistle him down once he made his speech, is all."

The girl's face brightened once again. "Oh! Now I'm upset that he's not coming too. I would have paid any money to see that."

"I would have whistled him down together with you," another female voice chimed in, in full seriousness, from behind Sophie's shoulder.

Sophie had to twist herself to shake hands with her comrade-in-arms.

"We still have Gauleiter Giesler," the new girl remarked, undisturbed. "I'm rather certain that that swine shall blurt out something worth whistling down."

Disappointed as she was, Sophie feigned appropriate cheerfulness as if she didn't feel as though the ground had just gone from under her feet. *In vain, all effort in vain*: she smiled through the bitter, stinging tears, and clapped mechanically after yet another professor's speech praising the students of the University of Munich. Failed, not through any fault of her own, but failed all the same, the stupid, naïve assassin-play-pretend. Sophie's nails dug so hard into her palms, red crescents stung each time she slammed her palms together—yet more senseless applause, yet another intolerable address to the student body.

But it was when Gauleiter Giesler took the stage that Sophie's rage finally found its outlet.

A self-professed *man of the people*, Giesler had already earned himself a reputation for his crude, outrageous remarks that didn't sit right with most of the population of Munich regardless of their political affiliations. However, that day he didn't even foray into a few minutes of obligatory niceties before unleashing the full torrent of his obscenities onto the unsuspecting professorial staff and their students. Whether Hitler's derisive remarks shaming Munich were to blame or Giesler simply didn't sleep well or had drunk too much cheap schnapps the night before and was therefore in a foul mood—it was anyone's guess. But his face said it all before he had even opened his mouth. *Pitiful herd, the lot of you.*

"The university is an integral part of the National Socialist society," he began solemnly, his red, fleshy face already shining with sweat under the hot mercury lamps. "Soon, new leaders shall be standing on the command bridges of German life." He roved his gaze around the auditorium and cringed as though the very thought of these students, who were presently eyeing him in mistrustful, resentful silence, replacing him at the helm disgusted him. "Therefore, it is imperative that institutions of higher education do not remain cloisters of puerile, intellectual thought."

"Of course, not. Why study at all? Let's just replace all universities with SS barracks—that shall help things," Sophie said loudly enough for the students around her to hear. She was surrounded by a like-minded crowd. There was nothing to fear from them.

A wave of excited, approving chuckles passed along their ranks. They began whispering Sophie's words down the line, passing them to those who couldn't hear.

"Twisted intellects and falsely clever minds are unacceptable and do not reflect real life." His excitement growing, Giesler was almost shouting now. "Real life is only transmitted to us by our beloved leader, Adolf Hitler, with his light, joyful and life-affirming teachings!"

"Have I drunk too much cognac before coming here or has that pig just really used the words 'joyful' and 'life-affirming' together with 'Hitler' in the same sentence?" Sophie also raised her voice, suddenly brave and giddy to some suicidal extent.

Such insolence instantly earned her delighted claps on the back and even hushed applause from the balcony crowd—the apparent misfits of the University of Munich.

Only the students in uniform narrowly avoided the Gauleiter's wrath.

"We thank you for your service and your sacrifice and salute those of you who shall head to the front shortly."

Just a thin trickle of claps joined Giesler's own enthusiastic applause. The uniformed students exchanged glances and stayed silent for the most part. Only a few greenhorns shouted an enthusiastic Heil Hitler and rose from their seats to salute. They hadn't seen their comrades being torn to pieces by Soviet rocket launchers yet. They still believed that a German man's greatest fortune was to receive a bullet in his guts and die for the idea.

"However—" Giesler swiftly recovered from such a lukewarm reception of his acknowledgement of a sacrifice he personally never had to make. He only knew how to send others to their deaths. "There are those among your ranks who are without talent or seriousness of purpose."

This time, Sophie burst out laughing herself. "I felt this was coming."

The laughter of the balcony echoed her own, so loud this time, it drew a wrathful glare from Giesler.

"They take away space and furnished rooms from those who are more deserving," he continued with barely contained anger, addressing the balcony crowd directly this time. "The university is not a rescue station for well-bred daughters and sons shirking their military duty."

"I told my brother the same very thing when he dared to return from the front alive to resume his studies," Sophie almost cried now, hysterical tears gathering in the corners of her eyes. Her nerves were escaping out after weeks of tension. She couldn't stop herself even if she wanted to.

Furious, their patience also finally exhausted, more and more girls shouted their protests at the Gauleiter, their voices joining Sophie's.

Much like most men of his type, Giesler refused to be out-screamed by those he deemed inferior to his sex.

"The natural place for a woman is not at the university, but with her family, at the side of her husband! You, women, should be fulfilling your duties as mothers and wives instead of studying!" Spraying his saliva—just as Alex had predicted—Giesler was shaking his fists in helpless ire.

More and more students, male this time, began shouting for him to shut his beer trap and quit insulting their esteemed comrades and future colleagues.

"What cave have you crawled out from?"

"Go to hell, you dung beetle!"

"Shut your mug! Our girls are smarter than your entire cabinet!"

Whole rows of students were on their feet now. At the doors, the SS guards tensed at their posts. Nervous and unsure which side to take, the professors were trying to mediate for peace, their voices all but drowned in the rising tide of anger.

"Women should present the Führer with a child every year!" Giesler bellowed at the top of his lungs, mad with fury and hoping —in vain—to mount at least some support from the nationalists present in the audience. However, even their approving cheers were strangled with deafening jeering and even cruder insults. Then, as if that wasn't enough, he decided to go in for the kill. "And for those women students who are not pretty enough to catch a man, I'd be happy to lend them one of my adjutants." An ugly leer creased his face into a grimace of hatred and utter contempt. "And I promise you that will be a glorious experience!"

There was a second of eerie silence, like one at the front before a bloodthirsty battle. Hans and Alex often recalled it with a tremor, for after it, the deadliest of salvos invariably came from the Soviet side, turning the ground and enveloping the sky itself in clouds of acrid, yellow smoke.

And then it came all at once—a wave annihilating everything on its way, sweeping row after row of the SS defenses as though they were mere slivers in the path of an unforgiving tide. Some of the adjutants rushed to the balcony to contain women with their guns drawn and aimed at their bellies. But Sophie, along with others, saw their faces pale with fear and pushed forward in spite of the violent threats, clawing and tearing at the hateful uniforms with their nails and teeth.

Fights broke out in the aisles. Overpowered and outnumbered, the SS were retreating closer to the stage. While Sophie was elbowing her way forward—the scuffle was a gift from the gods, she could swear!—someone was already whisking away Giesler and his closest entourage. By the time she had reached the stage, gun drawn, lungs bursting with excitement and fire, he had disappeared into the wings.

Someone tugged at her sleeve. Without turning around, Sophie yanked it free, clasping the gun tighter. But there it was again, much more insistent, imploring even. Sophie swung on her heel, teeth bared, ready to pistol-whip whoever lacked the sense to get out of her way, and froze momentarily at the pleading look of the familiar eyes. It was Huber, his hair in wild disarray, his robe torn at the shoulder, revealing a gray patch of his tweed suit. He made no sound, only tried to wrestle her hand, with the gun still enclosed in it, down; tried to direct it, though in vain, under the folds of her coat, away from the eyes of the SS.

A ripple of emotions creased Sophie's forehead, met the intensity of the professor's begging eyes—*go while you still can, there's nothing else to be done here, girl*. After a few seconds of inward struggle, Sophie's expression softened somewhat. She lowered the gun, nodding to Huber but already stepping away—away from his caution, from his logic, from everything that held so many Germans back.

There was no one else to shoot, that much he was right about, but he was mistaken on account of the other issue: something could still be done. The students' small rebellion didn't have to be confined to the museum's bowels. The embers of the revolution could ignite further, if guided by a proper hand, and Sophie was here to see to it.

Someone shot into the air, screaming at the students that they were all under arrest. Swiftly pocketing her own gun, Sophie turned towards one of the exits left open by the missing SS.

"Out of this rat trap!" she cried with all her might, waving her hand in the air for the students to see the escape route. Someone conscientious must have called the reinforcements already. It was only a matter of time until the police and more armed SS would arrive. "Take it to the streets! Let's show them where our place is! It's in the resistance!"

Not recognizing herself any longer, Sophie rushed outside and laughed like mad, drunk on frosty air and exhilaration and the fact that they followed her—that sea of excited, screaming, laughing faces—followed her like the leader she was.

A true leader, who didn't abandon her people like Hitler did with his men at Stalingrad.

A true leader who led by example, not empty words.

A true leader, who was ready to die along with them, if needed, instead of hiding out in his lair from his own people whom he could no longer trust.

"Link arms!" Sophie called and they followed. "Close ranks! Sing!"

Her high, clear voice soared above the Isar and floated along the ranks, growing into a chorus of voices, an ocean of singing students. As they marched along the river, more and more people stopped and stared in disbelief, more and more threw their windows open and gaped at such a remarkable parade of defiance and youth all wrapped in one.

On the corner, an elderly man pumped his fist in the air, his eyes swimming with emotion—he had long lost all belief that he would see such a glorious act of rebellion in the country he so loved and was about to lose.

From the tram station, men in workers' overalls waved and cheered; some joined the students' ranks and marched with them—to the devil with work. Let Hitler make those bombs himself.

Near Ludwigstraße avenue, prisoners of war clearing the rubble from the recent bombing slowly uncurled their shoulders and straightened to their full height, paying no heed—for the first time—to the enraged shouts of their Kapos and feeling no sting from the blows of their whips. Small, hopeful smiles began to form on their emaciated, begrimed faces. *Perhaps there was hope for Germany after all if this was her youth,* Sophie read in their expressions, and nodded.

Yes, there was.

The White Rose would die in seeing to it.

NINETEEN

FEBRUARY 3, 1943

It was only four in the afternoon and they were already well on their way to being thoroughly drunk. Though the occasion called for it: Christoph Probst had finally been permitted to return to Munich from his Austrian Luftwaffe base where he'd been serving.

"I've been pestering my commanding officer about my wife's condition until both of us were blue in the face." Christoph laughed, downing another shot of imported brandy Alex had commandeered from his father's well-stocked bar. "At last, he realized that it was easier to give me that transfer than listen to my whining for another day."

"When is Herta due?" Sophie asked, helping Alex with the samovar. Just as shamelessly as he'd commandeered the brandy, Shurik had requisitioned expensive Oriental tea leaves his father ordinarily saved for valued guests and high-ranking patients.

"Any day now." Christoph beamed.

"Will you be the attending physician as with the first two?" Alex gave him a wry wink.

"But of course!" Christoph even pulled back in mock offense. "I don't trust anyone else when it comes to my wife and my children."

"You should consider switching professions after the war,"

Alex said. "Become a gynecologist-obstetrician instead of a battle-field surgeon."

Christoph didn't laugh, only grinned wistfully. "To be frank with you, I wouldn't mind it one bit. I've seen enough guts and torn limbs to last me a lifetime. I would much rather bring babies into this world than announce to yet another soldier that he is now missing both legs. Or send them for a communal burial."

Except for the soft instrumental music coming from the radio, the room lapsed into silence. Everyone was thinking of what the war had taken from them. Not lives or limbs—not yet—but youthful innocence, to be sure, and along with it, trust in their leaders, in people in general. It scarred their hearts with suspicion and turned them into bitter skeptics long before they reached the age when such a nihilistic outlook on life was expected.

Only from the kitchen came an occasional burst of laugher and clinking of glasses and Traute's good-natured mocking of Hans' attempts to smear the cake she'd whipped up for the occasion with black-market honey.

"How's your stepmother, Christoph?" Willi suddenly asked.

Sophie felt Alex's hand pause next to hers, almost searing itself on the hot metal of the samovar's top. Without exchanging a word with him, she knew precisely what he was thinking. How rotten their situation must have been if they'd forgotten all about the half-Jewish woman who could have very well been dead by now. Preoccupied with their leaflets, they had not once visited her—the woman who had inspired one of those very leaflets.

"She's doing well, thankfully." Christoph's expression brightened once again. "Thank you for visiting her and for bringing her food and household necessities."

Under Sophie and Alex's stunned gazes, Willi looked down at his feet, color mounting in his cheeks. Moved by an impulse, Sophie crossed the room, wrapped her arms tightly around him and kissed Willi loudly on his temple.

"Willi, you Buddhist monk with your vow of silence! Why didn't you tell us anything? We would have gone with you or contributed some way..." She was stroking his hair in sisterly affection.

In his usual bashful manner, Willi only waved her off. "You were busy with other things. I had no wish to disturb you."

"Shurik, have you ever heard such blooming nonsense?" Sophie turned to Alex. "He didn't wish to disturb us!"

"You *were* busy, though." Christoph came to Willi's aid, grinning at Sophie. "Hans told me all about your leading the protest a couple of weeks ago like some Joan of Arc."

"Not like Joan in the slightest," Sophie countered. "There was no horse and no flag and, what's most disappointing, no body armor."

The atmosphere in the room lightened once again. After another round of brandy, laughter grew in volume; the cake, brought in by Hans and Traute, was met with raucous applause and cheers. They wouldn't have paid the slightest attention to the radio had it not been for the sudden beat of the drums that had filled the room instead of music, followed by the announcer's grim, funereal voice: "Citizens of Germany! We are interrupting our regular programming for a special bulletin."

"What now?" Hans groaned, expressing what everyone was thinking.

Lately, there hadn't been any good news coming from the official radio. Only Goebbels' lies and Göring's calls for the ultimate sacrifice. *Familiar rot.*

"Perhaps, we're in luck and Hitler got shot?" Alex suggested only half in jest.

Sophie gave him a warning look. She was grateful that he hadn't said anything to Hans about the gun she'd promptly returned to him, disappointment in her eyes quickly replaced by a rekindled fire after the successful revolt.

"You will not believe what had happened today," she had told him, still out of breath, her cheeks flushed from the wild sprint the students broke into after the SS reinforcements arrived.

"I have already heard everything," he had replied, admiration written all over his face, before covering her lips with his mouth. "You have set something formidable in motion today."

"It's not just me. It's the leaflets. I bet the seeds had been planted a long time ago, when the students read the very first one."

"Then let's go down to the cellar tonight and print more."

"Yes. Let's print as many as we can until the SS choke on them."

Now, Alex only looked back at her with the same admiration—at least for trying to go through with the assassination that many grown men were terrified to attempt—and pressed his lips together in a silent promise. It was their secret. He wouldn't betray her trust.

"That Falk Harnack fellow said that there were high-ranking Wehrmacht men who had avoided the Red Orchestra arrests," he ventured, busying himself with pouring tea into one of the cups out of the steaming Russian beast. "Maybe one of them lucked out and executed that bastard like he deserves."

"Fat chance." Hans accepted the offered cup with great skepticism.

"A man can dream." Alex shrugged, turning everything into a joke as was his habit.

As though on cue, the second movement of Beethoven's Fifth Symphony poured out of the speaker. Traute froze in her chair with a piece of cake impaled on a fork inches away from her mouth. Alex turned the samovar's little crane off, motioning for Willi to turn up the volume.

Hans and Sophie exchanged mistrustful, yet hopeful glances. *Could it be? Could it really be?*

Having turned the volume to the maximum, Willi clasped his hands next to the radio in silent prayer. It was blasphemy, to be sure, praying for someone's death, but as Sophie regarded his closed eyes, his eyelashes trembling faintly on his cheeks, it suddenly occurred to her that if Willi, the kindest soul of them all, had prayed for the madman's death, God would most certainly approve and forgive him.

And then, suddenly, the same grave voice: "The battle for Stalingrad is over. True, with their last breath, to their oath to the flag, the Sixth Army, under the inspirational leadership of Feldmarschall von Paulus, has been defeated. They died so that Germany may live."

A devastated moan echoed through the room—not for Germany's strategic defeat, but for so many lives wasted in vain, again, only because of Hitler's obstinate orders to stand to the last man instead of facing the humiliation of a retreat.

With one abrupt movement, Willi cut off the translation and sank back into his chair, burying his head in his hands. Hans cursed crudely and viciously under his breath. Next to him, Traute was trying to light a cigarette, but the matches kept breaking in her trembling hands. After hissing an emphatic *Scheiße*, she hurled her matchbook onto the floor and stormed off to stand and stare out of the window, hands jammed into pockets, looking just as stunned and helpless as all of them felt. Cupping his tea in his gentle healer's hands, Christoph was gazing at it tragically as though searching for answers among the swirl of aromatic jasmine leaves.

Scarcely suppressing an animalistic cry of pain, Sophie tore out of the room and rushed outside, into the snow-shrouded bleakness. She ran along the streets, hands pressed against her ears—even here there was no escaping the truth. The loudspeakers positioned strategically on every corner had seen to that, pouring their scathing accusations like acid on her nerves.

"Sophie!"

Having long lost her slippers, she welcomed the sting of the snow on her bare soles. Physical pain was always easier to tolerate than emotional. She didn't mind hurting herself one bit if it meant forgetting for a few blissful, pain-filled seconds.

"Soph!"

Sobbing—ugly hiccups and heaving chest and tears smeared all over her face—Sophie sank against Alex's arms as soon as he finally caught up with her and seized her tightly like a wild animal that could bolt at any given moment.

"What are you doing, you silly girl?" he cooed, cradling her against his chest. "It's colder than the North Pole outside. You'll give yourself pneumonia."

"I deserve it," she managed against his shirt, already wet with her tears. "I deserve everything and more."

"Rot."

"Not rot in the slightest. Fritz. Fritz is dead, because of me."

"He's dead because of that *Arschloch* Hitler, not you."

He said it loudly enough for people in the street to hear, but for the first time, no one scowled in disapproval. Their faces said it all. They'd heard the special bulletin too. Distant wails were already filling the streets of the city.

Everyone in Munich had lost someone that day—if not a relative, then a neighbor, a friend, a former classmate for sure.

Everyone was cursing Hitler's name along with Alex.

"He was there, fighting for us, and I—" Sophie couldn't finish, only muffled her anguished cry against Alex's chest. She felt as though a knife was twisting in her guts. She had long acknowledged to herself that she didn't love Fritz like she loved Alex, that she would break it off with him as soon as the war was over and he was back in Germany, safe and sound, but that didn't lessen the blow.

He was her first love, or so she thought. At one point, they were planning a wedding.

"He may still be alive, Soph," Alex said soothingly. He had just now noticed that she was standing there barefoot and gathered her effortlessly in his arms. "They can't be all dead. They'd been surrounded in Stalingrad for the past month or so. The Soviets wouldn't have just slaughtered the entire army group. They must have taken them prisoner," he kept rationalizing as he navigated the streets with Sophie in his arms. "As they process them all, their commissars will allow them to write home; I'm sure of it. You'll receive a letter before you know it. After all, if he'd been dead, his family would have gotten a notice and told your family; no?"

"He could have died in the last few days." The hysteria had

passed, slowly being replaced by a dull, throbbing pain in Sophie's aching chest. She sniffled quietly, suddenly empty and helpless in Alex's arms. "He could have died, and I was here..."

With you. She didn't say it, but he still understood.

"I'm sorry about your fiancé, Soph. I really am." Suddenly, he regarded her almost sternly. "But not about us."

Sophie wanted to look at him and say that neither was she, but discovered that she couldn't force a word out of herself, with the best will in the world. Her conscience still tormented her something terrible.

"I hate myself," she finally said with resignation, almost at the doors of their building.

"That's your right," Alex conceded with his usual ease, for which she loved him so. "I'll love you for the both of us then."

Next morning, just after the lifting of the night's curfew, Professor Huber knocked on Hans' and Sophie's door. Ghastly pale and trembling, his hair in wild disarray, he mutely handed Hans a sheet of paper with his shaking hand. He looked as though he'd aged twenty years in the course of one night.

"Herr Professor." Hans gestured for the man to come in.

But Huber only nudged the sheet into his hands with more urgency. "I was reluctant to write anything for you after our last collaboration." Even his voice sounded dull and dead. Just like Sophie's, Huber's eyes were bloodshot and full of unspeakable tragedy. He, too, hadn't slept last night. Sophie wondered whom he was mourning. "But after Stalingrad..." His voice trailed off, only the hand held out the leaflet with deadly persistence.

Nodding gravely, Hans took it from Huber and shook his hand for a very long time as the two said their goodbyes at the door, talking in undertones, as was the entire German population's habit now.

Hans read the leaflet aloud later, in the middle of the living room, when the White Rose gathered for their daily meeting.

"*Fellow students! Our people are deeply shaken by the fall of our men at Stalingrad. Three hundred and thirty thousand German men were senselessly and irresponsibly driven to their death by the brilliant strategy of our World War I corporal. Führer, we thank you!*" Huber's own sarcasm was palpable in Hans' words as he read. "*We grew up in a state where all free expression of opinion has been suppressed. The Hitler Youth, the SA, and the SS have tried to drug us, to revolutionize us, and to regiment us in the most promising years of our lives. A system of selection leadership, at once unimaginatively devilish and narrow-minded, trains up its future party bigwigs in the 'Castles of the Knightly Order' to become arrogant and conscienceless exploiters and executioners—blind, stupid hangers-on of the Führer.*"

A murmur of approval followed that statement.

"Soph, here's a part about you and your fellow revolutionaries." Hans grinned at his sister and went on: "*Gauleiters insult the honor of women students with crude jokes, and the German women students at the University in Munich have given a worthy response to the besmirching of their honor, and German students have defended their female comrades and stood by them. This is the beginning of the struggle for our free self-determination, without which intellectual and spiritual values cannot be created. We thank the brave comrades, both men and women, who have set us such a brilliant example.*"

Pallid and still not fully herself, Sophie managed a weak, grateful smile to the round of applause that followed.

"*There is only one slogan for us: fight against the Party! Get out of all Party organizations, which are used to keep our mouths shut and hold us in political bondage! Get out of the lecture halls run by SS corporals and Party sycophants. We want genuine learning and real freedom of expression. No threat can intimidate us, not even the closure of universities and colleges. This struggle is for each and every one of us, for our future, our freedom, and our honor under a regime that will be more conscious of its moral responsibility.*

"*Freedom and honor! For ten long years, Hitler and his*

comrades have squeezed, debased, and twisted those beautiful German words to the point of nausea, as only the ignorant can, casting the highest values of a nation before swine."

"I can't believe he called Hitler swine!" Alex cried in delight, almost leaping up in his seat. "Hans, don't you dare remove these words from the leaflet! Print it the way it is, or I shall divorce you and take the children!"

Even Christoph shook his head in amazement. "I did not suspect that Huber had it in him! Calling Hitler swine. Even we haven't gone that far."

"He must be really upset about Stalingrad," Traute agreed, appreciation also visible in her eyes. "Sorry, Hansi. Go on."

Hans obliged. *"In the ten years of destruction of all material and intellectual freedoms, of all moral fiber in the German people, they have sufficiently demonstrated what they understand by freedom and honor. The frightful bloodbath has opened the eyes of even the stupidest German—it is a slaughter that they orchestrated in the name of the 'freedom and honor of the German nation' throughout Europe, and which they start anew every day. The name of Germany will remain forever stained with shame if German youth do not finally arise, fight back, and atone, smash our tormentors, and set up a new Europe. Women students! Men students! The German people look to us! Up, up, my people, let smoke and flame be our sign!"*

Long after Hans had finished, Professor Huber's words reverberated through everyone's hearts. They felt doubly inspired—by the recent spontaneous revolt, by Huber's fiery involvement—and it showed in their restless pacing, their desire to do something—anything—before night would fall and it would be safe to go down to the cellar and print Huber's leaflet for the whole of Munich to read the very next morning.

"I just had another idea," Hans suddenly stopped in his tracks and snapped his fingers, "to make this leaflet's release particularly memorable for the Nazis. Shurik, you don't have any white and red paint in your studio by any chance, do you?"

Alex's lips slowly stretched in a wolfish grin. "Sure do."

The next morning, the city of Munich awoke to the walls of their stores, apartment buildings, and official agencies painted with the words "*Freedom*," "*Down with Hitler*," and "*Death to the Nazis*" in stark white. Under the SS men's mortified, cagy glares, Russian slave women workers were vainly trying to scrub off bloody red swastikas also crossed out with white paint.

And in the midst of all that chaos, Sophie and Hans walked toward the University of Munich, their faces a picture of innocence.

"Have you seen it?" One of the students nearly stumbled into them, his eyes open wide in utter excitement.

Hans only lifted his brows, feigning ignorance. "Seen what, my good fellow?"

Sophie pulled the scarf over the lower part of her face. Finally, she could smile again.

TWENTY

FEBRUARY 1943

Sophie was standing in line for their weekly ration of meat when the incident occurred. Preoccupied with her own affairs, she couldn't quite pinpoint what it was precisely that provoked the altercation. Perhaps the weather was to blame; wet snow had been falling since last night, turning the streets into slippery labyrinths of sleet-covered cobbles and sidewalks drowning in sooty puddles. This year's ration cards for footwear hadn't been distributed yet—it was anyone's guess if they would be at all—and the population's grumbles of discontent on account of their wet, frozen feet were gradually turning into open protest.

Perhaps it was Goebbels' recent speech and more sacrifices the German people had to make to aid the effort; his old, tired anti-Semitism blaming it all on the Jews—"What Jews?" People rolled their eyes. "There aren't any Jews left!"—or perhaps the general exhaustion from the war, from further reduced rations, from bombing and their glorious leaders driving around in their heated cars when people had no coal to even warm their house.

It began with the maid who someone in the line had recognized as Gauleiter Giesler's, who hurried away from the crowd with a thick bundle tied tightly with a rope. As people eyed her with great suspicion, the butcher's hoarse, loud voice boomed from inside the store: "No more ribs! We're out of ribs!"

A communal moan of desperation reverberated down the line. It shifted forward restlessly like a wave gathering momentum. Only the butcher's sharp knife raised threateningly in the air prevented them from pushing their way into the stall and raiding it as Sophie had suspected they were ready to.

"This is the second week that I'm left without any meat!" a woman began to protest loudly. "I'm a war widow! Both of my sons were lost in Stalingrad! And all you have to say is, *We're out of this, we're out of that, come again tomorrow!* My ailing parents need iron; they shall die without it!"

Something along the lines of "nothing I can do" reached Sophie's ears. Just as she imagined, the offhand remark only added fuel to the fire.

"You don't even follow the first come, first served rule!" a man's voice joined in. "You serve Party members before anyone else!"

"That's the law," the butcher grumbled, unimpressed, hacking at some pitiful remains. "Party members are to be served first."

"War veterans ought to be served first!" someone else shouted in indignation. "Look! There's a young man here on crutches; he's been waiting for over an hour, standing on the only leg he has left. Have you any conscience at all?"

"Conscience has nothing to do with it," the butcher countered with infuriating calmness. "The law is the law and orders are orders. When the Party passes a law to serve war veterans first, I shall serve them first."

At that very moment, a car pulled up near the shop. From the driver's seat, a soldier of a low rank climbed out and made his way straight to the front, unsuspecting of—or purposely ignoring—the beady eyes trained on him. The line had stilled itself, tensed visibly.

"Four sirloin steaks," the soldier said, handing the butcher ration coupons and money.

Without batting an eye, the butcher dove momentarily under the counter and laid out four fresh, thick slices of meat.

Sophie noticed a curtain twitch in the back seat of the car, concealing someone too important to stand in line for his own meal.

"You had sirloin hidden all along?" someone asked very quietly and viciously; Sophie wouldn't have heard the remark at all had it not been for the deathly silence now hanging over the line.

The young uniformed fellow, ignorant of the crowd's mood, turned to the voice with a bright smile. "Herr Sturmbannführer had it reserved," he offered by way of explanation. "Heil Hitler!" Even more cheerfully, he raised his arm in salute after gathering the wrapped steaks under his other arm.

"Tell your Hitler to go hang himself!"

A slap came out of nowhere, sending the soldier stumbling a couple of steps back. In his astonishment, he lost his grip on his precious goods. At once, a veritable riot broke out. The crowd was upon the steaks and the soldier before he could retreat back into the safety of his master's staff car. Within moments, the butcher and his helper were overpowered as well. Crawling over the counter, people began grabbing and distributing the foodstuffs as they saw fit.

"Here, war widow!" A red, juicy slice of steak made an arch in the gray air, promptly landing straight into the widow's hands. "To your parents, from Herr Sturmbannführer, with best regards, ha-ha!"

Not quite believing her good fortune, the woman made her escape before the police arrived.

"Here, soldier!" The same young man—Sophie thought she recognized a fellow student in him—ran up to the veteran on his crutches and pushed another great cut of meat into the bag hanging over his shoulder. "Thank you for your service. And now scram before the Gestapo haul all of our behinds into Dachau!"

The veteran didn't need to be told twice.

Even Sophie received her fair share—a nice set of flank steaks some other *Sturmbannführer* must have had reserved for his family dinner. In the distance, the whistles of the police could already be heard. But before disappearing into the side streets with her haul, Sophie searched in the sleet with her foot, found a suitable broken brick and, with a feral smile on her face, hurled her missile straight into the window of the high-ranking Nazi's car, breaking it on impact.

"From the White Rose, with best wishes!" she shouted, making use of the general commotion, certain that the man inside, whoever he was, would hear her.

Cheers still ringing in her ears, she ran as fast as her legs would carry her, lightheaded and overcome with joy.

"Hans!" she called, as soon as she burst inside their apartment, out of breath and rosy-faced with frost and her wild sprint. "You shall not believe what has just happened! They have just—"

Stopping herself mid-word, Sophie came to an abrupt halt on the threshold of the living room. Just across the room from her, flanked by Hans and Alex, sat a man of around thirty, handsome in some imperceptible, fine-boned way that betrayed aristocratic roots carefully hidden behind a regular army uniform. He had the face of an intellectual, with serious, deep eyes and a forehead prematurely lined with worry.

All three men rose to their feet at once, straightening their Wehrmacht tunics.

"Sophie," Hans said, looking at her in that special way he did whenever something grandiose was under way. "This is Falk Harnack. Falk, this is my sister, Sophie."

As they were exchanging handshakes, everything inside Sophie suddenly began to sing. Every cell of her skin appeared to tingle with excitement she thought she had long lost the habit to feel.

Falk Harnack—*the* Falk Harnack from Berlin, the executed Arvid Harnack's brother—was here, and that meant only one thing: everything was finally coming together for the German resistance. With a unified front, they would strike and then victory would be theirs. As Sophie looked into Harnack's eyes, she had no doubt of it.

The meeting of the White Rose was set for the evening of the following day. When it finally came, Sophie discovered that she couldn't sit still. Alex, who was one of the first to arrive, stood up each time the bell rang in the hallway, but each time, Sophie rushed past him to open it herself just to occupy her legs and hands with something. She needed to fill the excruciatingly long minutes of interminable wait with some mindless chatter and the assembly and reassembly of the pillows and the arrangement of food and refreshments on the table.

Alex, too, paced restlessly around the room and chain-smoked his pipe until the entire room was shrouded with gray, though not unpleasant, smoke.

Traute arrived but had to leave early—she had air-warden duty, which couldn't be skipped.

Willi had come straight from his fencing practice. He must have been starving but had entirely ignored the Russian meat pies Alex had helped Sophie bake, which stood currently in the middle of the dining table, spreading a mouthwatering aroma around the room.

"Have one." Sophie pushed the plate toward him. "Don't wait for Falk. He said he might be late."

Willi only shook his head. "Can't. My stomach has been in knots the whole day."

Sophie didn't press him. She understood.

At quarter to six, Professor Huber entered the apartment, as always looking odd and out of place among the students and their excited chatter, their long, restless limbs and eyes full of hope and wonder. Moving among them like an old raven, he perched on the chair in the furthest corner and began fumbling with the papers he'd brought, striking something from them and adding a line here and there.

"I wrote a draft of another leaflet," he explained when Hans approached him with a glass of brandy in hand, which he waved off categorically. "That fellow whom we're meeting tonight; you said he's with the Wehrmacht?"

"He is. With the highest-ranking Wehrmacht," Hans added.

That reassured Huber somewhat. After much fidgeting, he passed Hans his draft with another wave of the hand that, Sophie noticed, was shaking slightly again.

"You read it like you read the last one."

"Are you quite certain, Herr Professor?"

"Yes, yes," he said impatiently. "You do that. You have the requirements for it."

Hans looked at the professor. It was an odd claim coming from the man who never had trouble speaking in front of hundreds of students and now, suddenly, in front of just one man he had lost his nerve. But Hans took the paper all the same.

"As you wish, Herr Professor."

At last, Falk Harnack arrived. Her hands wet with sweat, Sophie welcomed the somber man warmly, marveling at how much older than his thirty years he looked. The shadow of his brother's death still lay around him like a dark mantle; in his gaze, the fire of revenge burned. With introductions out of the way, Harnack sat at the center of the table—the head of a small army of German resistance with students and an elderly professor in place of his generals.

"We're ready for the military putsch," he began without any unnecessary preamble, all business in his starched uniform, so unusually Prussian in his stiff collar and, yet, so utterly and fascinatingly rebellious under his field-gray disguise. "Allied invasion is also only a matter of time. That's why it's of paramount importance to carry out the assassination as soon as possible—to prevent more bloodshed from occurring. When I think of how many good men we lost with that rotten Stalingrad business..." Lips pursed in a sharp slash of disgust—at Hitler's "military genius," no doubt—Harnack shook his head before slapping his knees suddenly. "From what we've heard so far from our sources, the Allies shall cease fire as soon as the new provisional government occupies the Reichstag and announces the immediate cessation of all hostilities on our side—"

"Provisional government meaning the Wehrmacht?" Professor Huber interrupted him, suddenly suspicious.

Harnack glanced at him from under his heavy eyelids. "Provisional government meaning members of the three parties that shall represent the people of Germany in the new parliament: Marxists, Liberals, and Christians, all seated side by side in the Reichstag."

"Marxists?" Mortified, Huber gaped at Harnack, losing all faculty of speech for a few moments. "Surely, you're saying it in jest! I can understand the Liberal party, but not the Marxists!"

"Herr Professor." Harnack was in perfect possession of himself; that much Sophie had to give him. "You understand that we're at war with the Soviets, don't you?" Without waiting for a confirmation, he continued, "Then you must understand that when we sue for peace, we'll have to negotiate with the Soviet government as well, not just the allied western ones."

"But letting Bolshevists into the Reichstag!" Huber cried, clawing with his fingers at the edge of the table with such force his knuckles turned white.

"Would you rather have Nazis remain there perhaps?" Falk arched a sardonic brow.

It occurred to Sophie that Falk was the adult here and not Professor Huber, despite his advanced age. Perhaps, it wasn't altogether that surprising. Huber had a wealth of theoretical knowledge—"lots of bleating and not much wool," as her father loved to say—while Harnack had lived and fought through the years of persecution and the reign of the Gestapo. He was well aware who the real enemy was. The Bolshevists didn't execute his brother; the Nazis did.

"Herr Professor." Hans raised a conciliatory hand. "Let's discuss the question of the provisional government when the time comes. Now, we ought to concentrate our attention on more pressing matters."

"Yes." Sophie thrust her chin forward. "When are we shooting that bastard?"

Harnack didn't lift his gaze from inspecting his hands, but Sophie saw a grin he tried to conceal all the same. "It's not so simple, I'm afraid," he said, his tone much softer than before. "After Hitler discovered 'traitors' under his very nose, he's grown even more paranoid than before. He's surrounded by bodyguards at all times, and even his food has to go through several inspections before it is served to him. We can't just have an assassin barge into his quarters and kill him. The plan has to be foolproof." He looked up, suddenly brightening. "But that's not for you to worry about. You, my friends, shall help us establish our provisional headquarters here in the south while we're doing the same in Berlin. Scholl, didn't you say you had people in Hamburg too?"

Hans nodded. "Sophie and Traute established that particular liaison. They're printing our White Rose leaflets there now as well."

"Splendid. So, Hamburg is covered."

"We have also established small pockets of resistance in Austria." Alex purposely called Ostmark by its old, pre-Anschluss name. "In Linz, Vienna, and Salzburg."

"That's just grand!" Harnack's eyes gleamed even brighter. "It's always better to create a revolt from the bottom, not the top. People must assert their own power. The Wehrmacht's duty is to make it happen." He smiled at Huber this time, as one would at a pouting child. "But there shall never be a military rule in Germany again. Democratic elections and the majority's rule, as it should be. And then, you won't have to worry about your Marxists. If they're unpopular with people, people won't vote for them and they shall disappear on their own instead of being shipped to the camps."

"And if they prove to be popular?" Huber demanded, refusing to back down.

From Harnack, a shrug of perfect nonchalance. "If they do, it means their policies agree with the majority. But that's precisely what I'm trying to explain to you, Herr Professor. It doesn't matter if you or I like their policies—or any party's policies, for that matter. The majority shall decide. And we shall let them and respect their opinion. That's the entire point of democracy."

"He's an insufferable idealist!" Huber cried as soon as Harnack had departed.

The meeting in Berlin had been agreed upon; hands thoroughly shaken. Falk had other affairs to attend to. Now, it was just their immediate circle again—unchanged and yet transformed so completely after only two short hours of the Berliner's visit. Bubbling with enthusiasm, they paced, embraced, made plans and looked somewhere past the blackout curtains, somewhere into the future itself, just as bright and clear as their young, frank eyes.

"All of you are!" Only Huber remained seated, observing them from his perch with a mixture of wrath and confusion. "Democracy! You're too young to remember Weimar! It was Sodom and Gomorrah, your democracy! Cross-dressers and opium addicts on every corner! Is that what you want? Is that your idea of freedom?"

But no one heard him any longer. He was the voice of the old generation, the generation that had brought them to the brink of the collapse. Even with all his antagonism for their common enemy, he couldn't understand them, was too old to grasp their ideals of the new world that were already emerging out of the blood and ashes of the old one. It would be difficult, agonizing, tearing the material of the old at the seams, but deep inside, they all felt that whatever came in the old's wake would be fantastic and beautiful, untamed and wild. No one—not Huber, not Hitler and all of his armies—could prevent it from bursting into the world.

On Thursday, it rained the entire day. Moisture dripped off the skeletal tree branches, snaked along the windows crisscrossed with tape, soaked the boarded-up entrances to the houses whose inhabitants had left for the countryside, where the allied bombardments were rare and food still could be had. The air smelled of soot, wet wool, and despair.

Sophie didn't bother taking off her coat when she entered the apartment; the central heating was damaged beyond repair in most of Munich's homes. She and Hans had long grown used to sleeping in their overcoats, piling the blankets on top of themselves as though they were camping in the Baltic countryside once again—young, carefree, with their entire lives ahead of them.

"Hans!" she called in the general direction of the living room, shaking the umbrella free of raindrops. "Guess who's finally gotten his furlough?"

"Not Werner?" Hans' response came at once.

"The very same," Sophie confirmed and all but skipped into the living room, waving their sibling's letter in the air.

She came to an abrupt halt when she saw that Hans wasn't alone: Christoph Probst, pale as death and looking dazed, sat on a sofa, also in full uniform and even gloves.

"Christoph! What a grand surprise." Sophie's smile quivered, unsure, before she shifted her gaze to her brother. "Hans, some host you are! Not even coffee for our friend?"

Hans grimaced. "That chicory atrocity?"

Sophie moved a shoulder, undisturbed. "If you add enough cognac to it, it'll mask the taste just fine."

"It really is all right, Soph." Christoph was already on his feet, crushing his uniform cap in his gloved hands, backing out of the apartment with an odd air about him. "I only stopped for a few minutes. Herta is in the hospital, so truly I ought to be going. And please, I beg you, be careful while I'm gone. Those stunts of yours with the paint, that's just too dangerous."

"Oh, is she having the baby?" Sophie's face brightened at once. She didn't appear to hear a single word of his warning. "How exciting! But that certainly calls for a toast! You can risk one glass of brandy before you go to the hospital, can't you? Though, I thought you both decided on a home birth—"

"Soph." Hans gave her a look that stopped Sophie instantly in her tracks. "Let the man go back to his wife, will you?"

"Of course." Stealing one last glance at Christoph's red-rimmed eyes and tousled hair, Sophie stepped away to let him pass. "Give our love to Herta and the baby," she murmured to his retreating back.

Christoph nodded, smiled briefly over his shoulder, and disappeared into the darkened staircase, but not before Sophie had noticed his quivering lips and eyes brimming with tears.

"What happened?" Sophie was upon her brother as soon as the door had closed.

Hans only wiped his hands down his face with a suppressed moan. "Some complications with the delivery. The baby wouldn't come. Herta was losing too much blood. Just their misfortune, all the ambulances were on the other side of the city, busy with the victims of the recent bombardment. He had to flag a military vehicle down to bring her to the hospital. Thank God the Wehrmacht fellows took pity on them."

"Whatever was he doing here then?" Sophie sank into the sofa, incredulous.

Hans made no reply, only pushed a piece of paper across the table towards her. Instantly Sophie recognized Christoph's elegant handwriting.

Stalingrad! 200,000 German brothers were sacrificed for the honor and glory of a military fraud. The conditions of surrender set down by the Russians were not disclosed to the soldiers who were sacrificed. For this mass murder, General Paulus received the Oak Leaves. High-ranking officers escaped the slaughter in Stalingrad by airplane. Hitler refused to allow those who were trapped and surrounded to retreat to the troops behind the line. Now the blood of 200,000 soldiers who were condemned to death accuses the murderer named Hitler.

Christoph's words cut, sharp like a blade, deliberate and accusing. Anger laced every word, palpable, oozing out of the very soul of the man. His trust in his country had long been poisoned by the actions of his leaders, and he couldn't stay silent any longer after hundreds of thousands of innocent men laid their lives on the altar of their bloodthirsty Führer.

It was Hitler's war they were forced to fight. It was Hitler's debts they would have to settle, after all this was over.

The handwritten leaflet trembled in Sophie's hands, heavy with the predictions of what was yet to come—for them all if they didn't stop the madman now.

Tripoli! They surrendered unconditionally to the British Eighth Army. And what did the English do? They allowed the citizens to carry on living their lives as usual. They even let the police and public officials remain in office. Only one thing did they undertake systematically: they rid the great Italian colonial city of every barbaric leader. The annihilating, irresistible superpower is approaching on all sides with absolute certainty. Hitler is less likely than Paulus to capitulate: there will be no escape for him. And will you be deceived like the 200,000 who defended Stalingrad in a hopeless cause, to be massacred, sterilized, or robbed of your children? Roosevelt, the most powerful man in the world, said in Casablanca on January 24, 1943: "Our war of extermination is not against the common people, but against the political systems." We will also fight for an unconditional surrender. This is about the lives of millions of people. Should Germany meet the same fate as Tripoli?

Today, Germany is completely encircled, just as Stalingrad was. Will all Germans be sacrificed to the forces of hatred and destruction? Sacrificed to the man who persecuted the Jews, who eradicated half the Poles, and who wanted to annihilate Russia?

Sacrificed to the man who took away your freedom, peace, domestic happiness, hope, and joy, and instead gave you soaring inflation? This will not—this must not—happen! Hitler and his regime must fall so that Germany may live.

Make up your minds: Stalingrad and defeat, or Tripoli and a future of hope? And once you have decided: act!

"His wife and unborn child are in danger." Hans' voice cut into the torrent of Sophie's thoughts. "They could both die; the doctors told him that much. And that poor idealistic devil still made sure that we have the new leaflet." He chuckled softly, bit into his lip hard. "Just how damn sad such a state of affairs is, eh, Soph?"

For a long time, silence hung over the room. There was nothing else to say. In the dreary twilight of their apartment, with leaden skies weeping outside, they mourned their country on its deathbed until the darkness descended upon Munich, as though someone closed the giant coffin lid, burying them all alive.

"It's not fair," Sophie said to her brother's shadow, just visible against the window. "Not fair that Christoph has to suffer like this. That Herta has to suffer. That their children have to suffer." Her voice, at first quiet and even, was slowly gaining force and conviction. Unable to sit still, she leapt to her feet and began to pace the living room, bending her cold fingers one by one. "Not fair that *Vati* has to suffer. That *Mutti* has to suffer. That Fritz, and Alex, and Willi, and Traute suffer, and Werner at the front; that all of us have to suffer for that *Arschloch* Hitler's ambitions. He roped us all into this against our will. *Vati* has always been a liberal; he never voted for him! And now, because of Hitler, we're in this war we wished no part of; the bombs are obliterating our cities and killing us all indiscriminately, the Nazis and the ones who have resisted them from the beginning. We never wanted him as our country's leader. It's time we showed the Allies that much."

Hans' shadow tilted its head to one side, interested. "Without Harnack and his circle?"

Sophie only waved him off without once stopping her pacing. "We ought to mobilize all the forces now, Hans, so that when Harnack and his circle go through with the assassination, people join us at once and eliminate the rest of the Nazi leaders even before the Allies come. We'll show them that, just like Christoph has said in his leaflet, we aren't a hopeless nation, but simply a divided one. That once we are done with the Nazis, just like the Italians did away with their fascist leaders in Tripoli, we can be trusted to govern ourselves."

"And how do we do that?"

Her eyes shining with fiery determination even in the darkness of the night, Sophie lifted her index finger in the air—*wait here!*—disappeared into her bedroom and soon returned with a heavy suitcase, which she deposited triumphantly on the table in front of Hans.

His apprehension was almost palpable as Sophie watched him eyeing the suitcase with mistrust. "This is our monthly supply of Huber's leaflets," he muttered at last.

"That's right."

"...To be divided among us and distributed in different cities. Delivered to the Hamburg cell. To Harnack in Berlin..." Hans' voice trailed off.

Sophie lowered herself onto a cushion next to him and gathered his hands in hers. "Hans, don't you see? There's no time for that. It's taking too long. I say, let's take them to the university tomorrow. All by ourselves. Stuff them into every nook and cranny, litter the floor with them, make them drop from the ceiling on everyone's heads, so it finally hits them that the time for waiting is gone. If we want to get out of this alive and get our country back, we must act now. I want Herta to live to see it happen." Her voice softened with emotion and unshed tears in it. "I want Fritz's sacrifice in Stalingrad not to be in vain."

"Soph—"

"If you don't want to do it, it's all right. I'll understand. I'll do it myself."

His breath burned her eyelids where he kissed her with infinite brotherly tenderness. Sophie felt how his own cheeks were wet. "I'd never let you go alone. What sort of brother would it make me? I just... Sophie, I don't want you to die."

Sophie straightened, wiped her face with the back of her hand. "I'd rather die as a hero than live as a coward." There was steel in her voice; the Scholls' familial pride. "And if we get caught, I'll take all the guilt upon myself, so don't confess to anything. You're the Wehrmacht. They shall spare you."

"No, you don't confess to anything. I'll admit to everything instead. They won't execute a girl."

For a few moments, they stared at each other hard, competing in obstinacy like they used to when they were mere children, when their lives weren't at stake. When somewhere in the distance one of the countless Munich cathedrals chimed eight and it became obvious that neither one was about to surrender, Sophie leaned back, clasping her hands together.

"All right. A compromise. We both admit to the leaflets—one person would have never pulled it off at any rate—and cover for the rest of the team, so that they can carry on after our—" She stopped herself cold before she uttered the word "execution," but it still hung between them like a guillotine ready to drop at a moment's notice.

Hans brooded over the idea for some time but, at long last, heaved the heaviest of breaths and nodded. "It's actually not a bad plan. And if we're careful, we won't even get arrested in the first place."

"We're always careful."

"So, we'll live then."

"Yes, we will."

"And will join forces with Harnack for the assassination."

"And will sign an unconditional surrender right after."

"And end this war. Once and for all."

"Yes."

They sat in the unlit room and spoke late into the night, promising each other the future, in which fragrant nights existed for lovers and not bombers, in which booksellers sold books instead of mimeographs to the resistance cells, in which people were allowed to love whoever they wanted and speak their minds, and where women could lead countries and men fuss over children, just like their Christoph would love to do, and where peace and humanity were valued more than war and guns and hatred.

They didn't know if they would live to see it happen, but they would give their lives so that it would happen sooner rather than later for the others.

TWENTY-ONE

FEBRUARY 18, 1943

The grand body of the University of Munich towering before them, Sophie paused momentarily to recollect herself. Hans came to a halt as well, his hand clasping the handle of a worn suitcase. For some time, they stood side by side, brother and sister, gazing at their alma mater as the slight breeze, unusually warm for February, tossed their dark locks about.

"There's still time to change your mind," Hans said quietly without looking at her. "Go to the lecture. I can do it myself—"

"No," Sophie interrupted him, steel in her voice, and in her determined, brown eyes. "We'll do it together, like we have decided."

She moved a stray lock of hair out of her eyes. It had grown down to her shoulders, a thick, tangled mane neglected in the course of the past few months. No more rebellious, boyish haircuts for Sophie. In place of the defiant teenager who had arrived in Munich last May, a young woman now stood.

"Sophie," Hans began, this time turning to face her.

Sophie smiled gently at his imploring look—the same one he'd given her when she had just discovered the authors of the very first White Rose pamphlet. She cupped his cheek, and told him the very same thing she'd told him six months ago. "I can't hide behind your back, Hans. My conscience won't allow me. I can't sit still and do nothing when the victory—*our* victory—could be so very close."

"You heard what Christoph said when he came to visit."

"His wife was in the hospital after a difficult birth. He's all out of sorts because of it."

"He's afraid for his family's safety. He thinks we're being too reckless."

Sophie gave a shrug, unconcerned. They weren't reckless; they had simply tasted freedom and it had intoxicated them to the point where little else mattered. That was the reason why, instead of sleeping soundly in their beds, they had ventured into the city the first night after Harnack's departure and painted the words "Freedom" and "Down with Hitler" on the holiest of holy Nazi memorials—the plaque for the SA troopers killed during Hitler's failed putsch of 1923, which delayed the Nazis overtaking the power by ten years. While Sophie, clad all in black, her face covered with a scarf, had watched the SS honor guards standing rigidly on both sides of the memorial, her brother, Alex, and Willi had smeared white paint over the marble with a wonderful insolence about them.

No wonder Christoph had been mortified when he'd learned of it. Alex, meanwhile, had only shrugged and given him one of his disarming smiles. "Don't get your behind in such an uproar over it. We checked the wind before setting to work. It was blowing away from the SS—they couldn't smell the paint while we worked."

However, even the stunt with the SS was an innocent prank compared to what Sophie and Hans were planning to do now. This time, though, they acted alone. Somehow, without any actual discussion, it had been decided between the siblings that it was much too dangerous to involve the rest of the White Rose members. Even if they got caught, at least their friends should be safe.

"Christoph was only upset over that particular instance," Sophie said. "He still gave you the pamphlet he authored to print next."

Hans' free hand passed over the breast pocket of his tunic, in which the draft of Christoph's leaflet was hidden. His other hand, atop the suitcase's handle, was gradually turning white with nerves.

"I shouldn't have taken Christoph's draft with me," he muttered, more to himself than Sophie. "It was a mistake."

"No, it wasn't. We're going home to Ulm straight from the university," Sophie reminded him, nudging her brother forward ever so slightly. "We couldn't have just left it in the apartment. A bomb falls on the building in our absence, someone finds it—what next?"

"It's dangerous all the same."

Sophie exploded into laughter—unexpectedly even to herself—at those words. Inside the suitcase, they carried over a thousand copies of Professor Huber's Stalingrad pamphlet, which they were about to stuff all over the place, in the middle of the day, brazenly and risking being discovered at any moment. And here Hans was, fretting over one single draft that bore no signature, just text, which was typed, not even handwritten.

Hans was just about to hiss at her to quit that idiotic laughter before someone heard them, but then softened somewhat, caught her hand in his and squeezed Sophie's fingers in his tightly.

"Nervous?" He looked at her sympathetically.

Sophie considered the question for a moment. "Excited," she stated at last, feigning bravery for his sake and hers, before stepping inside the university's inner courtyard. From the glass dome above their heads, sun spilled its golden light as though crowning them with halos—two patron saints of the new Germany carrying its very future in their hands.

The courtyard stood still and deserted in the clear, crisp light of the early morning. They had calculated everything perfectly: the lectures wouldn't be over for the next twenty minutes. Plenty of time to do what they'd come for and disappear into the crowd before anyone discovered what it was precisely that the students were reading with such interest. Before anyone reported it to the authorities, they'd be long on their way to Ulm, an empty suitcase "accidentally forgotten" at the station in Munich.

"Ready?" Hans stopped—for the last time—at the foot of the grand marble staircase and searched Sophie's face for signs of hesitation. In vain—there were none; Sophie knew that much, felt it in her heart, in the pit of her quivering stomach.

"Ready," she said and made a resolute first step.

They hadn't even reached the middle of the staircase when, much to their astonishment, Traute and Willi appeared at the top, halting with just as much surprise on their faces as Hans and Sophie themselves.

Traute was the first to recover. "Skipping the lectures, you scoundrels?" she demanded playfully, giving Hans a kiss on his cheek when the two couples met in the middle.

"We're not the only ones," Hans retorted in the same key, avoiding a direct answer.

"We would never! We've been released by the professor, in fact," Willi said in mock indignation.

"We have a practical course in the medical clinic and it's at the other end of the city," Traute explained, her gaze lingering on Hans' suitcase. "What's with the luggage?"

"Just brought my lunch with me," Hans joked in the same light tone. Only Sophie saw him holding his breath, praying, undoubtedly, to all the gods for his girlfriend and Willi to let them be and just go along on their business and not get involved with his and Sophie's.

"We're going home straight from the lectures." Sophie quickly came up with an explanation before Traute could see through the charade. Hans was the dark, brooding type. He rarely laughed and joked even less, so unlike Alex in this respect. Traute knew him far too well not to begin to suspect something if she lingered any longer. "Just bringing laundry home. Sheets and pillowcases and such."

Willi, who had also been eyeing the suitcase suspiciously, was about to inquire further when Sophie probed him playfully in his back—"Well? Go on then; off with you two; you'll be late!"—already ascending the steps and pulling Hans after herself.

"We'll see you next week then?" he called after the siblings, uncertainty in his voice.

"Yes, yes, on Monday." Hans waved him off and all but ran up the stairs.

Only when they entered the safety of the empty hallway did Sophie release a breath of relief. "It's a good thing they're going. They'll be on the other side of Munich when—" She stopped abruptly and, instead of finishing her thought, gestured to Hans impatiently.

The amiable chit-chat had already stolen five minutes of precious time. They couldn't afford to lose any more.

Moving stealthily along the labyrinth of corridors and lecture halls, Sophie and Hans dropped stacks and stacks of leaflets on the doorsteps; scattered them about the galleries as they moved on tiptoes, muffling the echo of their steps on the marble floors; layered the subversive text atop the windowsills and pinned it within the frames of announcement boards.

As they worked side by side, beads of concentration and strained nerves breaking on their temples, their elation grew and along with it their very sibling bond, it seemed. To prevent being uncovered, they didn't exchange a single word; somehow, everything was understood between them on some telepathic level.

Wet with perspiration, chests heaving, they covered the vast grounds of the entire university complex before the bell rang, dismissing the students. White as ash, Hans froze at the top of the stairs—the same ones they'd taken—with a small stack of remaining leaflets in his hands.

"Give me half, quick!" Sophie demanded.

Before her brother could utter a single word of protest, Sophie leaned over the balustrade and hurled the leaflets over the enclosed courtyard, Hans following suit as soon as he recovered himself. From under the vaulted glass ceiling, freedom itself rained on German land that fine February morning, from the hands of the new generation that had refused to bow down to old savagery and outdated conservative values that had left the entire country writhing with agony.

Mad with joy, already losing herself in the crowd of students, Sophie thought she heard someone scream, "You're under arrest!" among the general commotion.

Hans close on her heels, she ran down the steps and was about to burst into the safety of the street when a pair of strong, hairy arms clasped her forearms with force.

"I said, you're under arrest!"

Lifting her stunned gaze, Sophie came face to face with the building custodian—the new one who had stared her and Alex down just a few weeks ago, the one with the Party pin displayed proudly on his ill-fitting overalls. Jakob Schmid.

"You too!" Schmid bellowed, seizing Hans' tunic with one hand while still holding Sophie with the other. "I saw what you did. With my own two eyes, I did. Spreading seditious materials on university grounds?" The man's eyes rolled wildly with indignation as though he had taken it as a personal affront. "Not on Jakob Schmid's watch! I don't hold a membership in the SA for nothing."

He was still ranting and raving, but Sophie didn't hear him any longer. With her eyes full of wonder and hope, she watched as students picked up the leaflets and read them on their way out of the building, how some quickly snatched entire stacks of them and concealed them under their clothes, how they went into the world carrying the White Rose's immortal words with them.

As Schmid was leading them down the corridor towards the rector's office, Sophie caught Hans smiling faintly to himself. He, too, saw what the students were doing. He, too, knew that their joint sacrifice hadn't been in vain.

TWENTY-TWO

GESTAPO JAIL, MUNICH. FEBRUARY 20, 1943

Serving an indictment was below his official standing (ordinarily, Mohr reserved this duty for his low-ranking underlings), but with the Scholl siblings, all of his work ethic, plus strict official rules and regulations, had long gone out of the window. With both full confessions signed, there was nothing else that he could do for them. The People's Court's presiding justice Freisler himself had expressed his interest in the case. After receiving orders from Berlin to send the case over to the butcher, whose hands were, undoubtedly, still bloody after executing the members of the Red Orchestra, Mohr had lost all hope of saving at least Sophie from death.

All that was left to do was to say goodbye.

An SS man standing guard by her door regarded Kriminalkommissar Mohr with surprise but quickly recovered himself, slammed his heels together and froze to attention.

His throat scratchy—*Must be the blasted cold making its rounds*, Mohr cursed inwardly—he silently gestured towards the door. It swung open with a groan full of desolate finality, revealing a narrow cell with two bunk beds and a tiny barred window, from which the sun poured in obscenely warm, golden light.

Sophie's cellmate (*What the devil was her name?* With the best will in the world, Mohr couldn't recall, neither her name nor the crime she was being investigated for) scrambled to her feet and froze by the bunk on which Sophie was presently sitting.

"Good morning, Herr Kriminalkommissar," Sophie greeted him warmly, as though he were a guest and not a Gestapo official with her indictment in his faintly trembling hands. "What a pleasant surprise." Oddly, there was not a trace of irony in her voice. She appeared to be genuinely glad to see him. "I thought Sunday was your day off."

"It is," Mohr conceded after clearing his throat. Something kept lodging itself in it, stealing his breath. Sophie's image swam in his eyes. In his rush, he had forgotten his damned glasses in his office. "I won't take much of your time. I'm only here to serve your official indictment."

Sophie's little, warm fingers accidentally brushed his as he was handing her the document. Mohr swiftly pulled his hand away and clasped it tightly with his left one behind his back. He remained in the same position while Sophie brought the paper to the light to read it. His expression unreadable, he was watching a tiny wrinkle form between her brows as her eyes were scanning the lines full of contempt and condemnation for her—*the traitor of the Fatherland, the enemy of the German people, the criminal*—

"I didn't write it," Mohr suddenly blurted out, surprising even himself.

Sophie looked up from the paper. There was so much kindness in her deep, brown eyes, Mohr's heart swelled painfully in his chest.

"I know you didn't," she said simply before resuming her reading, and all at once, Mohr felt as though he'd been absolved by the highest of priests of all his mortal sins.

At last, she reached the bottom of the page. As Sophie folded it carefully, Mohr saw the paper tremble in her hands. For some time, she stood silently, listening to the birds sing the songs of the approaching spring just outside the window. As if watching them fly as they pleased had grown too unbearable, she closed her eyes, a sharp slash once again cutting into her smooth forehead.

It took Mohr great effort to remain in his place when all he wished to do was to close the distance between them, grasp her in his embrace, and take her away from this prison, hide her in one cellar or the other perhaps—he had people who owed him a favor or two...

"Do you have a pen, Herr Kriminalkommissar?"

Lost in his frantic, ridiculous fantasies, Mohr blinked to recollect himself. When he looked at Sophie, her eyes were perfectly dry, hard as granite.

Swallowing with difficulty, he offered Sophie the fountain pen he carried in his inner pocket. Without hesitation, she slashed her signature under the indictment, smiling almost with pride this time.

"Such a beautiful, sunny day, and I have to go..." She took a deep breath, stealing one more glance at the painfully glorious morning outside. "But how many are dying on the battlefields, how many young lives full of hope..." Suddenly, she turned to Mohr, defiance back in her eyes. They were shining with it like never before. "What difference does my death make if our actions arouse thousands of people? The students will definitely rise up." With a shrug full of fascinatingly carefree nonchalance, she handed Mohr the indictment and his pen. "I did my duty. I shall die with my head held high."

"As you should," Mohr said softly, hoping that she would catch a double meaning behind his words. He couldn't quite condone her actions openly; not with a guard listening on the other side of the door and Sophie's cellmate (*Ilse? Else something?*) bearing witness to their conversation.

Sophie nodded—she had understood—and, rather to Mohr's astonishment, offered him her hand. After a moment's hesitation, he replaced the indictment under his elbow, grasped the girl's narrow palm tightly in his, covered it with his other hand, and shook it with all the emotion he couldn't put in words.

Her next words came as a mere whisper. "Remember what I told you during the interrogation, Herr Kriminalkommissar. It's not too late for you. It's never too late to do the right thing."

TWENTY-THREE

Sophie was in no mood for any more talking: conversations with Kriminalkommissar Mohr had bled her dry. It would have been easier if he were a typical Gestapo, if he raged and raved and slapped her about—that, she would have withstood much easier than those pitying, sympathetic looks of his and almost paternal pleas to save herself while she still could. Mohr had promised to testify in her defense in court. He had promised to teach her what exactly to say to the judge. All that Sophie had to do was to shift the blame onto her brother, serve a couple of years in one women's prison or another, and walk free before the war was over. Or—who knew?—maybe even less, if the Allies landed sooner and freed all of them, prisoners of the state. She had her entire life before her. Why die for nothing, if her brother himself would have been glad had she walked free? Why rob her mother not of one, but two children at once? Were they truly worth dying for, some idiotic leaflets no one read at any rate?

Kriminalkommissar Mohr was very persuasive indeed, with his searching eyes not devoid of kindness, with that tilt of the head Sophie had grown to loathe for it reminded her painfully of her own father whenever he reproached her for something, in the same mild voice, invariably appealing to her mind instead of issuing

empty threats. It was because Mohr reminded Sophie of her *Vati*
that it took her such great effort to say no to him. It was because he
reminded her of her father that she had to die to save him from
himself; to show him that yes, they were most certainly worth
dying for, some idiotic leaflets as he had called them, and that her
sacrifice wouldn't be in vain as long as he knew why she had
chosen to ascend the scaffold with her brother and her resistance
cellmates, why she had to martyr herself so that the others would
pick up their banner and carry it—all the way into the future
Germany, free of tyranny and hatred.

Sophie was in no mood for any more talking and that's why she
almost snarled at the guard when he opened the door to her and
Else's cell and informed her that Sophie's court-appointed defense
attorney was waiting for her downstairs.

"An attorney then?" She laughed mirthlessly, exhausted, on
the verge of tears. "Why, that's something new entirely. My indictment said I was the enemy of the state. Treason is punishable by
execution, no exceptions. Just what shall that so-called attorney of
yours do for me in this case, I wonder?"

Ignoring the poison in her voice, the guard shrugged evasively.
"I'm only doing my job," he said, casting his gaze about just to
avoid looking at Sophie.

"What if I refuse to see him?"

From the guard, another uncomfortable shrug. "I'll get an oral
reprimand from my superiors."

"Well, we can't have that, can we?" Sophie said, sarcasm dripping from every word, and instantly felt a sharp pang of guilt at the
guard's injured look.

He was a young man, of Werner's age maybe, just a few years
younger than Hans, but blond and clearly near-sighted judging by
his thick lenses. A bookish fellow, with the hands of a pianist, long
white fingers too sensitive to hold a rifle—an active army reject,
good only for minding defenseless prisoners. God only knew the
difficult time his family or friends or superiors were giving him on
account of his "weaknesses."

Heaving a sigh, Sophie rose from her cot, mumbled an apology and headed out of the cell. She was exhausted, her nerves ready to snap; all she wanted was a few hours of peace and quiet, just to forget herself in a dreamless sleep to collect herself before her final battle in the court, and they were robbing her even of that.

When Sophie sat on a hard wooden chair across from the attorney, separated from him by a metal mesh, she had no more patience left for the man himself or his valise stuffed with papers and law books, which he began demonstrating to Sophie with the uncertain look of an insurance seller on his first day on the job.

"I have prepared here a defense strategy based on similar precedents..." he mumbled, groping for something among his dusty stacks of folders. "Some date back to the Weimar and the laws have changed since then, but some don't, and if we stick to—"

"Am I going to be hanged or beheaded, what do you think?" Sophie asked in a voice so still and devoid of any emotion that the man froze where he stood, blinking at her like an owl.

"I beg your pardon?" he managed at last, tugging at his necktie —his only one, judging by its greasy, faded, threadbare state—as though it was suffocating him.

"I asked for your opinion concerning the execution method the court shall choose in my case," Sophie repeated in the same deadly calm voice. "Based on the similar precedents you have mentioned."

The attorney opened his mouth, closed it, opened it again and gaped at Sophie in the same manner, like a fish.

"And my brother, Hans," Sophie continued, picking at the mesh with her index finger indifferently. "Do you think it possible for him to get a firing squad instead of a noose? He's in the Wehrmacht, even if not on active duty. He'd rather prefer it, I should think. It's more honorable. Do you imagine you can ask for it during the hearing?"

When an entire minute passed during which the attorney— Sophie hadn't bothered to remember his name—still stood in front of her, shell-shocked and pale as death, Sophie finally turned to her guard.

"I believe I have rendered my attorney speechless." She chuckled. Her laughter echoed hollowly in the vast, unheated room. "Can I go now? I doubt he'll be of any use to me or anyone else anytime soon."

The walk back to her cell seemed somehow shorter—perhaps, because Sophie dreamt of her cot and the thin blanket that she'd pull over her head. But when the guard turned the key in the lock and pushed the door open, Sophie stopped in her tracks, bewilderment creasing her brow at the sight that presented itself to her eyes.

On the small wooden table, a veritable feast had been set up: smoked sausage and bread, a chunk of butter, cookies, and even a small pot of tea was steaming next to the stack of cigarettes Sophie's cellmate was arranging in an elaborate design.

Else gasped and broke into a huge grin. "We hadn't expected you to return so quickly," the young woman admitted, gesturing to the goods. "I thought I'd have more time to thoroughly organize everything. But no matter now. Come, let's make a toast. We couldn't get any alcohol on such short notice, but we'll toast with tea all the same."

"Who's we?" Sophie was still regarding the table with disbelief.

Else's grin turned wry. "Everyone donated whatever they could, as soon as they heard that the famous White Rose writers were incarcerated here. Don't worry, your brother and his comrades have their own share in their cells. We split it all evenly."

"Who's we?" Sophie repeated, her voice beginning to shake.

"Prisoners and guards," Else replied, stealing a glance at the blond warden at the door.

The young man never uttered a word, only shifted from one foot to the other, the color creeping up his downy cheeks.

Something caught in Sophie's throat. All at once, it was difficult to breathe. The guard's image swam in her eyes, together with Else's, until Sophie shut them tight, letting the tears—the very first ones she'd shed since her arrest—spill down her cheeks.

She swiped at them swiftly, already laughing and sniffling, and burying her face in Else's sisterly embrace. "Thank you. Thank you all," Sophie breathed into her cellmate's hair, hugging her back and biting her trembling lips when her eyes locked with those of the warden. He, too, was smiling bashfully before retreating back into the corridor and pulling the door closed after himself.

"Come, Sophie, quit it with the sentiments," Else said, producing a grubby handkerchief. "It's just sausage and tea. No big deal."

But it was a big deal. What Else didn't understand was that Sophie wasn't thanking them for the food; she was thanking them for proving her right and Mohr wrong; for showing that her sacrifice hadn't been in vain; that they were indeed everywhere, just like Sophie had told him they were—the people sympathetic to the cause.

Suddenly, all urge to sleep was gone. A new surge of energy coursed through Sophie's veins. She was ready for her final battle. She would go with her head held high.

TWENTY-FOUR

PALACE OF JUSTICE, MUNICH. FEBRUARY 22, 1943

Smoking his fourth cigarette in a row, Mohr paced the hall of Munich's neo-Gothic Palace of Justice waiting to be called any minute as a witness to the prosecution. There were two more such "witnesses" sharing a bench just outside Courtroom 216: Mohr's fellow interrogator Mahler and the University of Munich's custodian Jakob Schmid. Only the sight of Schmid's new, ill-fitting suit, which he had no doubt purchased with his three thousand Reichsmark reward money, pooled Mohr's mouth with acid. Quite a few times, the bailiff had offered Mohr to take a seat—the bench was wide enough for three of them—but the very thought of sharing it with Schmid was loathsome to Mohr.

From behind the closed doors, Presiding Justice Freisler's noxious screams rose in volume. Not even an hour ago, he had stridden past Mohr in his scarlet robe, carrying himself like some grand inquisitor from ages long past. He made a revolting picture with his hooded, droopy eyes full of icy scorn, protruding ears atop which his red biretta was sitting, and a thin mouth with corners turned invariably down as though in an expression of permanent disgust. But it was his shrill, slightly nasal voice hurling one insult after another at his victims that set Mohr grinding his teeth in helpless ire. Freisler was supposed to be the voice of justice, blindfolded and impartial, but instead he was the voice of his beloved Führer, just as coarse and hateful as his master.

But how was he, Mohr, any better? He came to an abrupt halt as the realization dawned on him. He, too, served the same administration. He, too, was the Führer's loyal dog.

No, he wasn't anything like that pig Freisler; Mohr tossed his head in horror, chasing the thought away. And nothing like that swine Schmid. He was only doing his job. He was still a mere policeman, still investigating crimes, interrogating criminals in the same manner he had been interrogating them for years, long before the National Socialists had taken power. He wasn't anything like some of the butchers who didn't mind beating the confessions out of their suspects. He even tried to help, help Sophie—

"Somebody had to make a start." As though on cue, her clear, confident voice sounded from inside the courtroom. "What we said and wrote are what many people are thinking. They just don't dare say it out loud."

Mohr bit into his lip, hard, to conceal a grin from Schmid's beady eyes following him like those of a hungry hyena's.

"Keep your mouth shut, insolent girl!" Freisler shrieked. Mohr imagined the blotches of red mounting on Freisler's drawn face. "Let's see how much you'll have to say once you ascend the scaffold!"

"I have already said everything I have to say in our pamphlets," came a perfectly collected reply. "The others shall carry my words."

How brave she was, that tiny slip of a girl! Mohr gazed at the shut doors, his face entirely unmoved—a mask he had long learned to wear before the others. Grown men trembled in terror before Freisler's wrath and here she was, mocking him openly to his face, serene and assured of the righteousness of her actions, unafraid to die for them—the new Germany's martyr.

A wistful sigh escaped Mohr's lips as he recalled the report of the government-appointed defense attorney. Ashen-faced and blinking rapidly, the poor fellow had claimed that the Scholl girl was mad, mad most certainly, because who, in their right mind, behaves in the way she did?

"I was assembling my papers, asking her what kind of defense line she was thinking to pursue and instead of..." The attorney had gestured with his hands helplessly. "She just... She goes and asks me if she shall be beheaded or hanged! And if that wasn't enough, she also demanded—in that unnaturally calm voice of hers—if I thought her brother Hans could get a firing squad in place of a rope since he served in the Wehrmacht! Who asks such things? No, she's mad, as true as I'm sitting here, she's absolutely mad!"

No, Mohr thought, lighting yet another cigarette. Sophie Scholl wasn't mad. Sophie Scholl was a hero living among too many cowards. They couldn't recognize her bravery because all they'd known their entire lives was blind submission.

His department's involvement with the White Rose case had ended when he'd served the defendants their indictment, but Mohr had still come to visit Sophie last Sunday. Officially, in a final attempt to make her reveal Alexander Schmorell's whereabouts in exchange for the possibility of a milder sentence. Unofficially, to smuggle her a paper and pen to write a letter home, which Mohr had personally posted, even paying extra for the expedited service.

In the courtroom, Christoph Probst was enumerating all the horrors he had seen as a medic on the Eastern Front, recounting the torn limbs, broken bones, and smashed skulls in all their gory detail. "Whatever I did, I did in the interest of my Fatherland. This bloodshed has to stop."

Mohr grinned, shaking his head to no one in particular. Probst was the most idealistic of the bunch and it showed; neither Hans nor Willi were trying to persuade those who had only seen battlefields from the safety of a private screening room what savagery and obliteration reigned there, dooming hundreds of thousands of young men like themselves to horrifying death.

"Day after day, with hundreds of men going through my medical tent, with their limbs hanging by tendons and bits of skin, with their guts spilling from their stomachs, with burnt flesh turned into a crust of red and black—I simply couldn't stand back in all good conscience and allow for this madness to continue. This needless, idiotic war—"

"Enough of that!" Freisler's annoyed shout once again. "I shall have none of this in my courtroom. Hiding your own cowardice behind the claims of patriotism! You are not a patriot; you're a pitiful traitor and criminal. Take your seat. No one is interested in your ridiculous claims."

"Ridiculous claims," Schmid repeated with a gleeful grin, revealing rotten, tobacco-stained front teeth.

Mohr shot him a death glare and turned away at once, disgusted.

"I don't think they shall be calling us," Mahler called softly to Mohr. "It seems the defendants are taking the stand for their final statements." He paused and listened with his head slightly cocked. "I thought we wouldn't have been needed," he continued when Mohr had made no reply. "After all, they did confess. There's no need for witnesses when there's a confession."

There was no need for witnesses at all in that circus calling itself a court, Mohr thought to himself poisonously. There was nothing left of the justice Mohr used to remember from the democratic Weimar days; justice had been replaced by Freisler and his carbon copies put in the presiding chairs they didn't deserve solely on Party-membership principle and devotion to the values of National Socialism.

And he, Mohr, was one of them.

Suppressing a painful groan with difficulty, he wiped his forehead with his handkerchief, wondering when his life had gone to the devil and how it was possible that he hadn't even noticed.

The commotion coming from the stairs pulled Mohr out of his unhappy musings. From the corner of his eye, he saw Mahler rising from his bench and craning his neck at the bailiffs holding an imposing, well-dressed man back. Behind his wide back, a small, painfully thin woman was sobbing openly into her handkerchief as a young soldier, faintly resembling Hans Scholl, supported her by her shoulders.

"If you haven't received official summons, you are not allowed at the hearing!"

"What do you mean, I am not allowed?!" the man bellowed in a voice of authority.

It occurred to Mohr that the man must occupy a position of power, either presently or some time ago. Judging by the absence of a Party pin on his lapel, some time ago it was. Long before Hitler had come to power.

"My children are there! Tell the Court, Robert Scholl has arrived to defend them!" With that announcement, Robert Scholl forced his way into the courtroom while the young man dressed in a Wehrmacht uniform—Werner Scholl, Hans' and Sophie's brother, Mohr realized—was reasoning with the two perplexed guards.

A small smile warmed Mohr's face. They had received their children's letters in time after all. Of course, it was ridiculous to hope that Herr Scholl's intervention would affect the outcome in any way, but at least Sophie and Hans would see their parents one last time. On far too many occasions, Mohr had witnessed the condemned pleading with stony-faced officials for one last visit from their loved ones just to be dismissed with a contemptuous smirk. "You should have thought of your loved ones when you were committing crimes against the Fatherland. Becoming a traitor to your country, you have forever waived your right to see them."

They were mere children, the Scholl siblings, not unlike Mohr's own daughter waiting for him at home. Helping to bring their parents to them to say their goodbyes was the least he could do.

For a few moments, it appeared as if Robert Scholl would succeed in persuading the court to testify in his children's defense. Somehow, with the fearless desperation only parents possess when their child's life is in danger, he made his way to Hans' defense attorney and whispered something in his ear.

His sense of order disturbed, the attorney rose unsteadily to his feet and approached Freisler. The judge towered over the courtroom from his raised podium like some ancient, bloodthirsty deity. The attorney had only begun to say something when Freisler rose to his feet and— performer that he was—made a dramatic gesture of dismissal with his arm draped in scarlet.

"Remove this man from the courtroom," Freisler said to the bailiffs, pointing at Robert Scholl. "Before I sentence him a second time. Apparently, he has already forgotten how leniently he was treated for his own crime. Quite a family of traitors we have assembled here; it's not every day you see something of this sort!" He snorted with great contempt.

From his place in front of the opened doors, Mohr saw Hans Scholl muttering something imploringly to his father, who appeared to have lost all faculty of speech. Werner Scholl, too, was already pulling his father away from the bench where his siblings were sitting. In a last desperate attempt, Robert Scholl reached for his daughter and clasped her hand. She smiled at him brightly and bravely, giving his fingers a parting squeeze.

"Go, *Vati*. I'll be all right. I have Hans looking after me."

Only after Freisler's threat did a guard sitting next to her make a half-hearted gesture to separate them.

"There is a higher justice!" Robert Scholl's roar, like that of a mortally wounded lion, drowned out even Freisler's frantic shrieking. "They'll go down in history." Struggling against the guards, he stared directly at the presiding judge's face. "And you shall die a terrible death for your sins!"

Much to Mohr's satisfaction, a passing shadow of fear glided momentarily over Freisler's distorted face.

"Out!" he squealed, pulling the ends of his robe around himself protectively.

"Werner!" Hans called after his brother. "Stay strong. No compromises."

Pausing at the threshold and swiping at the guards' hands in annoyance, Werner locked eyes with his brother and gave a grave, final nod.

Next to Mohr, Magdalena Scholl gasped faintly and would have most certainly dropped to the floor had he not caught her and, with Mahler's help, lowered her gently to the bench.

Shaken by the scene—he could only imagine the agony the Scholl parents were going through—Mohr stood at the entrance of the courtroom, not quite advancing inside, not quite retreating behind the tall ornate doors. The entire grotesque picture had a quality of a nightmare about it, in which he felt suddenly trapped, bathed in sweat, gasping for air and, the worst of all, unable to wake up, no matter how hard he pinched the skin on his left wrist.

Framed by the uniformed guards, the courtroom was shifting in and out of focus. His flaming scarlet robe moving about him as though it had a demonic life of its own, Freisler was screaming something, his face distorted, mouth gaping open—but no sound came. Something terrible was in motion: the presiding judges were leaving all of a sudden. Like horrific automatons, the spectators were instantly on their feet, arms high and straight—a mindless army of bloodthirsty fiends blocking Mohr's view of the ones he was desperately trying to keep in his sight. For some reason, he was certain that they were the only ones remaining seated, the free-dom-loving White Rose children, who disdained everything about this court and were absolutely right to do so.

The very name of the grim, stone-clad dungeon—the Palace of Justice—was a mockery. There was nothing resembling justice about accusing these students of high treason, when all they wanted was to stop the war and the ones waging it. There was nothing resembling justice in sending that pig Freisler down from Berlin to ensure that the sentence would be death.

Mohr saw that very verdict on Freisler's face as soon as Hitler's appointee returned to the courtroom, sneering like a snake—the same reptilian, beady eyes, the same cold blood in his veins.

"...For the crimes committed against the state, the People's Court sentences you, Sophia Scholl, to death by beheading."

With a rush of blood to his temples, where it remained, pounding violently. Mohr felt as though the sharp blade was hanging above his own head. It would have been better if it were; he would have taken the sentence for Sophie just then, without an ounce of hesitation he would—

"...sentences you, Hans Scholl, to death by hanging."

Suddenly, Hans was on his feet, his finger pointing at Freisler like that of an ancient seer. "You will soon stand where we stand now!" His voice reverberated around the courtroom as though coming not from an ordinary student, but some higher, omnipotent power.

And just as it happened with Robert Scholl, Mohr saw, to his great satisfaction, Freisler shrink away ever so slightly from Hans Scholl's frightening prediction. There was a moment of grave silence, the moment, during which Mohr suddenly felt he could see into the future, where the Scholl siblings' names were uttered with the reverence they deserved and Freisler's, Hitler's and—who knew?—perhaps his own too, spat out like curses, forever condemned to the dark, rotting well of history, precisely where they belonged. And for that single moment, Mohr felt that he could finally breathe again, that higher justice should prevail after all, and peace should descend once again upon the war-ravaged countries.

Later, after the sentences had been announced and the Scholl siblings led away in handcuffs, Mohr approached Robert Scholl. His namesake stood by the window, staring blankly into nothing, his hands buried in his pockets. All of a sudden, he looked as though he'd aged twenty years.

"Robert Scholl?" Mohr asked, offering the man his cigarette case.

"The very same." Scholl took one, moving slowly as if the menial task took all of his powers. "Are you here to arrest me?"

"No, of course not."

"You're from the Gestapo." It wasn't a question. He must have heard one of the bailiffs address him as Herr Kriminalkommissar.

"I was your children's interrogator," he confessed and, meeting Scholl's sharp look, added softly and sincerely, "they're both incredibly brave. You ought to be proud."

"I am. Thank you for not beating them, I suppose."

Mohr felt a flash of something, but quickly extinguished it. Scholl had every right to assume such things about him. He *was*, after all, from the Gestapo.

He opened his mouth, thought of saying that he was trying to save at least Sophie, that she had confessed to everything despite his repeated pleas, that it was him who had sent the letters, but then didn't. Instead, he stole a glance over his shoulder and slipped an official pass, already filled with his own hand and stamped by his own office, into Scholl's pocket.

"They were taken to Stadelheim Prison." Mohr scarcely moved his lips as he leaned toward Scholl. "Show it to the guards. They'll let you in for the last visit."

With Scholl gaping at him with a cigarette frozen within an inch of his mouth, Mohr swung sharply round on his heel and walked briskly toward Mahler, waiting for him by the staircase.

"Told him to leave town at once and not mess about with Freisler," Mohr muttered by way of explanation.

"Sound advice. Hopefully he'll listen if he knows what's good for him."

"Yes," Mohr said. "Hopefully."

TWENTY-FIVE

STADELHEIM PRISON, LATER THAT DAY

When the warden appeared in the door of her cell, a somber shadow against the fluorescent lights of the prison corridor, Sophie's heart momentarily dropped into the pit of her stomach.

"Already?" It was all she could manage, with her throat suddenly dry and scratchy.

She was aware that the sentences would be carried out immediately. On their way to Stadelheim Prison, Sophie and Hans had had their chance to say their last emotional goodbyes and ask Christoph for his forgiveness for dragging him into all this resistance business when he had a family and more important matters to take care of. He'd interrupted them with a violent toss of his head, his eyes burning with fiery determination.

"Nothing is more important than fighting injustice," Christoph had said gravely, clasping Sophie and Hans' manacled hands with his own iron-clad ones. "And it was my utmost honor to fight alongside you. Don't you dare apologize to me. I ought to thank you for granting me such a chance. Thanks to you, my children shall grow up in a free country."

There'd been such certainty in his voice that even Sophie had believed him. Despite the war still raging outside, despite the prison van rolling along the rabble-covered streets on the very last trip they would ever take, she had believed him.

That's why now, in her cell, it wasn't fear that gripped her, but something profound and monumental, as if her death would be the last one in a chain of disasters. After her final sacrifice, Germany's fortune would turn at long last and the beast calling himself the people's leader would be slayed by the ones following her and the White Rose's steps.

But the warden only smiled softly—a weathered, paternal smile full of infinite pity. All of the Stadelheim guards regarded them with the same expression, as though they, not ideological soldiers but ordinary men doing this rotten duty solely because they had their families to feed, couldn't quite comprehend how the world could have gone so mad that executing children for treason had become a state-approved activity.

"Not yet, girl. Your family is here. Would you like to see them?"

Would she like to see them? Sophie nearly threw herself on the warden's neck, ready to cover his lined face with kisses of gratitude. "Yes! Yes, of course!" She was about to say something else, but the man had already placed his warm, comforting palm on her shoulder and all her resolve, all her strength, had been reduced to nothing. She was so brave against the wickedness, so strong against the cruelty, but this sincere kindness had brought on the tears Sophie was certain she wouldn't shed.

His hand stroking the back of her head—the gesture of much-needed, almost familial support—Sophie wiped her face with the guard's handkerchief and nodded in gratitude for the time he had generously granted her to recollect herself.

"I'm all right. I'm ready now."

On the way to the reception cell, Sophie turned to her guard, making what use of his kindness she could.

"Do you know, have they arrested Alexander Schmorell yet?"

She held her breath, praying for a miracle. It was all over for her and Hans and Christoph, but he, her conflicted half-Russian, her fellow conspirator who'd refused to give a Hitler oath long before the entire White Rose business had come to exist, her tormented artist with his soul of a gypsy, if he lived, if he carried her memory in his heart, if he continued their fight, going into his invisible battles with her name on his lips, it was all worth dying for.

The warden shook his head, and the world around Sophie burst into colors once again.

"If he's a smart fellow, I bet he's already somewhere very far away," the guard mused out loud. "In Switzerland, maybe. That's where I would have gone. Has he any money?"

"His father is very rich. And he's smart. He's so very smart..." Sophie's voice trailed off, lost in the green pastures of Switzerland framed by snow-dusted mountaintops and rivers shimmering in the sun and blue sky untainted by the smoke of the aerial dogfights. All at once, the prison walls ceased to exist. She was already there, with him, two halves of one soul, united at long last—just like they'd dreamt countless times.

The same serene smile was still playing on Sophie's lips when she entered the reception room. Still in the grip of her dream, she saw, as though on a screen, her mother jump to her feet, her arms open wide; she felt, still vaguely, as if it was happening to somebody else, her father's lips on her temples and eyes; nodded at Werner when he was saying something, desperately trying to contain his tears, without quite hearing what it was precisely he was saying.

She kissed them back and laughed hollowly and said she didn't understand why they were crying.

"But, Sophie," her mother sobbed; she could barely manage to get the words out, "you shall never come through that door again..."

"Oh, *Mutti*." Sophie caressed her mother's hair that had turned gray overnight, suddenly transitioning from a child into a parent. "What are those few years anyway? I'm not going anywhere. I shall always be with you. You will easily find me: in the smile of a refugee welcomed into a new home after this war is over, in every dissenting opinion of the free press, among the crowd of protesters advocating for peace and love, in the reflection of a soldier refusing to carry out orders that go against his conscience—you shall always find me, if you just look closely enough."

"We'll be seeing your face on memorial plaques on every corner," Robert Scholl boomed, breathing heavily against Sophie's hair. "You and Hans. Our heroes. Germany's heroes. How proud I am—"

His voice broke off, replaced by suppressed, heaving breaths in his wide chest.

"No, no, *Vati*, we're having none of this." Sophie regarded him with all the love she felt for her father that instant. "I didn't cry when you were in jail. Proudly, I kept carrying out whatever acts of sabotage I could in your name's honor. And you do the same; you hear me? You don't give up. I forbid you to. You keep fighting for peace, and you too, Werner, my little baby brother. When you go back to the front, you start..."

Sophie was still speaking, and Werner was already nodding, fiercely, determinedly. Yes, he would. He would continue the fight, he promised. He would show them yet, what the Scholls were made of—

In the corner of the cell, Sophie noticed the same old warden hiding a grin of approval. *Good family*, his very expression seemed to read.

And then, suddenly, after Sophie had hugged all three of them for one final time, she saw, just outside the reception cell, the familiar outline of a civilian suit and the slightly hunched shoulders of Kriminalkommissar Mohr. He stood by the wall, in the darkest and furthest of corners, his face half-obscured by the shadow of his fedora, all but a shadow himself.

"Herr Kriminalkommissar!" Sophie raised her arm in a friendly wave. "Came to see me off?"

Mohr stared at her for one very long moment, seemingly caught off guard by the fact that she saw him, then swung sharply round on his heel, swiped at his face angrily and headed along the corridor in the opposite direction. His hurried steps echoed in the distance, and soon, silence enveloped the walls of the Stadelheim once again. Only the sole melodic, high-pitched song of a bird sounded somewhere outside, in the courtyard, where the guillotine stood. Her head slightly cocked, Sophie listened to it, her eyes gradually glazing over with the reflection of a Swiss paradise, where Alex would draw her against the backdrop of the mountains, sun-kissed and loved like no one else in the world.

"What a beautiful day," she whispered softly, tasting the sweet air itself on her tongue, savoring the last minutes of her short, but brilliant life. She had no regrets. If she were to start over, she would have followed the same exact path—resolutely and with her head held high. After the last deep breath, Sophie turned to the warden and smiled at him brightly—a fearless warrior, a noble leader to follow. "Let's go. I'm ready."

EPILOGUE

A FEW DAYS LATER

The enticing aroma of venison stew met Mohr as soon as he stepped through the doors of his apartment. Hearing the lock turn, his wife hurried out of the kitchen, wiping her hands on her apron, immaculately clean as always. With her kind, round face, warm smile and soft white hands, Helga was the very idea of home Mohr returned to like a diver rising from the dark, cold depths for a gulp of fresh air; an oasis of simple, domestic bliss in the ocean of hunger, war, and death. It was so uncharacteristic of him and yet, after the damned day he had had—Alex Schmorell, the last surviving member of the White Rose, had been apprehended and arrested at long last—it took Mohr all of his powers not to lower his head to her round bosom and weep in her loving, all-forgiving embrace. He ought to be celebrating; his superiors had hinted at a promotion and additional benefits for the successful elimination of the resistance cell, but instead, all Mohr wanted was to fashion a noose for himself out of his own tie and die like the dishonest criminal that he was. Only the thought of his wife and little Lisl prevented him from doing so.

A criminal and a coward, on top of everything. His lips trembled imperceptibly when he smiled at Helga.

"I thought they would never let you leave!" She began her

usual fussing over him. "Let me take your coat. Did you have a chance to have a little something? Of course not. They will work you to death one day, Robert, mark my words. How pale you look! Come, I'll pour you some wine to restore your color a bit. Magda managed to get venison; can you believe it? Thank heavens for your ration card. What would we have done without it?"

"We would have found something else to eat," he said, exhausted to the bone, and shrugged his way out of the heavy coat. "Where's Lisl?"

"In the library, studying," Helga said, searching his face.

Something had changed in him; they'd been married too long for her not to notice—Mohr knew that. For that very reason, he averted his gaze and went to kiss his daughter.

In the doorway of the library, he paused, studying her with a faint, tender smile. Immersed in her work, she hadn't noticed him enter. Only after he approached her, moving noiselessly across the carpeted floor, did she raise her startled gaze and slam the book so loudly that the sound echoed off the walls like a gunshot.

Puzzled by such unusual secrecy, Mohr regarded the papers she was presently covering with both her ink-stained hands, his smile slightly faltering. "What are you writing there?"

"A paper," Lisl replied, recovering herself and even holding his gaze steadily. "It's for school."

"Naturally, for school," Mohr said evenly. "You're too young to write love letters."

"*Vati*, I'm seventeen." She tilted her head with the coy grin she knew how to use on him all too well.

"You're still *Vati's* little girl."

She beamed at him, but her hands still covered the papers protectively.

"Do you need help with your paper?"

"No, *Vati*, thank you. It's a simple assignment. Just a short essay."

"What's the subject?"

"Making the right choice."

"Well, you shall ace that one."

"I hope so, too."

"You will. And now, come. Dinner is ready. Your *Mutti* is waiting for us." Rounding the table, Mohr leaned to kiss her on top of her head, right in the neat part in between two braids, and suddenly caught sight of familiar words peeking from under Lisl's crossed arms. *Support the resistance. Copy and distribute the leaflets.* And right under the brown sleeve of her school uniform, written in Lisl's own hand: *We will not be silent. We are your bad conscience. The White Rose will not leave you in peace!*

Lisl moved her arm slightly to cover them and looked up at him with her honest eyes.

For a few instants, Mohr stood still as a statue, his hand hesitating on the back of his daughter's chair. Then, he suddenly cupped her face, kissed the top of her head once again and pressed her to his chest.

"Yes, you will ace that one," he whispered. Then he released her and turned to take his leave before he changed his mind.

A LETTER FROM ELLIE

Dear Reader,

I want to say a huge thank you for choosing to read *The White Rose Network*. If you did enjoy it, and want to keep up to date with all my latest releases, just sign up at the following link. Your email address will never be shared and you can unsubscribe at any time.

www.bookouture.com/ellie-midwood

I hope you loved *The White Rose Network* and if you did, I would be very grateful if you could write a review. I'd love to hear what you think, and it makes such a difference helping new readers to discover one of my books for the first time.

I love hearing from my readers—you can get in touch on my Facebook page, through Goodreads or my website.

Huge thanks,

Ellie

www.elliemidwood.com

f facebook.com/EllieMidwood

A NOTE ON THE HISTORY

Thank you so much for reading *The White Rose Network*. Even though it's a work of fiction, I tried to stick to the facts as closely as possible as I've always considered it my duty, as a historical fiction writer, to not only write a compelling story but deliver lesser-known bits of history to my readers, only taking creative license where no witness accounts or historical sources are available.

Sophie Scholl arrived in Munich in the spring of 1942 to study at the same university—the University of Munich—as her brother Hans, with whom she shared a rented apartment in the bohemian district of Schwabing. At the time of her arrival, only one leaflet was circulating among the university students—the very first pamphlet written by the two original members of the White Rose, Hans Scholl and Alexander Schmorell. The circumstances of Sophie's identifying her brother as an author of the leaflet are true to historical fact, just like the fact that Hans was initially against Sophie's joining the resistance group due to his concerns for her safety. Eventually, Hans relented, persuaded by his best friend Alex's influence, and Sophie became a full member of the White Rose.

To bring Sophie, Hans, Alex, Willi, Christoph, Traute, Professor Huber, and Kriminalkommissar Mohr to life, I relied on historical sources and their own surviving correspondence and diary entries to paint them as authentically as possible. In this respect, *Hans and Sophie Scholl: at the Heart of the White Rose* (edited by Inge Jens)—the collection of diary entries and letters written by the Scholl siblings—was my biggest source of inspiration and a true wealth of information concerning their beliefs, moods, and just ordinary facts of life that I tried to transfer into this novel with as much accuracy as I could.

It was through these diary entries that I learned of Sophie's conflicted feelings for Alex Schmorell and her fiancé Fritz Hartnagel, who was at the time serving on the Eastern Front. I felt it was an important plotline to investigate as it compares two very different men (traditional and very "Prussian" Fritz and bohemian rebel Alex) and the gradual change in Sophie's own personality under the influence of those conflicted romantic feelings. Sophie's diary entries testify to the fact that she struggled between her passion for Alex and her long-standing relationship with Fritz.

However, her own romantic feelings definitely took second place to Sophie's priorities, the first and foremost being the White Rose. In a few short months, Sophie progressed from being a relative novice to the group's official treasurer and active participant. She helped compose, print, and distribute the pamphlets and indeed took a dangerous trip with Traute to Hamburg, which resulted in the forming of Hamburg's branch of the White Rose. While Hans, Alex, and Willi had gone to serve on the Eastern Front and the printing press had been shut down for the time being, she contributed to the resistance cause in her own way, sabotaging production at the factory where she was forced to work and helping Russian slave-laboring women as much as she could. Her father, Robert Scholl, was indeed arrested and sentenced to serve time in prison at approximately the same time, so one can only imagine the stress she was under. The instances of Hans, Alex, and Willi getting into fights with the Party members and the SS are also based on fact, just like the story with Hans offering a Jewish girl his rations and a flower.

Sophie's return to active participation in the White Rose activities as soon as Hans, Alex, and Willi returned from the front testifies to her selflessness and ultimate bravery. Personally witnessing how the regime treated such minor crimes as making one remark against Hitler (the "crime" that landed Robert Scholl in prison), Sophie was well aware what awaited her and her fellow resistance members if they were uncovered. Still, she persisted and one can only admire her for never backing down even in the face of mortal danger.

The historical events surrounding the plot all really took place on the dates added to the beginning of each chapter, including the very first bombing of Munich and the students' uprising.

While writing this novel, I decided to give special attention to the interrogation chapters. I found it incredible and fascinating at the same time that Kriminalkommissar Mohr, who was a real former police detective turned Gestapo agent, hoped to help Sophie by persuading her to shift the blame to the male members of the White Rose, thus sparing her life. I wondered what moved him and what could have possibly motivated his compassion and so, by digging deep into whatever historical sources that were available, I constructed one of the most contradictory characters I've ever written.

We'll never know the real Mohr's motives, but to me he personifies all of those government officials who perhaps weren't bigots or ardent supporters of National Socialism. They took up the positions because they were well-cushioned and provided support and comfort to their families in times when ordinary citizens were suffering from food shortages and rationing that was growing stricter and stricter as the war was progressing further. Naturally, even such "passive" involvement for the sake of the benefits doesn't excuse him in any way. It is because of government officials like Mohr that the Nazi machine could proceed with its persecutions of millions. Bureaucrats, who never personally hurt anyone, were just as guilty of crimes against humanity as SS men who actually pulled their triggers. As Elie Wiesel said, "The opposite of love is not hate, it's indifference." Perhaps, Mohr finally realized what his personal indifference to the fate of the persecuted led to only when he faced Sophie Scholl, but it was too late at that point for him to change anything, no matter how much he tried. That was the reason why I let him redeem himself through the epilogue, in which his daughter—the symbolic embodiment of the new generation—picks up the White Rose flag and carries it to the new age in the name of a new Germany.

Mohr, however, isn't the main reason why I was looking forward to writing interrogation chapters. As had been agreed among them beforehand, both Sophie and Hans simultaneously confessed to the same crimes (writing and distributing the leaflets) in order to protect their friends. Despite all of Mohr's efforts, Sophie continually declined to shift the blame onto the others, even though it meant her own execution. It was her personal bravery and willingness to sacrifice herself for the ideals the White Rose fiercely believed in that made writing the interrogation chapters such a profound experience. While writing them, I tried to stick to the facts as closely as possible to show the true extent of her heroism. That's why Sophie's final words uttered in her cell— *"Such a beautiful, sunny day, and I have to go... But what difference does my death make if our actions arouse thousands of people?"*— are a direct quotation, just like her defiant remarks thrown at Roland Freisler in court.

For the same reason, the text of the real leaflets is used in the novel largely unchanged, if slightly shortened to keep the pace steady.

Just like the members of the Red Orchestra before them, the White Rose paid with their lives for standing up for freedom from tyranny and ending the war that took millions of lives. However, their legacy didn't die with them. Unfortunately, Falk Harnack never met Hans on the appointed date in Berlin (Hans was already in custody), but Harnack's resistance circle, with high-ranking Wehrmacht officials in it, eventually carried out the most daring assassination attempt in the history of Nazi Germany—the so-called July coup of 1944. Only due to unfortunate circumstance did Hitler survive the attempt, but the fact remains—the German resistance (I used the umbrella term for all different cells that existed) members sacrificed their lives in the name of freedom and it's so very important to remember these brave people's stories in order to prevent the same atrocities from happening again.

Thank you so much for reading these heroes' stories. I can only hope that their memory shall live on in our hearts forever and inspire us to be better people and stand up to injustice just like they did—to honor their legacy and ensure that they didn't perish in vain.

ACKNOWLEDGEMENTS

First and foremost, I want to thank the wonderful Bookouture family for helping me bring Sophie Scholl's story to light. It wouldn't be possible without the help and guidance of my incredible editor Christina Demosthenous, whose insights truly bring my characters to life and whose support and encouragement make me strive to work even harder on my novels and become a better writer. Thank you, Bookouture family, for all your help and for making me feel welcome and at home with your amazing publishing team. It's been a true pleasure working with all of you and I already can't wait to create more projects under your guidance.

Huge thanks to my family for believing in me and showing such enthusiasm for each one of my new book babies. Thank you for raising me a free spirit, for letting me choose my own way and supporting me on every step—I am where I am now thanks to your unconditional love and unwavering faith in me and my abilities. Love you to death.

A special thanks to my fiancé and two besties (sisters from other misters, as I call them) for their love, support and understanding when it comes to missed dinners and lunches because of my deadlines—I promise, I'll make it up to you!

Huge thanks to all of my fellow authors whom I got to know through social media and who became my very close friends—you all are such an inspiration! I consider you all a family.

And, of course, huge thanks to my readers for patiently waiting for new releases, for celebrating cover reveals together with me, for reading ARCs and sending me those absolutely amazing I-stayed-up-till-3am-last-night-because-I-just-had-to-finish-your-wonderful-book messages, for your reviews that always make my day, and for falling in love with my characters just as much as I do. You are the reason why I write. Thank you so much for reading my stories.

And finally, I owe my biggest thanks to all the brave people who continue to inspire my novels. Some of you survived the Holocaust and WWII, some of you perished, but it's your incredible courage, resilience, and self-sacrifice that will live on in our hearts. Your example will always inspire us to be better people, to stand up for what is right, to give a voice to the ones who have been silenced, to protect the ones who cannot protect themselves. You all are true heroes. Thank you.